NOW THAT I'VE FOUND YOU

~ The New York Sullivans ~
Drake & Rosa

Bella Andre

CHAPTER ONE

There was someone out on the cliffs. *His* cliffs.

Drake Sullivan watched as the person crossed the cliffs just beyond the trees surrounding his property. In the six years he'd owned this cottage on twenty acres at the northern tip of Long Island, few people had ever trespassed. Sure, his siblings and cousins often showed up out of the blue, but most people didn't know the lone private parcel in Montauk Point State Park existed—even locals. The trails dead-ended a mile from the edge of his property, and even sailors out on the water couldn't see his small cabin through the trees.

A black cap flew off the person's head, and long, dark hair blew out. She didn't try to catch the cap, didn't actually seem to notice it was gone. Instead, she kept her head down as she walked along rocks that could be treacherous when wet. One wrong step and she could slip and fall on the sharp, unforgiving slate that rose up from the sand below.

The closer he looked through his cottage's living room window, the less steady she appeared. The wind had kicked in big-time earlier that morning, and he could see her legs were shaking. Not just her legs: all of her. Anyone else out in this biting wind would have been wearing a jacket—a heavy one. Her T-shirt and jeans weren't much better than being naked out there in the elements, especially now that the rain had started coming down in sheets.

Surprise shifted to concern as he realized she might not just be a hiker who had somehow found her way onto his property. Someone out to enjoy the outdoors would actually have been *enjoying* it—the growing swells of the surf, the violent dance of the storm clouds as they took over the sky, the golden beach such a surprising contrast to the dark gray cliffs that jutted up so abruptly. But this woman obviously wasn't having a good time—barely seemed to notice where she was, in fact.

Was she trying to hurt herself by going out on the wet rocks when the wind was kicking up like this? Or did she just not know any better?

He was already heading out to see if she needed help when she suddenly dropped down onto the rocks. His innate protective urges had him flying out the door and crunching quickly through the pine needles on the forest floor to go and help her.

But as he got closer, he realized that though she was definitely crying, it didn't seem to be because of a fall. From what he could see, she was sobbing the way his sister, Suzanne, and his numerous female cousins did when their hearts had been shattered. Sitting in a little ball near the edge, the woman's arms were wrapped around her knees, her head tucked against her legs as she wept.

Though he still wanted to make sure she didn't come to any harm, Drake made himself stop where he was, hidden in the trees. He knew enough about women to understand that when one was crying like this, the very last thing she wanted was for someone to witness it.

Especially a stranger.

As he watched over her from the forest, Drake finally noticed all the things he hadn't seen when he'd thought she might be about to harm herself. The way her slightly wavy hair went from light brown at the roots to a darker bronze at the tips. The elegant curve of her neck. The long line of her spine as she hugged her legs. And, most of all, the surprising strength in her slender arms.

Sobbing this hard should have reduced her in some way. Should have diminished her. But she had such strength—a magnificent power that only seemed to magnify as he watched over her.

The last thing Drake expected was to feel something stir in him. Something that hadn't stirred in a very long time: an urge to paint.

Since he was a kid, he'd always carried a small sketchbook in his pocket to make sure he could capture inspiration whenever and wherever it came. It wasn't until he reached into his back pocket and came up empty that he remembered he hadn't touched it in weeks, his dearth of inspiration having already killed his longstanding habit of slipping it into his pocket.

Most people came to Montauk for the wide-open beaches or to be *seen* in the Hamptons. But Drake came for silence. And inspiration.

Two months. That's how long he'd been waiting for some damned inspiration to strike. Instead, he'd reached the point where he could barely see a reason to open a sketchbook or set up his easel. All this beauty around him, an ocean that seemed to stretch on forever, old fishing buildings throughout town that had more soul than any modern buildings would ever have—and still nothing sparked.

Until now.

Until *her*.

As Drake stood in the thick copse of trees, he had only his memory with which to capture the image of the woman on the cliffs. His visual memory had always been borderline photographic, yet despite his ability to remember fine details that most people never even saw, he still wished she were sitting in his studio now so that he could stare, learn, discover.

His brain skidded to a halt. *What the hell was he thinking?*

Drake didn't paint women. Ever. It was his one hard-and-fast rule. Oils and acrylics, pastels and watercolor—he was open to it all. But he had never brought a woman into his studio, and he never planned to.

Besides, even if he didn't have a hard line about painting women, he shouldn't be thinking about work right now. He should be concentrating on making sure this woman didn't decide to leap from the rocks during her crying jag.

At first her grief had rivaled the storm. But the storm within her seemed finally to be subsiding, calming by degrees. As if she controlled the weather, the wind that had been whipping the ocean and the forest into a frenzy just moments earlier suddenly died away, the storm clouds parting to reveal blue sky—and a stream of sunlight that landed on the woman like a spotlight.

When she lifted her head from her knees and turned to face the sun so that he could finally see her profile, Drake's heart stilled in his chest—stopping as surely as it might if a knife stabbed it, or a bullet pierced it.

He needed to paint her.

* * *

Rosa Bouchard—not *Rosalind*, no matter how much her mother insisted on using her legal name because it sounded "classier"—hadn't cried in years. Not since her father had passed away when she was ten and she'd lost one of the most important, loving people in her life.

But today she couldn't stop.

There was so much water around her already— waves crashing, salt water spraying up onto the clifftop to soak her shoes, her clothes, her skin. What was a little more salty liquid to add to it? Especially when her tears were barely a drop in the bucket compared to the huge, wide ocean in front of her.

It was almost a relief to let the tears flow through her so hard and fast that she couldn't concentrate on anything else. Rosa didn't want to think right now. Didn't want to have to make any big decisions. Didn't want to keep remembering what had happened. Not just the horrible pictures, but all the awful comments from strangers that had followed. And, worst of all, the things that the people who were supposed to care about her most had said.

Unfortunately, nothing could stop her mother's voice from playing on repeat inside Rosa's head: *"That horrible man who hid those cameras in your hotel room and took those pictures of you won't stand a chance against our lawyers. They'll nail him to the wall for sneaking and selling those pictures. But you shouldn't feel bad about what people are seeing, honey. Your body isn't anything they haven't seen before. Why don't we let the lawyers go after him while we look on the bright side—we've gained over a million followers on every single social platform in just a matter of hours!"*

In the end, that was what had cracked Rosa's heart in two—realizing that her body had been nothing more than a trade for a few million new social media followers for her family's brand. That her pride, her privacy, her utter lack of consent to the nude photos were simply a good way to increase their worth to advertisers who wanted the Bouchards' endorsements for their makeup and fashion lines.

As a new wave of misery rose within her, Rosa could feel the rips and tears clawing at her heart. The ocean crashing on the rocks swallowed up the sound of her tears, but instead of continuing to be glad for the cover, anger suddenly flooded her.

She was so tired of being muted. So damned sick of always being told what to say and how to say it by the cable network's publicity team.

A roar of fury was rising in her throat when she was jolted by a sudden flood of unexpected warmth. Lifting her face from where she'd had it buried on her knees, she was shocked to realize that the gray clouds had parted and a beam of sunshine was coming through.

Shining straight on her.

For one blissful moment, both her brain and her heart cleared so that she could appreciate the sound of the waves crashing and feel the warmth of the sun on her wet face and arms.

But the moment passed way too soon, and when it did, everything that had happened in the past twenty-four hours came crashing right back.

Rosa hadn't thought about where she was going that morning. She hadn't awakened at four a.m. and had her bags packed with a clear destination in her GPS. She'd simply had to get out. Had to get away from everyone and everything that was hurting her. So she'd snuck out of the house to her car. Not one of the fancy ones the car companies gave them to drive for the free publicity, but the old car she'd bought with the money she'd saved up from babysitting in the years before reality TV made her life completely unreal.

She'd driven through the night and kept driving as the sun rose, until she'd found herself in Montauk, a town nicknamed THE END. It was the perfect description for how she felt—all the way at the end of her rope.

She'd been to Montauk once before with her dad on one of their special yearly father-daughter trips. Rosa remembered driving past the long stretches of beach and wondering when her dad was going to stop so that they could go outside and play. But she'd trusted him to know the best place—she'd trusted him about absolutely everything—even when he'd pulled into a forest instead of the beach.

They'd hiked a winding trail, laughing as they'd skipped over some puddles and splashed through others, then come to what looked like a skateboarder's big concrete half-pipe. Her father had told her that it was an old storm drain that was no longer used, but that it would take them to one of the most spectacular places he'd ever seen, one hardly anyone knew about. As they'd walked together along the cracked concrete, she'd been so excited by the adventure that when the trees suddenly opened up to reveal dark gray cliffs and the endless ocean beyond, she'd gasped in wonder.

Rosa always had fun playing in the sand and surf, but it was the turbulent ocean that had always touched her most deeply. Though she hadn't ever said the words aloud to her father, he'd understood.

That special day so long ago, he'd taken her hand and told her they needed to walk carefully over the slick clifftop because he couldn't stand the thought of her falling and getting hurt. She still remembered the warm, steady grip of his hand, how sure she'd been that he'd always be there to take care of her, to make sure she was never hurt. And how excited she'd been when he promised that they could come back to this spot the following year on their special trip.

A month later he was gone in a helicopter crash that took the lives of his entire radio traffic reporting team, and she'd never come back to these cliffs that she'd always thought of as their special place. But on that one perfect afternoon, he'd told her all about the currents, the tides, the marine life. And then, for a long time, they'd simply sat quietly together and appreciated the beauty all around them.

Her dad had been so good at being quiet, and letting her be quiet too. Rosa hadn't needed to be the pretty one with him. The bubbly one. The fun one. The exciting one. The risky one. She could just be herself.

Whoever the hell Rosa Bouchard was now...

Just that quickly, the sun disappeared, its warmth gone as if it had never been there at all. The wind picked up again too, but strangely, she wasn't cold. Or maybe she'd just been cold for so long she didn't notice it anymore.

The rain came again, pouring down so hard that it stung her eyes, her skin. She wished it could wash her clean, but after all she'd consented to during the past several years as a reality TV star—and the horrible pictures she hadn't consented to—she was afraid nothing would ever wash her clean again.

She'd turned off her cell phone hours ago, but she could still feel the unyielding weight of it against her hip in the back pocket of her jeans. She always had her phone with her and would have felt naked without it.

Naked.

She still couldn't believe that the whole world had seen her naked on their phones.

Again, she didn't think. Didn't plan. Just jumped to her feet, grabbed her phone out of her pocket, and threw it as hard, and as far, as she could.

Despite the countless hours of yoga and Pilates she'd put in to keep her naturally curvaceous figure in line, her phone barely made it to the sharp edge of the cliffs. Still, she could see the screen had shattered as it teetered back and forth, back and forth, back and forth... before finally falling over the edge.

Disappearing, just like her.

CHAPTER TWO

She was leaving.

When the woman on the cliff had hurled her phone against the rocks in obvious fury, for a moment, even with the heavy rain drenching her, she'd almost seemed relieved. But then her shoulders had slumped again, her long, wet hair covering her face as she walked back along the clifftop toward the forest.

Despite the rain pelting her, she moved with innate grace, like a dancer or a runway model. And though there was no audience to impress, and she was still clearly upset, it was impossible to miss the sensuality in the slight sway of her hips. She was drenched from head to toe, and her jeans and T-shirt clung to her like a second skin, revealing a figure that would have made the hands of Rodin himself burn with the desperate need to sculpt her.

But the sex appeal that fairly dripped from her wasn't what drew Drake, wasn't what made it so hard to stop staring, to stop itching to paint her. He'd been with plenty of gorgeous women, and he'd never felt like this before.

Light seemed to surround her, follow her, cling to her, even beneath thick gray clouds and pouring rain.

Jesus. He was starting to lose it out here in his remote cottage, had obviously been staring at a blank canvas for far too many weeks. But even after he shook his head to clear his vision, that halo of light continued to surround her as she headed for the old storm drain that must have been her way in.

He didn't need to keep watch over her anymore to make sure she didn't fall—or leap—from the rocks. He should head back into his cottage and make himself paint something.

Anything but *her.*

Even if he were stupid enough to break the one hard-and-fast rule he'd always been careful to live by, he couldn't chase this woman down and ask her to sit for him. Not when she'd just been sobbing as if her whole world had ended. Only a total douchebag would put his art above a person's feelings. Sure, there were plenty of painters who felt justified in doing or saying anything to get what they wanted onto their canvases. But Drake had never hurt anyone in the pursuit of art, and he wasn't planning to start today.

Still, as she disappeared into the trees and out of his line of sight, it took a hell of a lot of self-control to stop himself from running to the storm drain to find her.

To ask for her name. To beg her to come back one day when she wasn't sad anymore. If only so that he could feel this spark again, this insanely strong urge to paint that he'd taken for granted all his life.

As Drake forced himself to head back to his cottage, he finally noticed that he too was soaked through. He'd been so intent on the woman—and fighting his crazy urge to paint her—that only now did he realize how low the temperature had fallen during the storm. He had his shirt off by the time he got to his front door and stripped off everything else in a wet heap before he opened the door and walked inside.

Oscar looked up from his big, soft dog pillow in the corner, lifting his dark brows as he took in his naked and dripping owner. "Some guard dog you are. You just slept through a stranger out on the cliffs and one hell of a storm."

Drake loved the big furball anyway, of course. Oscar only looked like a guard dog—part German shepherd, part Boxer, part Akita. Inside, the mutt was a sleepy ball of Jell-O. As if to reinforce his lazy reputation, Oscar yawned and buried his muzzle beneath one big paw.

Drake dried off with a towel, then grabbed a dry pair of jeans and a shirt from his bedroom and headed back into his combined living room and kitchen. He'd trimmed the tree limbs surrounding his cottage so that light streamed in through the windows that took up three walls. This had always been his best studio space, better even than his west-facing New York City penthouse that looked out over Central Park. Having his studio, kitchen, and bedroom within a dozen feet of each other had been the ideal way to keep himself fed and rested while on a painting jag.

Lately, the whole setup felt like it was mocking him.

Drake knew he wasn't the first painter to lose his spark. Thirty years ago, his father had lost his spark too. But Drake had always assumed it would never happen to him if he was careful. If he didn't make the mistake of pinning all his inspiration on one person the way his father had. If he didn't let his heart get too attached or dive too deeply, not just with anything he painted—but with any woman at all.

William Sullivan had once been the hottest painter in the country. Back in the eighties, his work had fetched six figures—and even more at the end. Because that was what happened the day Drake's mother, his father's ultimate muse, had walked out on William and their four kids and taken her own life. William's passion for painting, and his brilliant talent, had ended. He'd never picked up another paintbrush, never set foot in his studio again. Simply let the canvases gather dust, the paints dry up, and his paintbrushes be replaced with hammers and nail guns as he eventually turned to building houses instead.

Drake had been only six months old the day his mother left. While his older siblings had talked with him about it in the years since, it was mostly other artists and dealers who never tired of rehashing the tantalizing details of personal destruction. Because when William Sullivan quit painting out of the blue, it hit the art world in the same way his death would have, with most of his remaining unsold works jumping to nearly ten times their original value. Even his oldest paintings, which were little more than dreamy love letters on canvas to the woman he had been obsessed with, became priceless collectors' items.

Drake knew enough about psychology to understand why he personally preferred his Montauk cottage to his New York City penthouse. His father's fame—and the legend of how love gone wrong had made one of the greatest modern-day painters abruptly put down his brush forever—had always made Drake's life too much of an open book. Sure, Drake could play the game in the city at galleries and with art investors, but he preferred not to. Especially now that he was at the point in his career where he could hole up and focus on painting full time, letting his agent take care of the deals. Because while Drake honestly didn't care what the world thought about him, his family, or his paintings, that didn't mean he was going to help feed people's glee over rehashing the past either.

During the past few weeks, his siblings and several of his cousins had been asking when he was going to head back to the city, but he refused to go back until he'd done what he came here to do: create a dozen great paintings.

Telling himself to just forget the woman on the cliffs already, he picked up his nearly empty sketchbook. After all, he didn't even like painting people, apart from deliberately silly portraits of his cousins' kids, who were all so full of life and laughter. Even when they were naughty, Drake couldn't resist the playful twinkle in their eyes.

But as the pencil in his hand seemed to move of its own volition over the page, it wasn't a stormy ocean vista that formed—it was the woman on the cliffs. If only her face hadn't been obscured by the distance and rain. If only he'd gotten closer...

His phone rang and Oscar made a grumpy half-growling sound at having his nap interrupted. Drake cursed as he dropped the sketchbook as though it were on fire. *What the hell was he doing? Where was his self-control?*

He normally kept his phone off, but he'd needed to check in with his agent earlier that morning before she came to Montauk and hunted him down. Seeing Candice's name on the screen, he picked up.

Dispensing entirely with pleasantries, his agent said, "Drake, I need those paintings."

"Soon."

But they'd worked together long enough for Candice to know when he was full of it. "I've already bought you two extra months. You're a hotshot talent, Drake. Which is why the top gallery in NYC is thrilled to give you their entire space next month. Please tell me you've at least started something."

He looked down at the sketchbook before forcing himself to shut the cover on the beautiful, enigmatic face that stared up at him. "Their walls won't be empty."

"Good. I hope you're taking care of your gorgeous self all the way out there in the wilds."

"The Hamptons don't count as wild, Candy."

He could practically see his agent shiver with horror at the thought of being more than a hundred feet from the latest fashions, gourmet coffee, and must-eat-at restaurants.

"Call me as soon as you've shipped the paintings."

Drake shut down the phone, knowing that although his agent had played it fairly cool, both she and the gallery were clearly freaking out that he hadn't delivered any paintings yet, with the show barely two weeks away.

It was long past time to kick his muse in the ass and paint. Especially now that he could see at least a dozen new paintings in his head already, images bursting with passion and emotion, visions that centered around the beautiful stranger he couldn't stop thinking about.

Cursing, Drake told Oscar to keep sleeping on his dog bed in the corner, then grabbed his car keys to get the hell away from his sketchbook, paints, and canvas before he dug himself into a hole he might never be able to escape.

CHAPTER THREE

Rosa pulled up to a general store that looked to have seen better days. She'd passed a new grocery store a mile back, but she figured the odds of getting in and out of a store without being recognized were more in her favor if she went somewhere teenagers were likely to avoid.

When she'd climbed back into her car fifteen minutes ago, she'd immediately soaked the seat. Unfortunately, she didn't have any dry clothes to change into. And her growling stomach reminded her that she didn't have any food either.

But just because she hadn't prepared for this trip to Montauk didn't mean she was ready to go home. How could she go back to a life where there was a "bright side" to people sneaking naked pictures of her and then selling them so that the entire world could see her completely exposed?

Her chest hurt and her stomach cramped every time she thought about the pictures. She hadn't known anyone was filming her as she'd stripped off her clothes in her hotel room, that they were taking one shot after another of her getting into the bathtub, that even more shots were taken while she'd dried off before slipping on a robe. She had thought she was finally off the clock for a precious thirty minutes in a steaming tub without cameras following her.

She'd been wrong.

Tears started to come again, but she forced them back. She didn't want to keep falling apart, was determined to pull herself together. Because if she didn't, then it would *really* feel like they'd won. Everyone from the guy who'd taken and sold the pictures, to the strangers who said such awful things about her online, to a mother who was just so damned thrilled by how high their social media numbers had jumped in the wake of the scandal.

No, Rosa definitely wasn't going back. Not until she had made a decision about her next step. But she needed her head to be clearer as she worked to figure that out. She couldn't stay hidden forever, but she also wouldn't let herself rush or panic again. She might only have a high school diploma, but she'd been accepted to a great university before she'd chosen reality TV instead. If she'd learned anything from the legal teams her family had worked with over the past five years, it was that a well-drawn plan was always better than something carelessly slapped together.

Which meant that right now, since she was still

reeling and hurting too much to make any good decisions, she simply needed to get some clothes and food, then find a place to stay for the night without alerting anyone as to her whereabouts. If she remembered correctly, the motel where she and her father had stayed when she was a kid was only a mile or so up the road.

Fortunately, Rosa carried a stash of cash in her bag at all times. Her just-in-case money. No one in her family liked to talk about the downside to being so famous, but another reality TV star had advised her early on that using cash instead of credit could help buy her a little freedom if she ever needed it.

Of course, back when they'd signed on to do the show—both because their family desperately needed the money and because it sounded so exciting—Rosa had never expected to need that freedom quite so badly.

Grabbing her bag from the passenger seat, she checked to make sure there was no one around before she got out of the car. Fortunately, the heavy rain seemed to be keeping people at home. She was about to put on her sunglasses when she realized that would only make her look more conspicuous.

Her heart pounding a million miles an hour, she stepped into the empty store. A gray-haired woman was sitting behind the register watching a soap opera on the TV that hung in the corner.

"Hello, honey." The woman looked at her kindly—and with zero recognition. "The storm caught you, did it?"

Rosa nodded. "It did."

"Well, it's warm and dry in here, so you just let

me know if you need help with anything."

Rosa tucked her head down so that her wet hair fell over her face just in case anyone came in, then grabbed a hand basket and started looking for essentials. A toothbrush and toothpaste. Some apples, oranges, and microwave dinners. A couple of tourist T-shirts. A sweatshirt and a pair of sweatpants with *Montauk* written down one leg. And a pack of white cotton underwear and socks.

Hoping this would be enough food and clothes to make it a few days while she hid and figured out her next steps, she was heading to the register when she walked past an aisle containing sewing supplies. Unable to resist them, she ran her fingers over the beautiful blues and greens, reds and yellows on the spools of thread. Even when she was a little girl, she'd been totally drawn to playing with her mother's needles and thread. Not to make clothes, but because she loved to watch patterns and pictures emerge from her stitches. The quality of the thread and yarn here wasn't great, and there was no embroidery floss, but she could make do by doubling or even tripling the thread. She couldn't help throwing some spools and a pack of needles into her basket.

Rosa didn't realize the magazine and paperback section was on the facing side of the aisle until she turned and flinched at her own face staring back at her. Her stomach twisted when she thought about how excited she'd been the first time she'd landed on the cover of a magazine. But back then she'd never dreamed there'd be headlines that shouted, *America's Favorite Bad Girl: Nude Photo Scandal? Or Another Brilliant Business*

Move for the Bouchards?

Rosa was doubling down on her prayers that the woman working the register wouldn't recognize her without her usual makeup and couture clothes, when the bell over the front door clanged and shook her back to reality. She needed to buy her supplies and get away before someone spotted her.

Fortunately, the gray-haired man who walked in didn't look as though he'd be any more likely to know who Rosa was than the woman behind the register. He leaned over the counter and gave the woman a sweet kiss before saying something that made her giggle like a schoolgirl in love.

Love. It was something Rosa had once longed for, but as her fame grew, she'd quickly learned that the odds of finding it in the middle of her crazy life were so low there was no point in even trying. Not when every guy she'd been out with over the past couple of years only wanted to be with her to become famous himself.

Her chest felt tighter than ever as she walked up to the register and put her basket on the counter. The woman hummed softly as she rang up each item. At the end, when she put a freshly baked chocolate chip cookie into the paper bag "on the house," that little bit of unexpected kindness had Rosa nearly bursting into sobs again.

Her hands shook from the effort of trying to hold her emotions at bay as she drew out a few twenty-dollar bills. Just as the woman was making change, the door flew open and the loud laughter of three teenage girls filled the store.

Oh God, they were going to recognize her.

Rosa's heart started pounding so fast that she was glad her stomach was empty, or she might have thrown up all over the counter. As it was, she was so lightheaded from the quick rush of blood pounding through her that when she grabbed the bag, she tripped over herself making a dash for the door.

"Honey, you forgot your change!"

It was change she'd need, given that her cash was likely to run out soon and she couldn't risk being tracked down by using her ATM card. But right then, it was more important to get out of the store as fast as possible.

She kept her head down, the grocery bag clasped tightly to her chest as she rushed through the pouring rain toward her car. She wouldn't feel safe until she was back inside with the door locked. Wouldn't even feel safe then, actually. Not when she no longer felt in control of anything in her life.

She was so out of control, in fact, that the next thing she knew, she ran straight into a wall. The chocolate chip cookie tipped out of her bag and landed—*plop!*— in a muddy puddle, a couple of apples following it a moment later. But as she blinked the rain out of her eyes, she suddenly realized she hadn't hit a wall.

She'd slammed into a man with a very broad and muscular chest.

Rosa needed to hightail it to her car before he recognized her, but when he picked up her dropped groceries, then straightened to give them to her, she couldn't get her legs to move.

He was *gorgeous*. But not in a slick Hollywood

way. The total opposite, actually, with his bristly jaw and muscles flexing beneath wet flannel and denim.

What was she doing? This was the very last moment she should be drooling over some guy. Especially considering that, unlike the lady behind the register, he was the right age to know who she—

"It's you." He looked stunned. "I can't believe I've found you. Here at the general store."

Oh no. She needed to get into her car and start driving again. Somewhere far away from here. But when she moved to the side to skirt around him, he shifted his big, rugged body into her flight path.

"You were just on the cliffs outside my cottage in the rain. It's private property, so I'm not used to seeing anyone there."

Wait...*that* was why he recognized her? Because she'd been on the cliffs outside his house? Not because she was a star whose naked pictures were currently plastered all over the media?

The way he was looking at her—not as though she was some reality TV sideshow freak, but as though he truly couldn't believe how lucky he was to have run into her in the general store's parking lot—made it hard to think straight. So instead of hightailing it away from him, she found herself saying, "I didn't mean to trespass. Back when my dad and I—" The words stilled in her throat as she choked up. "Last time I was there, I didn't know the cliffs were on private property."

"It's okay." The look he gave her was as gentle as his voice. "It looked like you needed to be there. I know we've just met, but if you need any help, maybe I can—"

Oh God. Of course he'd witnessed her meltdown. Her endless, wracking sobs, which had ended with her throwing her phone off the cliff.

"I'm sorry I trespassed," she said again, her gut twisting at what a fool she must seem to him. She supposed she shouldn't have any pride left at this point, but somehow she still did. "I need to go."

He held out her food. "Don't you want these?" She shook her head as she finally managed to get around him. "At least tell me your name."

Shock sent her skidding through a puddle. *He really didn't know her name?* Was he for real? But she couldn't risk his finding out as she yanked open her car door and threw herself inside.

Only, before she slammed it shut, she heard him say, "If you want to come back to my cliffs, you can."

Her heart was leaping as she gunned her old car out of the lot. But even though she wouldn't let herself look for him in the rearview mirror, his invitation played over and over in her head.

If you want to come back...if you want to come back...if you want to come back...

She wanted nothing more than to go back—to watch the tides shift, the sky change colors, the seabirds swoop down to the sand. She wouldn't even mind the rain, not when it was just part of the natural ebb and flow of the seasons.

But this wasn't a vacation. She might have fled home without thinking things through, but if she didn't want her family or the network to find out where she was and drag her back into the middle of the madness, she needed to stay hidden.

She also needed to take a shower, put on some dry clothes, and eat something. A little sleep would probably do her a world of good. But first, she needed to get out of Montauk and find a new town to hide out in. One where gorgeous men in general-store parking lots didn't make her heart race even when she knew better.

But when she pushed her foot down harder on the gas pedal, her car suddenly began to make noises. Really bad, loud noises.

This couldn't be happening.

Her car couldn't actually be breaking down on top of everything else, could it?

CHAPTER FOUR

The woman from the cliffs had peeled out of the parking lot in her beat-up old car faster than she should have. Drake didn't know her—didn't even know her name—but he was worried nonetheless.

He'd seen that kind of bleak look before. Whenever his mother's name came up, even after all these years, all the color would drain from his father's face. Thirty years after her disappearance and death, William Sullivan's pain hadn't dimmed.

Likewise, whatever had happened had obviously hurt this woman deeply. Especially considering how spooked she'd seemed by every word out of Drake's mouth.

He'd never thought he would see her again, never thought he'd get to drink her in up close, never thought he'd have a chance to memorize the perfect, exotic planes of her face. He'd already done more than he should have by sketching her, then had left his cottage to make sure he didn't give in to the pull to bring her to life on a canvas. But now...

Now the itch to paint her had spun into deep desire. The kind of urgent drive to paint that an artist waited his whole life to feel.

Drake didn't realize he was still holding the woman's apples and cookie until the cookie crumbled in his fist. Wet dough and chocolate chips were smushed between his fingers as he walked over to the garbage can by the front door and threw the cookie away. After he let the rain wash away the crumbs on his hands, he dropped an apple into each pocket and finally headed inside.

"Drake, sweetie, we haven't seen you all week."

Mona Agnew had manned the general store's till for the past thirty years, ever since she and her husband had opened the doors. Despite the fact that she was a tad on the nosy side—particularly when it came to his love life—he far preferred shopping here to the new chain grocery store just up the road. Drake had always appreciated places with some life to them, which was why the old hunting cabin at Montauk Point suited him perfectly.

"How are you, Mona?"

"Just fine. I've saved one of those fresh-baked apple pies you like so much. Why don't you take care of your shopping while I get it out of the back for you?"

He grabbed a hand basket and was picking up his usual chicken and veggies when his gaze caught on a magazine cover. Stopping dead, he put down the basket and grabbed the glossy magazine, hardly able to believe his eyes.

The girl from the cliffs was on the cover.

In most ways she barely looked like the woman wearing tons of mascara and blood-red lipstick and dripping with jewelry—but he'd just stared into those eyes and he couldn't be mistaken.

As much as he sometimes wished he could, he didn't live under a rock, so he knew the Bouchards were the reality TV family on the networks these days. He'd never seen their show, however, and had never met any of them in person either. Not until—the magazine said her name was Rosalind, which didn't seem quite right, though he couldn't pinpoint why—Rosalind showed up out of the blue on the cliffs this morning.

His gut clenched as the headline finally registered. *America's Favorite Bad Girl: Nude Photo Scandal? Or Another Brilliant Business Move for the Bouchards?*

Was that why she'd been crying? Why she'd hurled her phone over the edge? Why she looked so bleak?

He'd never taken naked pictures on his phone, but he knew plenty of people did it. Had some sexy photos she'd taken for a boyfriend been hacked into and broadcast for the whole world to see?

Drake had enough brushes with fame—and enough famous relatives—to know there was likely less than ten percent truth to anything written in this magazine. But where he'd just barely managed to keep from painting her, now there was no way he could stop himself from flipping open the magazine and reading the article.

It took less than a paragraph to make him angry. According to the article, someone on one of her TV crews had secretly placed cameras throughout her hotel room on location in the Virgin Islands—and then the scumbag had sold them for an "unverified but hefty" sum to the worst gossip site on the Web, which had then resold the pictures everywhere possible. Evidently, her family was "furious" and "working to prosecute the man who took and sold the pictures, to the furthest extent of the law." Rosalind was "recuperating from the shock" and couldn't be reached for comment.

Recuperating? Like hell she was. She was sobbing and shivering on a clifftop fifteen hundred miles from Miami.

In this magazine, the stolen pictures had been reprinted with red stars over the most private parts of Rosalind's body, but they didn't really hide anything.

And Drake hated himself for looking.

He slapped the magazine shut and shoved it into the back of the stand behind an issue of *Log Home*. But her beautiful face—and barely covered body—was on the covers of half a dozen others.

As soon as he'd seen her walking along the cliffs, he'd known something was wrong. If only it had just been a bad breakup. Because Drake couldn't imagine how eviscerating it would feel to have something like this happen. A muscle jumped in his jaw as he brought his groceries over to the counter where Mona was waiting with his apple pie.

"Anyone you're planning to share this pie with?"

she asked as she rang him up.

Unbidden, Rosalind's face popped into his head. "Not unless one of my siblings drops by unannounced. I'm here to focus on painting, just like always."

"I suppose a strapping young man like you must have all the girlfriends you can handle in the city, don't you?"

He forced a smile. "I'll see you in a few days, Mona."

Rain was still coming down as he headed back out to his car. He hadn't seen a storm like this in years. Visibility was so bad as he pulled out of the parking lot that he wouldn't be able to drive safely at much more than fifteen miles an hour.

He'd been planning to head straight back to his cottage to force himself to get some work done even if it killed him, but he couldn't stop thinking about Rosalind. Her family had told the press that they were helping her through her ordeal. But was that actually true? From what Drake had seen, it sure didn't seem to be.

What's more, he doubted someone from Miami would be used to driving in this kind of fog, with its low visibility. Hating the thought of something else happening to her, he turned left out of the parking lot in the same direction she'd gone a few minutes earlier, rather than heading back toward home. It wasn't likely that he'd run into her again, but he couldn't live with himself if he didn't at least check to make sure something hadn't happened to her or her car in the storm.

Less than five minutes later, when he saw her car on the side of the road, he knew his gut had been right.

He pulled up behind the old car and got out, expecting to see her sitting inside waiting for help. But she was nowhere to be seen.

Was she actually walking on the side of the road in this weather?

Cursing, he ran back to his car, put it into gear, then pulled back onto the narrow two-lane road, squinting through the thick rain and fog in which his windshield wipers and headlights were barely making a dent. Finally—thank God—he saw her walking a hundred feet ahead with her head down and her shoulders hunched against the force of the rain.

The last thing he wanted to do was accidentally skid into her, so he carefully pulled to the side of the road again before jumping out of his car. "Rosalind!"

Even through the fog, he swore he could see how big, how scared her eyes were as she turned at the sound of her name. A beat later, she started moving even faster down the road, away from him.

He didn't blame her for running, considering what had happened. But that didn't mean he could let her stay out here on a seriously dangerous stretch of road in the middle of a storm.

For the second time in one day, he went running after her. Only this time he didn't stop halfway there. Not when he knew precisely how much she needed someone to help her.

He didn't know what he expected her to do when he caught up to her and put a hand on her arm, but it definitely wasn't dropping the bag she was holding and whirling around with her fists raised as she yelled, "Go away!"

My God, she was beautiful. And so damned fierce, even when scared and soaking wet, that he now knew for sure exactly where her beauty came from. Not the perfect lines of her jaw. Not the lush curves of her mouth. Not even her incredible figure.

No, it was *strength* that underlay every other part of her. So much strength that she literally took his breath away.

But just because she was strong didn't mean she wouldn't be worried about being out in the middle of nowhere with a man who was a good foot taller and eighty pounds heavier.

"I'm not going to hurt you," he promised her in a voice loud enough to carry over the rain hammering the pavement. "But walking on the side of the road in this storm isn't safe."

"I've been fine so far."

Drake had no doubt whatsoever that she would be fine again one day soon, but sometimes it didn't matter how strong you were—you still needed help to get over the worst parts. "I saw your car on the side of the road a half mile back. I can help by taking you where you're trying to go."

He could see how much she hated needing to accept his offer. But no one could deny the danger in their spot on the side of the narrow road.

Still, she didn't answer him with words, simply bent down to pick up her soaked bag. Since it had already torn most of the way through, the slightest touch was all it took for the brown paper to split completely. Everything rolled out, with a pack of underwear landing on his foot, followed a moment later by a couple of oranges.

Maybe it was the last straw on a terrible day, because she simply stood there and stared at the mess. Moving quickly, Drake bent down and picked up everything. The TV dinners, tourist shirts and sweats, and especially the underwear, toothbrush, and toothpaste, told him that she hadn't planned this trip. She'd obviously needed to get the hell away from Miami and had somehow ended up in Montauk.

The only items that didn't make sense were the colorful spools of thread and the sewing needles. If the magazine article was to be believed, she didn't have any skills or interests apart from her growing beauty empire. Then again, given the ridiculously embellished stories he'd read about his father and mother over the years, Drake knew better than to believe anything he read.

Hoping she'd follow him now that he had her things, he headed for his car. Fortunately, by the time he opened the passenger door and threw her things in, she was only a step behind him. He held open the door for her until she was safely inside.

It wasn't until he was behind the steering wheel that he realized just how small a car could be with only two people inside it, especially with the windows steaming up on the inside.

"I'm Drake Sullivan."

It was a little strange to finally tell her his name when it felt like they'd already been through so much together today. But that wasn't actually true, was it? *She* was the one who had been through the wringer. All he'd had to deal with was his painter's block...and the relentless urge to end it by capturing her face and body on canvas.

"You acted like you didn't know who I was at the grocery store."

"I didn't. I saw your face on a magazine, and that's when I realized who you are."

"*Please*." She turned to him in supplication. No longer fierce. No longer furious. "Please don't tell anyone I'm here. I'll give you whatever you want. As much money as you want, just to keep this quiet."

"I don't want your money." How could she think he would? Then again, she didn't know him, did she? Didn't know anything at all about him—even though he'd just seen pictures of her getting in and out of a bathtub. "I'm sorry for what happened to you."

"You feel sorry *for* me?"

"Not sorry for you." He wanted to make sure she understood that. He didn't pity her. She was clearly too resilient for his—or anyone else's—pity. "But what happened to you? It was wrong. Really wrong. If something like that happened to my sister—" He gritted his teeth. "I'd want to kill the guy who took those pictures."

"You've—" The word broke, and she slumped back into the seat in a defeated pose. "Of course you've seen them. The whole world has seen them by now."

"If I could take back looking at them, Rosalind, I would."

"Rosa." The one word from her lips was so quiet he almost couldn't hear it. "Rosa is my real name."

"Rosa." It fit her so much better than Rosalind. "Rosa," he said again, just to feel her name on his own lips.

Had anyone ever tugged at him like this? If so, he couldn't remember. Then again, these were some pretty crazy circumstances, weren't they?

Of all the cliffs, in all the parks, in all the world, she'd walked onto his.

"I can help. My family—"

"No!" The word *family* seemed to snap her back to life. Back to *fierce*. "I don't want your family involved. I'll figure things out on my own. All I want right now is somewhere to clean up and rest for a few hours before I make my next move. When I was a kid, there was a motel pretty close to here. It would be great if you could take me there."

"The Seaside Motel is still there. But there are nicer places in town."

"No!" The word was infused with panic. "The Seaside Motel is good enough."

Even if the magazine article had been ninety-nine percent lies, Drake knew one thing for certain—the woman in his passenger seat was rich. Really rich. One-thousand-thread-count sheets had to be her standard, not whatever faded cotton was on the ancient beds at the Seaside Motel. But instead of pushing her on it, he said, "I have a friend who can help tow your car. Joe won't ask any questions. And he can fix it for you too."

Her "Thank you," was heartfelt, but soft. Almost as if she felt she didn't deserve his kindness. As if she actually thought it was her fault some creep had taken and sold those pictures of her.

"I have money, but I can't really get to it right now without people tracking m—" She cut herself off as though she suddenly realized she was saying too much. "All I've got on me right now is some cash, so hopefully your friend's work on my car won't be too expensive."

"Don't worry, Joe doesn't rip people off."

Finally starting his car and pulling onto the road, they drove the short mile to the motel in heavy silence. When he pulled into the parking lot, she asked again, "You won't tell anyone I'm here, will you?"

He understood the urge to get away from real life. It was part of the reason he'd bought his cottage. Yes, it was a quiet place to paint, but more than that, it was the perfect way to escape from the pressure that came with his painful legacy as William Sullivan's son. Even so, he didn't have the first clue how to deal with her situation.

"I won't tell a soul, Rosa."

He wasn't prepared for her small smile—or for the way his heart turned over in his chest at the pure sweetness of her beauty.

"There's an extra car key hidden under the driver's seat." She licked her lips, biting the lower one before saying, "I owe you. Big-time."

With that, she gathered up her things in her arms and got out of the car. He waited until he was sure that she'd arranged for a room on the second floor before slowly driving back to his cottage.

He'd tried like hell to forget her this morning, but now that he'd met her and knew even the smallest details of her situation?

There was no chance at all he'd ever forget her now.

And there was no way he wasn't going to try to help, even if they never had more than that five-minute conversation. First by calling Joe to take care of her car, then with a second call to his cousin Smith, who just happened to be one of the biggest movie stars in the world.

Drake knew how busy Smith was writing, producing, and starring in movies. But when it came to family, his cousin always made it a point to pick up the phone.

"Drake, great to hear from you."

"How's Valentina?"

"Beautiful, like always."

Drake could easily hear the love—and the pride—in his cousin's voice when he spoke of his fiancée. Valentina and Smith worked together on all their movies now and were currently in the running for an Oscar for their first co-venture, a love story set on Alcatraz.

Not wanting to waste his cousin's limited time, Drake got right to it. "I've got a favor to ask."

"Sure, what do you need?"

"Have you heard of the photo scandal involving Rosalind Bouchard?"

"Who hasn't?" Smith sounded disgusted. "Hollywood can be a good place to work, but you wouldn't know it from looking at what can happen to people like her. Why do you ask? Is she a friend of yours?"

"No, she's not." A five-minute conversation in

his car didn't make them friends. But that didn't change the fact that Drake felt compelled to help her. "I'd still like to know if you, or anyone else, has the power to make those pictures disappear."

Smith made a frustrated sound. "Honestly, it's unlikely. Once pictures are out on the Internet, they're pretty much impossible to pull out of circulation. But I would think her family is already dealing with it."

"Whether they are or not," Drake said, his words growing more agitated despite himself, "if there's anything you can do, I'd appreciate it. I wish I could explain more right now, but I'm afraid I can't."

"I'm on it."

And that was it. No more questions. No hedging or waffling. Just Smith's promise to help in any way he could. That was the magic of being a Sullivan—they were always there for one another, no matter what.

Drake wished like hell that Rosa could say the same about her own family.

CHAPTER FIVE

When Rosa woke the next morning, she was momentarily surprised by the faded drapes, the old diamond-pattern wallpaper, and the double bed with the orange and gold comforter.

Too soon, everything came back to her. The photos. The things her mother had said. Getting in her old car and driving nearly twenty-four hours straight, only stopping for gas a couple of times along the way. Crying out on the cliffs. Her car breaking down.

And then, Drake Sullivan.

A little sigh escaped her, just from quietly saying his name in her head.

He'd been right—walking on the side of the road hadn't been smart. But she'd had to do *something*. Had to at least try to save herself, instead of giving in at the first sign of adversity. Especially when the truth was that she'd already given in for far too long...

Drake had been her knight in shining armor, modern-day style. And amazingly, even through her haze of frustration and panic, she'd been unable to ignore her reaction to him. He was simply that sexy, even by Hollywood standards, his muscles defined by the wet clothes that stuck to him. Yet again, she worked to shake him out of her head. She had so many far more important things to worry about than some hot guy.

Yesterday, she'd headed straight for the warm shower as soon as she'd checked into the motel under a false name, paid in cash, then dead-bolted the door behind her. She'd stood beneath the spray until the water had started to go cold. The new clothes she'd just bought had been too wet to put on after falling out of her bag, so she'd simply wrapped a towel around herself, wrung her clothes out and hung them up to dry in the bathroom, then heated up one of the TV dinners in the microwave. Even in the midst of this mess, she was starved, which was clearly why her body would never be anything but curvy. After wolfing down her food, she'd planned to blow-dry her clothes, but she was so tired that she crawled into bed instead.

Every single second she'd been in the room, she'd had to work like crazy to ignore the TV set on the scratched dresser across from the bed. It was crazy, wasn't it, that even when she knew no good could come of turning it on and seeing what the various entertainment shows were saying about her, it had only been the sheer magnitude of her exhaustion that had actually kept her from doing it? She was tempted to ask the guy at the front desk to take it out of her room so that she didn't give in to temptation. But since she couldn't risk drawing unnecessary attention to herself, she would just have to control her self-destructive impulses.

Now, as she came fully awake, she reached for her phone on the nightstand to see what time it was. But she didn't have her phone anymore. It felt so weird to be without what had essentially become her security blanket over the past five years. But there was something freeing about not having it too. For once, she couldn't go online to see what people were saying about her and end up with her stomach twisting at the horrible things they so often said. This morning she didn't have to document her every move—what she was eating, putting on, looking at.

For a few precious moments, she could just *be*.

Surprisingly, she'd had a better night's sleep in this dingy motel room than she'd had in any five-star penthouse suite. Feeling halfway normal again, she grabbed an apple and took a bite out of it as she went to the window and pulled back the curtain a couple of inches. It was still drizzling, but she could tell that it was early morning, rather than late evening.

Had she really slept for more than twelve hours?

Finishing her apple, she tossed the core into the wastebasket, then got back in the shower. *God, that felt good.* She'd never take feeling warm for granted again. Her clothes were almost dry, but instead of putting her too-tight jeans back on, she fluffed her new Montauk-themed sweatpants and sweatshirt with the blow-dryer and slipped them on over a new pair of cotton undies and her bra. Her clothes from the general store were a little big, but it was actually nice to wear something that didn't cling to her skin like plastic wrap.

She heated up another microwave dinner, made a cup of coffee in the coffee maker, and sat on the bed to have breakfast and come up with a plan. All the while, however, she couldn't forget about the darned television.

What would it really hurt to turn it on just for a few minutes? After all, if she was going to make a plan, it would probably help to have more data as to just how bad things were, right?

No, a voice inside her head warned her, *don't do it!*

Normally, when the press said nasty things about her, she was able to tell herself that they were simply talking about a character she'd been playing for the cameras. Rosalind Bouchard, who liked glittering parties and front-row seats at international fashion shows, not the real Rosa, who was happiest in a quiet room with a needle and thread.

But she hadn't been Rosalind in the pictures that guy had taken without her consent—hadn't been posing, hadn't had her mask on, her armor to face the public. She'd already stripped all that away by the time he took the pictures. And in some ways, that was what made her feel the most naked of all. Not just exposing the parts of her body that the public had never seen before, but the real version of herself that she had always been careful not to give away to anyone she didn't know and care about.

Turning on the TV would only lead to more

regret. Regret she simply couldn't deal with right now on top of the shame that had fueled her every move so far. Which was why she got up off the bed, went into the bathroom, and came out with a dry towel to drape over the screen. It wasn't a perfect solution, but it helped a little bit, at least.

Sitting back down with her slightly congealed microwave meal, she took a deep breath and tried to focus on what her next step should be. The problem was that she didn't yet know what, precisely, she wanted. Because turning back time so that the naked photos had never been taken wasn't a plan she could actually act on.

Could she go back to her current life, or was it time to make a change? If so, what kind of change could she possibly make when the entire world thought she was only capable of being a "bad girl"? And if she did leave reality TV, how deeply would it affect her family? Would they lose the show? Would she lose them?

Or had she already lost them long before now, when their TV show and brand had become more important than protecting one of their own from true harm?

For eight years after Rosa's father passed away, her mother had worked double shifts at the two hospitals in town as a nurse to try to make ends meet. Unfortunately, it simply wasn't enough to withstand the crushing debt their father's death had left them in when his aerial reporting company failed after his death. The day the casting agent had "discovered" their family in town had seemed like manna from heaven.

But none of them could possibly have imagined

how five years could change everything yet again. Still, the fact remained that, whichever way she chose to go, Rosa wasn't sure if she could forgive her mother for selling her out.

Voices in the parking lot outside her room drew her off the bed and back to the window. Peering out from between the curtains, she was surprised to see her car parked at the edge of the lot. She wanted to thank the guy getting back into his tow truck—Drake had said his name was Joe—but she couldn't risk being recognized again. While she hoped she could trust Drake to keep his promise about not disclosing her whereabouts to anyone, she knew the odds were low that a second person would be willing to keep her secret.

Maybe it was foolish to trust Drake when she'd been betrayed so many times recently. Maybe she was mistaking his good looks for a good heart.

Or maybe it was just that she *needed* to believe in something—anything—right now.

In any case, as great a refuge as this motel room had been last night, she couldn't spend the whole day here. Especially with the TV set still beckoning to her to turn it on and see exactly how bad the fallout from the pictures was.

With the sky having cleared, for a little while at least, maybe she could find a stretch of empty beach somewhere nearby without too much risk of discovery. Somewhere she could stretch her legs a bit and hopefully get her brain working again.

As she caught sight of herself in the mirror on the back of the bathroom door, she nearly broke out laughing at how ridiculous she looked in her head-to-toe Montauk gear. One thing was for sure—no one would even think of looking for Rosalind Bouchard in these clothes. No makeup or hairstyling helped too.

Only her purse—next season's Versace satchel—might give her away. Slipping some twenties into the pocket of her sweatpants, she grabbed her car keys and left her purse in the room. Feeling a little like she was in a spy movie, she made sure no one else was in the parking lot before going to her car. She'd been lucky that the guy manning the motel office last night had been a contemporary of the woman behind the register at the general store, and she hoped he would remain just as uninterested in her today as he'd seemed yesterday.

She was about to unlock her car when she stopped with her key still in the door. There was an envelope on the seat. Her brain immediately raced with a dozen possibilities—most of which centered around her fear that Joe, or someone else at his garage, had figured out who she was and was now interested in seeing exactly what he could squeeze out of her for his silence. It wouldn't be hard to run her plates, but she'd hoped that Drake's kindness would extend to the guy he'd called in to help her.

Her hands were shaking as she finally unlocked the door and picked up the envelope. She'd never seen a blackmailer's note in person before. Then again, she thought as she pulled out the note, the past couple of days had contained plenty of terrible firsts for her.

The bill for repairs and towing is taken care of.

Call if you have any other problems with the car. - Joe

Relief swept through her. Not only because it wasn't a blackmailer's note—but also because she hadn't been wrong about Drake being a good person.

Actually, her feelings about Drake weren't entirely about relief. Rather, she was feeling an emotion she couldn't quite pinpoint. Some combination of gratitude and attraction.

Well, now she knew what she needed to do next. She needed to find Drake and pay him back. Sure, she could find his address in the phone book and mail him the money, but the truth was she couldn't resist seeing him again. Couldn't stop herself from wanting to know if he was as handsome and kind after her full night's rest as he'd been when she was freaking out and losing it.

Her car started right up, and as she headed toward the cliffs again, if she tried really hard she could almost pretend that she was on vacation and simply enjoying a beautiful day in a seaside town. She couldn't pretend forever, but she wouldn't begrudge herself a few minutes of forgetting in the car.

She entered the state park, then parked in the same spot where she'd left her car the day before to head toward the cliffs via the same unused storm drain her father had showed her so long ago. She hadn't seen a house in the woods yesterday, but she hadn't been looking for one either. Now, she scanned the trees until a small brown cabin finally came into view. It didn't take her long to get to Drake's front door, at which point she suddenly realized that just as she should definitely not turn on the TV in her motel room, she probably shouldn't have given in to the urge to come here either.

But before she could turn around and hightail it out of there, the door opened.

"Rosa?"

Oh my. She definitely hadn't exaggerated his good looks yesterday. Or his rugged physique. Or the concern in his eyes as he said, "Are you okay?"

No, she wasn't okay. Not by a long shot. So rather than answering his question, she said, "I wanted to pay you back for the car repairs and towing."

"Don't worry about it. You don't have to."

But she'd stopped listening a couple of words back, because to his left she could see a couple of canvases up on easels in the living room.

And her likeness was painted on both of them.

CHAPTER SIX

"Why are you painting me?"

Drake was so surprised to see Rosa standing on his doorstep that his brain pretty much stopped working—just the way it had every other time he'd looked into her eyes. Which was why it took him far longer than it should have to realize that she was pointing at his canvases.

At *herself* on his canvases, damn it!

Even worse, every answer he could think of sounded lamer than the next.

I was blocked until I saw you.

These paintings are just studies to see if I can get my mojo back.

You're the most beautiful woman I've ever set eyes on.

No, he definitely couldn't tell her that. Not when he knew for a fact that her beauty had brought her more bad than good, at least in the past week.

She'd pushed past him by then and was standing directly in front of the painting he'd just been working on. She stared hard at it for a few long moments before whirling back to face him. "Why?"

In the end, he didn't have anything for her but the truth. "I couldn't help myself."

His honesty seemed to disarm her a little. "Oh!" She jumped as a wet nose pressed into her hand. She looked down to find Oscar gazing up at her in his characteristically serious way. "Where did you come from?"

"That's Oscar."

Most people who met Drake's dog took one look at his big body and sober expression and assumed he was vicious. But Rosa immediately got down on the ground and began to stroke his ears. "Aren't you sweet?"

Oscar's eyes were all but rolling back in his head from the extreme pleasure of having such beautiful hands stroking his fur. As woman and dog connected with each other, the bright halo of fiery color that Drake always saw when he looked at Rosa began to shift to a calmer blue-green. But instead of continuing to let herself relax, she gave Oscar one more sweet stroke over his big head, then stood to face Drake again.

"Normally, I would be flattered that someone as talented as you had painted me. But the way things are right now, I just can't allow you to—"

"I'm not going to sell them." He needed her to know he wasn't looking to exploit her the way everyone else was. "I promise you that's not why I'm painting you."

She frowned. "Why else would you do it?"

He hadn't admitted to anyone just how bad his block had become. Yes, his siblings and agent knew he wasn't exactly having a good run of it, but he hadn't actually told anyone that inspiration—hell, even the urge to paint—had completely dried up.

But Rosa was going through more than enough crap already. He'd never forgive himself if he added to it. Which, unfortunately, meant that he was going to have to take the truth yet another level deeper.

"When I saw you out on the cliffs—that was the first time I've wanted to paint in months."

"I don't understand." Her frown deepened. "You said you didn't know who I was, that you only learned my name because of a magazine. So why would seeing me on the cliffs make you want to paint again?"

He ran a hand through his hair, tempted to pour himself a shot of Irish whiskey before answering her. But then she'd probably think he was an alcoholic stalker, rather than merely fixated on painting her.

"I've been painting since I was a kid. I was sixteen when I had my first major show. Painting was never work for me, never a struggle. It was just something I always loved doing." None of this was meant as bragging, just the facts, so that she'd understand where he was coming from. "I never thought I'd hit a block. I was careful to make sure I didn't." He knew that part wouldn't make any sense to her, but it was nice, for once, not to be judged by his mother and father's tragic love story. "But it didn't matter how hard I tried to make sure inspiration didn't slip away. It still left. I've been here for two months trying to get it back. Praying for it. Yesterday I had all but given up on it." Holding her gaze, he was struck to the core again from nothing more than being in the same room with her. Even in her Montauk sweatshirt and sweatpants, she was hands down the most beautiful woman he'd ever set eyes on. "And then there you were."

She didn't say anything for several long moments, just stared at him. "You could paint someone else."

"I don't paint people. Ever." When she raised an eyebrow in the direction of his canvases, he had to laugh at himself, though there was no humor in the sound. "I tried like hell to keep from painting you. I swear it. But I couldn't."

Oscar hadn't left her side, and she began to stroke his fur again as she asked, "What about now?"

He knew what she was asking him—if he'd stop painting her now that she'd caught him in the act. But just having her standing in his cabin had already put a dozen new paintings into his head. More than anything, he wanted to study her longer, wanted to explore the varying shades of brown in her hair, the way her expression changed so quickly from frustration to curiosity, the sensual tilt of her exotic eyes and cheekbones, the way she dampened her lower lip when she pulled it between her teeth as she listened closely to what he was saying.

"I should stop. For both of us." He didn't want to lie to her. But he didn't want to hurt her either. "It's not good enough to tell you I'll try. I know that." And yet, he couldn't get the words out to promise her that he'd stop.

"You're a really successful artist, aren't you?"

She held up the hand that wasn't buried in Oscar's fur. "Actually, you don't need to answer that. I can see how good you are."

He'd been praised a thousand times in his career. But no compliment had ever hit him the way hers did. As though he'd just passed the most important test of his life.

"I do all right."

"Save me your modesty," she said with a roll of her eyes, an expression that seemed more relaxed than anything he'd seen so far. "So collectors are probably lining up to buy your work, but you're promising not to sell these paintings of me you've started."

"Yes."

"And you want to make more?"

In a decade and a half of serious painting, he'd kept his vow not to paint women. But he'd never seen Rosa coming. Never realized that he'd one day come to a point where the only thing he could say was, "I do."

Oscar made a soft snorting noise as he shoved his head even harder under her hand. She looked down at his dog. "You're a glutton for pleasure, aren't you?" she said as she knelt on the floor to give him some serious loving.

Drake had never been jealous of a dog, had never even thought it could be possible. But Lord, if he wasn't wishing he could change places with his lazy furball.

After a good sixty seconds of focusing on Oscar, she stood and turned her attention back to Drake. "You've stood by everything you've promised so far, but—" She stopped in mid-sentence. "I want to trust you. I mean, you were so great about my car and not telling anyone

I'm here. In fact, that's why I came." She pulled a bunch of twenties out of her pocket. "To pay you back. And to thank you for being so kind to a stranger."

"You don't need to pay me back."

"I do. And I know this can't possibly be enough to cover the repairs and towing, but I didn't want you to think I wasn't good for it. As soon as I can get access to more money, I'll—"

"I don't need your money."

His words came out louder than he intended, and Oscar actually bared his teeth a little. As though his own dog felt he needed to protect Rosa from his owner.

Damn it, just because not picking up his paintbrush and painting Rosa while she stood in his living room was one of the hardest things Drake had ever done, that was no excuse for being an asshole.

But before he could apologize, she said, "If you won't take my money, how can I possibly pay you back?"

"You don't owe me anything."

"I do. Tell me what I can do, Drake. Tell me what you want."

As a rule, Sullivans tended to be pretty stubborn. Especially about making sure they didn't take advantage of anyone else. Rosa was clearly no shrinking violet either when it came to doing what she felt was the right thing.

"I want to paint you."

The words were out before he could stop them. Before he could remind himself just how bad an idea it was for a Sullivan to paint a beautiful female muse—if his mother and father's destructive history was anything to go by.

Drake's only saving grace in his dearth of self-control was his utter certainty that she'd say no. Rosa was a reality TV star in hiding. Sitting for a painter would be the very last thing she'd want to do.

But she wasn't shaking her head. Wasn't looking at him as if he'd lost his mind. Instead, she was petting Oscar again, scrunching her fingers in the fur on top of his head while he gave the happiest dog moan Drake had ever thought to hear.

"I can't believe I'm about to say this," she finally said, "but if you want to paint me, I'll let you."

Drake had never wanted anything so badly. *Never*. But at the same time, he couldn't stand the thought of being just another person to carve his pound of flesh from her. "Having your car towed and fixed was no big deal. You don't have to offer to be my muse as a trade. I couldn't sleep at night if I thought I was forcing you to do something you don't want to do."

"That's a first for me."

Those five words were all it took for fury to rise up in him again. He'd never felt this close to violence, never wanted to hunt someone down as badly as he wanted to track down the guy who'd taken and sold those pictures of her and tear him to shreds. Not just that guy. *Everyone* who had hurt Rosa, who had made her this cynical, this afraid to trust. Family was supposed to be there for you, but she obviously hadn't gone running to hers. She'd run in the opposite direction instead.

But before he could force himself to let her go, she said, "Maybe a trade for your help with the car and keeping my presence in town a secret isn't the only reason I want to stay." She turned back to his paintings, looked first at one, then the other. "Maybe it's because the woman on your canvases isn't the one on any of the magazine covers."

He finally took the risk of moving closer to her, close enough that he could see her gnawing on her lower lip again as she tried to explain her motivations for offering to stay and let him paint her.

"People have been taking pictures of me for years. But they've always wanted me to look a certain way. It was fun at first to feel like I was putting on a show, playing a character. But then, somewhere along the way, that character became the one everyone thought was real." She shook her head. "God, listen to me. I really should have put my tiny violin away before I said all that."

"It can sit next to mine." He'd just done plenty of his own complaining about losing his muse and inspiration, but since no one had taken and sold naked pictures of him without his knowledge, he figured he was the lucky one here.

Her soft laughter—so unexpected and beautiful— rocked through him. And not just as the guy who wanted to paint her.

No, right now it was the guy who wanted to *kiss* her who was standing front and center.

He hadn't been able to keep from asking her to let him paint her, but the urge to kiss her was so strong he had to force himself to take a step back. And then another. She'd agreed to sit for him, not to sleep with him. And when her stomach growled, he felt like a total idiot. Why hadn't he thought she might be hungry? He'd seen what she'd bought at the general store. It hadn't had enough nutritional value to keep a fly alive.

"I've got a lasagna in the freezer. I can heat it up for us. And Mona from the general store saved me an apple pie."

Her lips quirked up at the corner in a surprised little smile. "I am pretty hungry."

"Then I'll go put the lasagna in."

"And I'll get ready to pose." She scrunched up her face. "Or not pose, if that's what you want."

He could still hardly believe she'd agreed to sit for him. Or that he was actually going to paint her when it went against every professional and personal vow he'd ever made.

"Are you sure about this?" Even as he said the words, he knew he was asking more than that.

"Honestly," she said in a soft voice, "I'm not really sure about anything right now." Oscar leaned even harder against her legs, and she wobbled while trying to stay upright. "Apart from how awesome your dog is. But I do know that I don't want to leave your cabin. Not until I've had some real food. So if you want to paint me while I'm here..."

He all but ran to the freezer, grabbed the lasagna, shoved it into the oven, then grabbed a sketchbook. "It'll be enough today just to make some drawings."

Her eyebrow rose at his use of the word *today*, but all she said was, "Will it work if I sit over there?"

The leather club chair by the fire was where he

sat and read at night. Her scent would cling to it—hell, her gorgeous essence had already permeated the entire cabin. "Sit. Stand. Pace the room if you want. Whatever you do will work for me."

She headed over to the chair with Oscar tripping over her heels. As soon as she sat, he climbed up into her lap and dwarfed her while she laughed, a louder, stronger sound this time.

"Oscar," Drake warned, motioning for his big lump of a dog to get off.

"He's okay."

"I've never seen him like this." Oscar had always been a fairly aloof dog. He liked people, but didn't cling. Not until today, when he seemed desperate to be as close to Rosa as possible. The thing was, Drake couldn't really blame him—she was the kind of woman you couldn't help but want to be close to.

"If your legs start to go numb, or you just want to shove him off, say the word and I'll make sure he knows your lap is off-limits."

When Oscar lifted his head and gave her a woeful look, she said, "Don't worry, cutie, you can stay right where you are for as long as you like."

Cutie? Had she just called his one-hundred-and-fifty-pound behemoth of a dog *cutie*?

She turned back to Drake. "Do I need to look at you while you sketch?"

Having already begun to draw, it took him a few moments for her question to register in his brain. "You don't have to look at me if you don't want to. Just having you here is more than enough." So much more than he thought he'd ever get. And he couldn't stop staring and drawing. Staring and drawing. Staring and drawing.

"I've never met anyone quite like you." She truly did sound perplexed. "Easygoing and intense at the same time. Safe, but also kind of dangerous."

"Dangerous?" His hand stilled over the sketchbook. He'd heard both *intense* and *easygoing* before, but *dangerous* was a new one. The last thing he wanted was for her to feel as though she was in any danger from him.

She rubbed a hand over her eyes. "Sorry, none of that was supposed to actually come out of my mouth. I think I'm still tired, or loopy, or something. I didn't mean *dangerous* in a bad way. I meant it more in a se—" Her cheeks colored as she cut herself off. "Never mind, forget I said anything."

She'd almost told him she thought he was sexy. How was he supposed to forget that? Sure, plenty of women had said that over the years. But he hadn't been trying like hell to resist any of them.

Only her.

"I've never met anyone like you either, Rosa." A woman who was soft and fierce, broken and strong, all at the same time.

"You mean you haven't had any other run-ins with reality TV stars whose naked pictures are plastered all over the media?"

He hated the sarcastic tint to her voice, hating most of all that the vitriol was clearly aimed at herself. "You didn't ask that douchebag to take those pictures of you." He didn't bother to contain the heat behind his words. "Don't you dare blame yourself for it."

"See," she said softly as sparks jumped high and hot between them, "that's the dangerous side I was talking about."

It took everything he had to stay where he was and draw her, when all he wanted was to steal her away from his dog, drag her into his arms, and kiss her until both of them forgot why they shouldn't.

CHAPTER SEVEN

For the past five years, everything Rosa did, everything she said, every picture taken of her, every meeting—all of it was intended to build up her media profile so high that she could guarantee her family would never be on the verge of ruin again.

But the past forty-eight hours couldn't have been more different from the life she'd become accustomed to. Driving all night from Miami to New York in an old sedan. No cell phone. Deliberately staying out of sight of the paparazzi. Sleeping at a roadside motel after eating a TV dinner.

And now *Drake*.

Technically, she wasn't doing anything more than sitting on a leather club chair staring out at the ocean. Maybe it shouldn't have felt like she was breaking all the rules. Maybe it should have felt like no big deal.

But it didn't feel like no big deal.

It felt *huge*.

Forty-eight hours ago, her agreement to pose for a painter would have come with a twenty-page contract and a price tag in the multiple hundred thousands. And she wouldn't have been sitting here in too-big sweats— she would have been dressed to the nines, in couture and full makeup. Her PR team would have been hovering over the painter, watching every stroke of his brush to make sure she looked good enough that the painting couldn't possibly harm her future net worth.

She was breaking every single rule that her mother had set up early in the game to benefit all of them. Only, in many ways, hadn't those rules stopped making sense once they had more than enough money in the bank to ensure they'd never need to worry about where their next meal was coming from? And if so, why hadn't Rosa and her mom and two younger brothers sat down together and made some positive changes? Changes that would have given them all more time to truly be themselves—or, in Rosa's case, time to figure out who she was now that she was no longer a frightened eighteen-year-old willing to do whatever it took to keep her family together.

This was the first chunk of time, the first bit of space that she'd had in five years in which to make some big decisions about her future. And if she was going to make a big change, she wanted it to be the right one. Not some rash reaction because she was mad or sad or scared. Or helplessly attracted to a gorgeous painter.

Fact was, so much had happened in the past forty-eight hours that she wasn't sure she could trust any of her instincts at the moment. Not even when the warmth of the fire felt so good...and Drake's hot gaze felt even better.

She stole a look at him from beneath her lashes, then felt herself flush as he caught her checking him out. How could he not, when he was watching her so closely? But it was more than just watching. It was as though he was drinking her in, one slow, sweet glance at a time.

The absolute last thing she needed right now was to get involved with a guy. Of course she wasn't going to do anything *stupid*. Her world already had way more than its fair share of stupid in it at this point. But that didn't mean she couldn't be curious, did it? And since she was already sitting here, what could it hurt to learn more about the man drawing her as though his life depended on it?

"Why don't you paint people?"

More than a little discomfort registered on his face as his pencil stilled over the sketchbook. "It's a long story."

"I like long stories." Everything in her life had been boiled down to thirty-minute episodes, two-minute interviews, six-second video clips. An actual story that took a while to tell felt wonderfully fresh by contrast. "The promise goes both ways, you know. You won't tell anyone about me and I won't tell anyone about you."

His gaze grew sharper, even more intense. "My story has never been a secret."

"What do you mean?"

"My father is a painter too. A really well-known, respected artist. At least he was until my mother walked out on him six months after I was born, then took her life. The story is up for anyone to see on Wikipedia, timeline and everything."

He said it as if he were totally over it, as if it not only didn't bother him that his mother was gone— but also that a major part of his life story was clinically detailed on an Internet encyclopedia site as if there were no human beings with feelings behind it. But how could that be? Rosa might have big issues with her mother right now, but at least her mom had made sure they stayed a family even in those difficult years after Dad had passed away and they hadn't been able to figure out how they were going to keep paying the mortgage *and* the grocery bill.

"I'm sorry, Drake." Though she barely knew him, she ached for his loss. No child should ever have to lose a parent so young. And she knew firsthand how hard it was to deal with people writing about you on the Internet.

"My siblings, and especially my father, were destroyed when she left and passed away. I always figured I was the lucky one because I never really had a chance to know her."

She hated that he'd had to try to find the silver lining. "How many brothers and sisters do you have?"

"Two brothers and a sister."

"You're close, aren't you?"

He smiled. "How'd you guess?"

"Your voice, your expression—talking about them clearly makes you happy."

"We're a pretty tight unit," he agreed. "We had

to be."

"I lost my father when I was a kid." Suddenly, she needed to share that with him. "So I know how hard it can be to get by with only one parent left. Your cliffs were my special place with my dad." But since she still wasn't yet ready to dig too deeply into her own story—past, present, or future—she asked, "Is that how you found this spot? Because of your father?"

"No."

His voice was clipped. Definitely different from the way he spoke about his siblings. Did that mean the tight unit didn't extend to his father?

"My cousin Mia is a Realtor in Seattle. She got a tip about this place coming up on the market for the first time since it was built as a hunting cabin fifty years ago. She's the master of knowing just what people need."

"I could use someone like her in my life right about now." Though Rosa said it softly, she already knew that Drake didn't miss a thing. "How long did it take your father to recover from losing your mom?"

"He hasn't."

Her eyebrows went up. "But it's been thirty years."

"Exactly. She was his muse. His obsession. His *everything*. He stopped painting the day she left. And that's why I always swore I wouldn't ever paint women. Because I never want my art, or my life, to be tied that closely to just one person." He looked down at the sketchbook in his hand. "You're the first woman I've ever painted. The first woman I've ever *had* to paint."

If someone else had said something like this to

Rosa, she probably would have been flattered or creeped out, depending on how weird the guy was. But with Drake, she felt as though warmth infused her, way down deep inside where she'd grown used to feeling so cold.

"These are extenuating circumstances," she supplied for him, not wanting him to feel bad about breaking his rule—and not wanting to let herself build this up into anything more than two strangers hanging out together for a couple of hours. "I'm sure painting me isn't about anything more than getting your juices flowing. After I leave, you'll be off and running again like you were before, and then you can throw that sketchbook into the fire."

"I promised you I wouldn't show these paintings to anyone. But I won't burn them, Rosa."

She licked her lips and tried to calm her racing heart. She should get up and leave before the sexual tension sparking like crazy between them combusted and made her life even messier—and his too. But leaving was the last thing she wanted.

What she really wanted was to walk over to Drake and beg him to put his shockingly talented hands on her already overheated skin.

The dinging of the timer on the old red enamel oven broke through her inappropriate thoughts. "The lasagna is ready," she said. "I'll get it out."

But her voice was full of far more suppressed lust than an Italian dish warranted.

CHAPTER EIGHT

Drake's cabin didn't have a dining room table. He'd cleared out most of the furniture when he'd moved in so that he could fit more easels into the space. If the weather was good, he ate at the picnic table outside. If it was bad, he sat in the leather chair by the window and unfolded a small card table for his meals.

Since the rain had come in again, he set up the table, then went and got a couple of folding chairs out of the closet. Rosa had served up the lasagna on the chipped brown and orange plates that had come with the cabin, and he ripped off paper towels to use as napkins.

His kitchen was small enough that they kept brushing up against each other. Just little touches that wouldn't normally have registered—an inch of her hip against his, the tip of his elbow across her stomach—but with Rosa, nothing was *normal*. And when they suddenly found themselves face to face between the fridge and the peninsula, neither of them moved. Hell, he wasn't even sure either of them breathed.

All he could do was stare.

And *want*.

Drake wanted to run his fingertips over her flushed cheeks so that he could finally find out just how soft her skin was.

He wanted to trace his tongue over the full curve of her lower lip to finally know if she tasted as sweet as she looked.

He wanted to run his nose along the curve of her neck and into her silky hair so that he'd never be able to forget her scent.

He was so far gone, in fact, that he didn't notice when Oscar walked into the kitchen and suddenly leaned—hard—against Rosa's side. Clearly, she didn't see his dog coming either, because where she'd been able to keep her balance before, this time she was so surprised by the heavy weight that her knees buckled.

Drake reached out and caught her before she could hit her head on the corner of the kitchen counter, and it was pure instinct to pull her against him so that their bodies were flush and tight and their faces barely a breath apart. Her lips parted and her hands tightened on his waist where she'd reached out as she fell.

"Rosa." He couldn't form any other word but her name, couldn't think about anything but *her*.

His mouth was nearly on hers when the sketchbook he'd put on the counter fell off and hit the floor, the metal rings holding the sheets together making a surprisingly loud slap on the wood floor. Loud enough, anyway, to startle Oscar into barking. Which, of course, sent Rosa jumping from Drake's arms.

She bent down to pick up the sketchbook and was about to put it on the counter when she stopped with it still in her hand. "Can I see?"

Most people didn't wait for his answer. But though Rosa should have felt his sketches were fair game given that her face and form were inside, she obviously wouldn't look if he said she couldn't.

"Sure." The lone word was raw with unquenched desire from coming so close to tasting her mouth...but not nearly close enough.

She opened up the sketchbook on a drawing he'd done a few weeks back of Oscar having a moment of silliness rolling on the moss outside and laughed. "You've captured him perfectly!" Her laughter was such a pretty sound that it actually made headway into Drake's frustration. "And wow..." She'd turned to a sketch he'd done of the rolling ocean waves. "How are you able to make everything come so alive with only a pencil?"

But before he could answer, she was turning to his first sketch of her, when she'd sat on the leather seat in the corner looking wary and unsure about her decision to let him paint her. He couldn't read her expression as she went to the next drawing—her laughing while a too-big Oscar tried to climb into her too-small lap. In silence, she turned the pages one by one on which he'd wanted to show all her different sides—her joy and empathy, her bravery and fear, her strength and her softness. But it wasn't until she reached the final sketch that he realized he'd also captured *desire*, the flush that had been in her cheeks before she'd popped up to take the lasagna out of the oven mirrored by the flush that colored them now.

"You really are an amazing artist." She closed his sketchbook and put it back on the counter. "And your lasagna is probably getting cold, so we should eat."

Drake had always been the rare kind of artist who was confident enough in his own vision to not particularly care what other people thought of his work. But, yet again, things were different with Rosa. "You don't like my sketches of you."

She was halfway to the folding table when she stopped and turned. "It's not that." She shook her head. "You see so much. Too much. Even things I'm not sure I see myself." She seemed to battle with herself for a few moments before finally turning to meet his gaze. "I've spent years in front of cameras and endless hours in editing booths watching myself on screen, but what you drew on those pages is really different." She ran a hand through her hair. "God, I'm doing it again. Tripping over both your dog and all my words. It's probably best if I fill up my mouth with some of your great-smelling lasagna instead of continuing to say all the wrong things."

He wanted to tell her she wasn't doing or saying anything wrong, wasn't feeling anything she shouldn't. He wanted to admit that he was falling for every one of the facets of her that he'd drawn. He wanted to say that he already knew fifty years wouldn't be enough to capture them all.

But, unfortunately, he also knew just how fast—and far—she'd run if he did that. Especially when just looking at his sketches had made her so uncomfortable. Hell, he should be uncomfortable too, shouldn't he? Wasn't this exactly the kind of connection he'd been fighting his whole life—one where it already seemed far too likely that creative interest could spin into obsession?

Thankfully, as she sat down and tucked into her food, she seemed to forget all about his drawings for the moment. "This is *so* good." She forked another bite into her mouth before she'd even finished chewing the first. "Did you get it at the general store too?"

"I made it."

She stopped with another forkful halfway to her mouth. "How?"

He knew she wasn't asking about sheets of dried pasta and meat sauce. "My dad wasn't much of a cook. If we wanted to eat a meal that didn't come out of a box, we made it ourselves."

"All of your siblings can cook?"

"Alec and Harry are the oldest, so of the four of us, they're the best cooks." Alec, in particular, liked to use his kitchen prowess as an ace in the hole with women. He often bragged to the rest of them that nothing made a woman hotter than a billionaire who turned out to be even better in the kitchen than his French chef. "But Suz and I can hold our own when we need to."

Whenever he talked about his siblings, Rosa got a wistful look on her face. Her current situation was so off-the-charts crazy that he needed to tread carefully, but since she hadn't been shy about asking him questions, he figured it would be okay to ask one. "How many siblings do you have?"

"You really don't know that I have two younger brothers?"

"I'm not a reality TV fan." When she winced, he belatedly realized just how insulting his comment had been. "Rosa, I didn't mean—"

"It's okay. I know what I do isn't exactly Shakespeare." When she put down her fork, Oscar decided that meant it was okay to put his big muzzle in her lap. She stroked his head as she sighed and said, "You said those pictures aren't my fault. But they are."

"How the hell can you say that?"

"Because I've done dozens of photo shoots where I'm barely covered at all. My mother was right that it isn't anything people haven't seen before."

Her mother said that? Drake didn't have a prayer of pushing his fury away. "First of all," he said as his fork hit his plate with a clang, "you made a decision to do those photo shoots. You looked at yes, you looked at no, and you chose yes. But the guy who snuck the pictures in your hotel room didn't give you a choice, did he?"

"Well, no, but—"

"No buts. Just *no*. As for your mother—" He should get up from the table, go outside, and cool off in the rain. But, damn it, he couldn't stand the thought of Rosa's mother having said that to her. "She should be protecting you, doing whatever it takes to keep you safe, down to her very last breath."

"It's not that simple."

"It is."

"No, it isn't. After my dad died, we nearly lost

everything. I know most people think reality TV is a joke, but it saved us. My mom did what she needed to do to make sure my brothers and I had food on the table for every meal and a roof over our heads and clothes for school. She did what she thought was best."

"Including condoning people selling naked pictures of her daughter?"

Rosa pushed back from the table and stood. "I shouldn't have come here. And I definitely shouldn't have stayed. Thanks for the lasagna and for towing and fixing my car. I hope your painting goes well from now on. Take good care of Oscar."

Damn it, she was saying good-bye. Because he couldn't leave well enough alone. Because he'd pissed her off by sticking his nose into her family business. Because he hadn't made sure to tread carefully when he knew it was exactly what she needed when everything was this raw.

Oscar stood in the middle of the room looking like his world was ending. He turned baleful eyes to Drake as if to say, *Fix this, you idiot, or she'll never come back.*

"I shouldn't have pushed so hard." Drake was on his feet now too, barely keeping himself from leaping in front of the door and begging her to stay. "It's just that I hate what happened to you. And I hate that you're willing to take the blame for what everyone else did to you."

She stopped with her hand on the doorknob and turned to look him in the eye. "I'm not a victim." Her expression shifted as if she'd just had an epiphany. "I'm not a victim," she said again, her voice firmer this time.

"You're right that I didn't have any control over the guy who snuck the pictures of me in the bathtub, but I could have said no to being on the show at any time if I thought it wouldn't hurt my family for me to leave. And if starting over wasn't the hardest thing in the world."

"Why do you think it has to be hard?"

She looked a little startled. "Why do I think starting my life over and trying to be taken seriously in a new field would be harder than being wined and dined all over the world while I'm filming my show?" She looked at him like he was nuts. "You're kidding, right?"

"I'm not."

"Because you're such a reality TV expert?"

"You're right, I don't know anything about the world you've been living in. I have family in the entertainment business, but that doesn't mean I understand what your life has been like. All I know is that something about you makes me want to break all my rules. You make me want to risk the very thing that completely destroyed my parents. That's how strong you are. That's how much power you have. The power to do, to achieve, to have absolutely anything you want."

Her jaw dropped at his impassioned soliloquy, and she stared at him for several long moments. "Do you know what the most dangerous thing about you is? How much you *care* about everything, even a stranger who hasn't ever done anything good enough to deserve it."

She held his gaze for a long moment in which he silently prayed she'd decide to stay instead of go. At last she said, "Good-bye, Drake," and walked out the door, closing it quietly behind her.

CHAPTER NINE

Rosa hadn't thought things could get any more complicated. But she'd never seen Drake Sullivan coming. And she'd never met anyone with so much passion that it simply overflowed from him. Not only onto his sketchbooks and canvases, but also to his mouthwateringly good lasagna.

And especially to every single hungry look he'd given her in his cabin.

She'd never felt so tempted by a man before. She could so easily lose herself in him and temporarily forget her worries in his arms. But she wouldn't let herself do that. And not because staying away from a potentially complicated relationship was the smartest thing to do at this juncture.

She would keep her distance—would handcuff herself to the old scratched-up bedpost at the motel if that's what it came to—because she wasn't good enough for him.

I'm not a big fan of reality TV.

Only eight little words, but they spoke volumes. He hadn't said them in a mean way. Hadn't even said them in a judgmental way. But she'd been called plenty of bad things over the years—*trash, one step down from a stripper, media whore*—so it wasn't hard to read between the lines.

She didn't need to know about the art world to guess how prestigious Drake's work was. All she'd needed was to see his paintings for herself.

Drake Sullivan was talented beyond measure *and* he was clearly close to his family, who all sounded really great and normal. He could have anyone. A nice girl without a nutso career making duck faces for selfies and oversharing "personal" things with utter strangers.

She hadn't yet figured out her next step, but she knew one thing for sure: Drake should be with a girl whose naked body hadn't been viewed by millions of people on cell phones and computer screens and TV sets and magazines all over the world.

Which was why she needed to make herself forget him. Needed to forget the heat in his eyes. Needed to erase that too-potent visual of how strong and sexy his hands were as he speed-sketched her in one moment, then served her lasagna the next. And especially needed to forget how he'd leapt to her defense when she'd overshared about her mom.

He'd been her knight in shining armor more than once. First on the wet road, then by getting her broken car fixed without blowing her cover, then again in his fury over what her mother had said after the naked pictures came to light.

She understood his fury—it was a large part of why she'd fled. But as she'd told him, things truly weren't that simple. Rosa knew her mother loved her. And even though Rosa had run from her family and was deliberately hiding out in Montauk, the feeling was mutual. But somewhere along the way, things had gotten weird. Worse than weird—downright bad. And now, Rosa had no idea whether she could ever make them good again.

Could she be a part of the Bouchard family without being on their show? Or did leaving the show also mean leaving the people who meant the most to her?

After forty-eight hours of distance, her family had to be worried about her. She hadn't called or texted, hadn't given them any information at all about where she was, didn't even have a working cell phone so that they could trace her whereabouts. Guilt pooled in the pit of her stomach, thick enough that even though she wasn't ready to go home, she had to at least let them know she was okay.

She was almost past the general store's parking lot when she decided to pull in. She'd had good luck going incognito yesterday, and she was pretty sure she'd seen prepaid cell phones for sale. It was fairly easy to track a call from a cell phone, but could she use it to connect to her email without giving away her location?

The truth was, she hadn't actually missed her phone at all. If there was any other way she could think of to get an immediate message to her family, she would have chosen it, if only to have more than a two-day respite from the ever-present technology.

Rosa kept her head down as she headed through the parking lot and into the store, but the woman behind the counter obviously remembered her. "I'm so glad you're back! You forgot your change yesterday." She reached under the counter and handed Rosa several bills and coins.

Rosa made herself smile as she said a quiet, "Thank you," before she hurried toward the rack with the phones and quickly chose one that said it was Web mail–enabled. She picked up a bunch of grapes and a couple of bananas on her way back to the register, the cash she hadn't given to Drake still in her pocket.

She knew he didn't care about the money, but now that he wasn't painting her, she wouldn't feel right if she didn't pay him back. Of course she wouldn't make the mistake of going back to his cabin—she couldn't trust herself around him. Not when he made her want so much more than she deserved. As soon as she could, she'd mail him the money in a simple thank-you note.

"You sure do look familiar," the woman said as she rang up Rosa's purchases, "and not just because you were in yesterday. Have you recently moved to town?"

"No," Rosa said, praying the woman couldn't tell just how hard her heart was pounding. "I'm just taking a little vacation."

"Sorry the weather isn't better for you." The woman cocked her head. "I could swear I've seen you somewhere, though. I wouldn't normally forget a pretty young woman like you."

Blood was rushing hard and fast into Rosa's head as she said, "You're very sweet, but I hear that a lot. I must have one of those familiar faces."

Fortunately, the woman simply smiled and said, "People always used to tell me that I looked like Jackie O."

Rosa tried not to grab her change too fast. Looking like she was panicking would only make the woman more suspicious. "I can see why. You have the same bone structure."

"We do, don't we?" The woman looked extremely pleased. "I'm Mona Agnew, and I hope I see you again soon."

Rosa picked up the bag with her phone and fruit and headed for the door before saying, "It's so nice to meet you, Mona."

Her heart was racing as she drove back to the motel and jogged up the stairs to her room on the second floor. The good news was that Mona hadn't actually recognized her. But how long would it be before the nice woman restocked the magazines and realized that the face staring back at her didn't simply resemble the woman who'd come by her store twice—but was one and the same?

Rosa had spent years with camera lenses on her every time she stepped out of a building, but she'd never felt this paranoid. Then again, she'd never actually wanted to hide before. Never truly needed a few days out of the public eye to completely reassess everything.

Drake's cabin had been so much warmer and

cozier than Rosa's motel room with its faded bedspread, old carpet, and outdated wallpaper. But this too-quiet room was far safer than his difficult questions—and the heat between them. She'd turn on the cell phone, send a quick email to her mother, then shut it down so that she could sit in her safe, quiet room and finally figure out her next step.

But as soon as she stepped inside, Rosa realized safety was nothing but an illusion. The bed was made and the towel she'd placed over the TV screen had been folded neatly on the bathroom counter, so Housekeeping must have been in while she was gone. Unfortunately, the person who'd tidied up her room must have turned on the TV and forgotten to shut it off when he or she left.

And right now Rosa was looking straight at her own face—and barely clad body—on the screen.

"As the nude photo scandal over reality TV's It Girl continues," the entertainment show host said, *"we've brought in two Hollywood experts to weigh in on where we should draw the line between private and public life. Selma, I know you're not a huge fan of Rosalind and her family, but does she have your sympathy now?"*

Selma Laskey was one of the nastiest gossip journalists in Los Angeles, and even though it was like standing in front of an oncoming train, Rosa's eyes remained glued to the screen as the too-thin woman said, *"Are you kidding? I just can't believe she hasn't posed for nude pictures before this."*

"But she didn't pose for these," the host said. *"Or do you believe she orchestrated this situation in some way for her own gain?"*

"I don't believe that for a second," John Canyon put in before Selma could respond. He was a well-known Hollywood lawyer, but not someone Rosa had ever personally dealt with. *"Just because she's a public figure doesn't mean these pictures aren't a massive violation of her rights. While she wasn't hacked, she was attacked online, so calling this a cyber-attack is certainly in the ballpark, and I hope her lawyers are hitting the perpetrator with everything they've got."*

"There's nothing an exhibitionist wants more than to have every eye on her," Selma tossed back with a flip of her hair, dismissing the idea of a cyber-attack with a roll of her eyes. *"I guarantee the fact that the entire world is talking about her makes everything better."*

Finally coming unfrozen, Rosa leapt at the TV to turn it off.

She'd known people could be cruel, but what had she ever done to Selma to make her think she deserved something like this? No woman did, not even one who had opened so much of her life to cameras. A reckless mix of anger and frustration drove her to yank the prepaid cell phone from its package so that she could call the studio and make them put her on the air to defend herself.

Fortunately, by the time the phone booted up, a tiny bit of sense had set in. Making a rash phone call would only open the floodgates to a tsunami of questions and requests that would sweep her back into the world she'd only just barely escaped. And the truth was that Selma hadn't said anything Rosa hadn't heard a million times. All things considered, exhibitionist was one of the kinder insults people had thrown her way over the years.

Rosa desperately wished things were clearer and that she had all the answers she needed to move forward. But right now, the only thing she knew for sure was that she needed more time to think. Time to breathe. Time to figure out exactly what *she* wanted, rather than the easiest path or what would make her mother the happiest.

She'd been barely out of high school when she'd agreed to do the show. But she wasn't a kid anymore. She knew a heck of a lot more now than she had at eighteen. So even though the cell phone felt like a hot potato in her hand and she couldn't wait to be free of it again, she had to at least get a message out to her family as soon as possible.

As she went online and logged into her email, she worked to ignore the tight clench of her chest and the knots in her stomach. But when she saw hundreds of new emails waiting in her inbox, there was no point in even trying to be calm and collected. Not when there were media requests from every major outlet in the world, everything from *People* magazine to the *London Times* newspaper to *US Weekly*. Even *Time* wanted to talk to her.

Her hand shook as she clicked on only one email from her mother's private account.

Rosalind, I'm praying you're okay! Please contact me! We're all so worried.

Rosa's throat swelled with emotion, and her eyes were already full of tears as she typed:

I didn't mean to worry you.

She paused with her fingers over the phone. She didn't want to make any promises about when she'd be back, but she didn't want to cut ties forever either. After a half-dozen false starts, she finally settled on:

I promise I'll be back in touch soon. I hope you and Aaron and Lincoln are doing okay. I love you all.

Rosa had hoped sending the email would make her feel less guilty. But, if anything, knowing how worried her mother was made her feel worse than ever. And more than that, she realized just how much she wanted to hear her voice.

She was just about to switch over from email to the phone so that she could call home, when a new email appeared on her screen.

Thank God you're all right! I was so worried when you didn't pick up any of my calls or answer my emails. I know how upset you were about the pictures, but by now I'm sure you can see that the public is more on our side than ever. Absolutely everyone wants to interview you and the network is ready to do a two-hour special in the top time slot. We can turn something terrible into something amazing, honey, but we can't do anything with these incredible opportunities without you. I'm waiting by the phone. Everyone here is ready to jump on a plane and come right to you, wherever you are.

Rosa felt as if a bitter, cold wind had whipped into the motel room.

Had she actually been stupid enough to think that her mother was simply worried about her?

How could she have forgotten that, although they'd agreed to do the reality show five years ago to save their family, now the cameras, the interviews, the *opportunities* always came first?

Her stomach roiled, but she didn't give in to the urge to be sick. Or to cry. Or to scream. Instead, she methodically logged out of her email, shut down the phone, and placed it on the bureau next to the needles and thread she'd bought at the general store.

She had always been able to think most clearly while her hands were busy, and as she picked up the spool and rubbed the glossy thread between her thumb and forefinger, the steady scratch of wound cotton against her skin helped her feel less numb. Less empty. Less like she was teetering on the edge of a cliff with nothing but a long dark hole beneath her.

Fiber art had been Rosa's secret escape during the past five years. No one outside of her family knew that she made crazy pictures with thread and, honestly, that was just fine with Rosa. She liked having something that was all hers, something she didn't have to broadcast via photos and video clips, something she didn't have to pull out for late-night talk shows like a performing monkey. Fiber art was her quiet place. Her time to unwind.

She wasn't actually an artist—not like Drake— but in the same way that she'd heard writers say they got their best ideas in the shower, she'd always had her best ideas with a needle in her hand. Her hobby had kept her sane, so maybe if she could stitch something she'd be able to get a handle on her racing heartbeat, her anger... and most of all, her hurt that even now her mother was focused only on the *opportunities*.

Rosa's hand tightened around the spool so tightly that the plastic edges bit into her skin as a hot rush of powerlessness rose up inside her again. Unbidden, Drake's voice sounded in her head, as if to provide a counterpoint to her shame, to how painfully vulnerable she felt.

Something about you makes me want to break all my rules. You make me want to risk the very thing that completely destroyed my parents. That's how strong you are. That's how much power you have. The power to do, to achieve, to have absolutely anything you want.

She didn't know how he saw what he saw when he looked at her. Couldn't even begin to figure out why he felt what he felt when he was with her.

All she knew was that she wanted so badly to go back to him, to his cabin that had seemed like a refuge in the storm howling all around her.

She wanted to keep looking at the sketches he'd drawn, where she actually looked strong and powerful, until she somehow started to believe it could actually be true.

And, most of all, she wanted to rewind to the moment when they'd almost kissed in the kitchen, just be able to close her eyes and forget about everything but how good it would feel to press her lips against his.

But if she went to Drake and used him to bury her pain for a few blissful hours in his arms, wouldn't that be proof that she was all the horrible things people had called her over the years? Rosa didn't want to be that woman. Couldn't stand the thought that Selma Laskey might be right about her.

Which meant that instead of rushing out the door and over to Drake's cabin to lose herself in him for a few sinfully hot hours, she needed to pick up her Montauk sweatshirt, thread a needle, and take a few stitches.

She wasn't going to be able to stitch her life back together anytime soon—especially not when she was still reeling from what she'd seen on TV and in her email. But she could at least make a start by not ripping anything or anyone else to shreds.

Because the only thing that could possibly be worse than what she was already dealing with would be falling for a man whom she already knew was too good for her...and then ending up with a broken heart when he figured it out too.

CHAPTER TEN

Drake was beyond captivated. Miles past enthralled.

He was full-out *consumed.*

Painting as darkness fell outside his windows, he kept painting until the sun rose again. He didn't stop to eat. Didn't need to sleep.

Not when all the inspiration he'd been lacking over the past months was hitting him in a hard, fast rush. His hands and shoulders began to ache, and Oscar was looking at him as if he'd lost his mind, but Drake couldn't stop. Couldn't focus on anything but working out the different tones of Rosa's skin—paler when she was scared, darker when she was mad, rosier when she was laughing, and a beautiful combination of all three when she'd been looking at him with barely suppressed heat.

As long as he was painting, Rosa was still there with him. But if he stopped, even put down his brush for five minutes?

He'd be in his car before he could stop himself, driving to her motel, slamming down the door to beg her to come back. To come sit in the leather chair again so that he could keep memorizing every line of her face, the slope of her nose, the curves of her ears, the hollow at her throat.

And, most of all, so that he could kiss her breathless. And just keep kissing her until neither of them remembered why they shouldn't.

When it started raining again, the hail hitting the roof and the porch louder than he'd ever heard it, he immediately saw Rosa sitting on the cliffs in the rain, strong even as she buried her head on her knees. Yanking another canvas up onto the easel, he painted even faster, more consumed than ever despite having worked for nearly twenty-four hours straight.

But when the hail continued to come down harder and harder, he finally realized it wasn't hail. Someone was outside knocking on his door.

Rosa.

He dropped his brushes and lunged for the door, throwing it open. But the woman standing beneath an open umbrella wasn't the woman he'd been obsessing about.

"Suzanne."

His sister's eyebrows rose all the way up under her bangs. "Holy crap. You're a mess."

He hadn't looked in a mirror, but he had no doubt

that she was right. He hadn't slept, eaten, shaved, or changed his clothes. And he'd been painting so fast that splatters of color covered his hands and arms, clothes and shoes. His hair too, probably.

"I've been working."

"That's good." His sister smiled. "I know you've been hoping inspiration would strike. Looks like it finally has."

She pushed past him to come inside out of the rain, closing her umbrella and leaving it just outside the front door. Oscar got up from his pillow to give her his usual greeting. Suzanne and Oscar had always been good buddies, although it struck Drake as he watched the two of them that it wasn't quite the level of adoration his dog had given Rosa.

As Suzanne gave Oscar a good rubdown, she said, "I really need to get myself a dog one d—" She looked up and finally caught sight of the dozen canvases lined up all around his living room and kitchen. "Wow." She moved closer to one that was still wet. "These are amazing, Drake. Absolutely breathtaking. But—" She turned to him. "You never paint people."

He'd promised Rosa that no one would ever see his paintings of her, but he hadn't counted on his sister dropping by unexpectedly from New York City. "They're just something I'm messing around with. I'm not planning on anyone ever seeing them."

"You're not going to show or sell them?"

"No. I promised the woman that I wouldn't. You aren't even supposed to see them."

"Don't tell me this is some weird commission

where you're painting these for this woman's collection so that she can stare at herself all day in every room?"

"Not even close." The words came out more impassioned than he'd intended. Then again, given that he'd just spent nearly twenty-four hours painting Rosa in a reckless rush of inspiration, he clearly didn't have a speck of self-control where she was concerned. "She asked me to burn them when I'm done."

"You can't!" Suz looked and sounded horrified. "I know the art world can be really weird, but how could anyone possibly ask you to *burn* these incredible paintings?"

He ran a hand over his eyes. Eyes he finally realized were burning from lack of sleep and too many hours of laser focus. "It's not that simple." They were the same words Rosa had used to describe her relationship with her mother, and though he'd argued with her, the truth was that he understood *not that simple.*

It was how he'd felt about his father his entire life.

"Wait a second." Suz turned back to the paintings as if something had just clicked into place. "I know her. That's the reality TV girl. The naked one."

"Those pictures weren't her fault." His growl caused his sister to gape at him in shock. Oscar looked just as offended, as if the dog could actually understand her.

"You know I didn't mean it like that." Suzanne held up her hands. "It's just that it's all over the news right now, and I spoke without thinking. What's happened to her is horrible. Beyond horrible. If I could figure out a way to write a program that would erase all those pictures off the Internet for her, I would. I've actually thought about this before—about creating a tech task force that would help women protect themselves from Internet stalkers and trolls." She put a hand on his arm. "But why didn't you tell any of us that you know Rosalind Bouchard? Or that you're painting her?"

"I only met her yesterday." He wouldn't give away any of Rosa's secrets, but he needed his sister to know one important thing. "No one knows she's in Montauk, so you can't even tell Harry or Alec."

"Is she okay?"

Rosa was one of the strongest people he'd ever met. But she clearly wasn't *okay* with anything happening in her life right now.

"She'll figure things out." He was sure of it. If only he could be as sure about everything else.

Yes, he was fired up to paint Rosa right now. But would that fire translate into anything he could actually show in the NYC gallery in two weeks? And even if it did, how the hell was he going to keep from tracking Rosa down in the future when he simply couldn't imagine never seeing her again, never feeling her laughter resonate all the way through his body, never watching Oscar worship at her feet?

Damn it, he needed to stop thinking about her, at least long enough to ask his sister, "What are you doing here?"

"If you ever bothered to turn on your cell phone," Suzanne replied with a little scowl, "I wouldn't have to drive three hours to talk to you in an emergency. It's so much easier to reach you when you're in the city."

"Emergency?" Now he was the one reaching for his sister to make sure she was okay.

"I'm fine. But Dad isn't."

Of course. He should have guessed the emergency had to do with his father. Suz had always been the one to take care of him. Harry too. Alec was usually too busy knocking heads with him.

As for Drake? The truth was, he'd never had much of a relationship with his father. Maybe because Drake had been one kid too many in five years for their mother to handle? Maybe because William Sullivan thought Drake was the reason his mother had left—and his father had never been able to forgive him for it? Or maybe it was because Drake had his mother's eyes and had always been too painful a reminder of all his father had lost?

His mother and father's tragic story might be up on Wikipedia for all to read, but Drake and his siblings didn't actually know much more about their parents' marriage than that. Their father had never sat them down to talk about what happened—and none of them had ever felt they could ask. As the years went by without anyone broaching the subject, the wall between their father and his kids had only grown higher and thicker.

"What's wrong with him now?" he asked his sister as exhaustion finally hit him like a brick. Heading into the kitchen, Drake pushed the start button on the coffee maker, while Oscar went back to his dog bed in the corner and flopped down on it, watching brother and sister.

"Dad called to ask if I wanted any of his paintings. Evidently he also called Harry and Alec and asked them. I'm assuming there's a message waiting for you on your phone."

Drake wasn't in any frame of mind for family drama right now, but he still needed to clarify something. "He wants to give us his paintings of Mom?"

"Yes, and I told him of course I wanted them. That I was sure we all would. He said I had until the end of the month to collect the ones he'd put aside for me."

"I don't get it," Drake said as he tried to make sense of this hugely unexpected news. "He's been holding on to those paintings for thirty years. What could possibly have changed?"

His sister looked just as bewildered. "I don't know, but I'm heading to the lake now to pick them up. I'm hoping he'll explain things once I'm there. Do you want to go with me? Harry and Alec said they're both going to make some time to head out to the Adirondacks in the next week or so."

Thank God the coffee maker dinged right then—Drake was going to need to drink the whole pot before he could begin to make heads or tails of this. He poured both of them a cup, then chugged his. Suz drank slowly from hers, watching him over the rim in a mirror of Oscar's watchful pose while Drake willed his brain to push through the sludge of exhaustion.

"You're not going to come with me, are you?"

It had been so long since he'd felt this kind of creative inspiration, he worried that if he left in the middle of the rush, it might pass. And there was still so much he wanted to paint, so many different visions of Rosa that he wanted to bring to life on his canvases.

But even as he tried to tell himself that his work was the main reason he didn't want to head to his father's house in the Adirondacks with Suzanne, he knew he was lying to himself. Even his strange relationship with his father wasn't the main reason.

No, the biggest reason Drake wanted to stay in Montauk was because of a woman he barely knew. Odds were pretty high that she'd left the Seaside Motel yesterday after he'd pushed her too hard about her mother, and hit the road again.

But if Rosa was still here? If there was even the barest chance that he could convince her to come back to sit for him again...

"Jesus." He put his head in his hands. "It's finally happened. I've turned into *him*."

It was clear Suzanne knew he was talking about their father. "Why are you saying that? Because you want to paint Rosalind Bouchard?" She waved her hand in the air as if his statement were utterly ridiculous. "Sure, you're brilliant painters. And I love you both. But you're not Dad."

Suzanne and Harry had always been the rational ones—the computer genius and the brilliant academic. Alec had a fairly well-earned reputation as a hothead. As for Drake? While he'd certainly been willing to play the *artiste* card when it suited him, at his core he'd always thought of himself as a fairly even-keeled guy.

Until now.

Until Rosa.

"That's what I've always thought." Or at least it was what he'd always told himself—that he and his father were totally different people. That he didn't have any of the inner torment William had nursed for thirty years. "But I've got twenty-four hours of paintings staring me in the face telling me I'm full of it. Even though I know I need to stop thinking about her, need to stop painting her, I can't."

The last thing he expected Suzanne to do was laugh. "It's called a *crush*, Drake. Everyone gets them." She looked at the paintings again. "Rosalind is a stunningly beautiful woman, and not in a typical, boring way. If I were a painter, I'm sure I'd be just as excited about painting her. But it's not like you're in love with her or anything."

In love with her?

Of course he wasn't.

There was no way that he could have fallen in love with Rosa at first sight, out on the rocks in the rain. No rational reason that talking with her while eating lasagna on chipped plates at a card table on folding chairs could have cemented those crazy emotions.

"Oh, my God." His sister was staring at him as though she'd never seen him before. "You *are* in love with her!"

Thirty years of practice at keeping love at bay had Drake instinctively telling himself that he was simply captivated. Obviously enthralled. Definitely consumed. Yes, he was tempted to break all of his rules for her—was already doing it, for God's sake. Had been riding the edge from the first moment he'd drawn her in his sketchbook.

But did that mean he was in *love* with her?

Drake deliberately turned his back on his paintings. "I told you—I just met her yesterday."

Suzanne actually had the nerve to smile. "At least half of our happily married cousins can attest to the fact that love at first sight is real."

"When did my computer genius sister become such a romantic? Is there a guy you haven't told us about?"

"Don't try to turn this on me." She wagged her finger at him. "We're talking about you right now and what you're going to do about the fact that you're in love with Rosalind Bouchard."

"Her name is Rosa." Of all the things to correct his sister on right then, Rosa's name shouldn't have been at the top of the list. And yet, he couldn't forget how she'd looked as she'd said, *Rosa is my real name.* Working to shake that vision out of his head, along with the others that had all but hypnotized him from the first moment he'd seen her on the cliffs, he said, "Trust me when I say that the last thing she needs right now is some new guy in her life."

And the last thing *he* needed was to fall in love with a woman who could too easily become an obsession. A woman who had already brought him far too close to the kind of deep feelings he'd made it a point his whole life to avoid so that he wouldn't repeat his parents' destructive cycle.

"Are you sure about that? After all, she let you paint her. Maybe you're *exactly* what she needs. And maybe that goes both ways."

His sister had the same determined look that she got when a computer program she was writing wasn't doing exactly what she wanted it to do. Drake knew for a fact that she'd always beaten the computer, every single time.

"I understand if you don't want to head to the Adirondacks with me right now to see Dad. But I won't understand if you don't do something about Rosa. I've never seen you like this, never seen you paint like this either. Your work has always been amazing, Drake, but these paintings?" She put a hand over her chest. "They make my heart spin around in my chest, in the best kind of way. And if my heart feels like this just from looking at your paintings, then I can't even imagine the way *yours* must feel when the two of you are actually together."

Lack of sleep had him admitting, "It's like nothing I've ever felt before." Now that he'd finally said the words aloud, it was suddenly impossible to keep the next ones inside. Especially when Suzanne was one of the only people on the planet who could fully understand where he was coming from. "But that's exactly the problem, Suz. Our mother wasn't just Dad's muse, she was his *obsession*. And that obsession didn't just destroy him." He ran a harsh hand through his hair. "It destroyed them both."

"Yes, it destroyed them. But it didn't destroy *us*. And I refuse to believe that you and I and Harry and Alec are destined for the same horrible-ever-after ending."

Suzanne spent so much time inside her head that people often made the mistake of assuming her passions didn't run deep. But Drake knew firsthand just how wrong they all were. His sister had one of the biggest, most caring hearts of anyone he knew. Especially when it came to her brothers. They would fight to the end for her, and she would do the same for them.

Just the way she was right now.

Her eyes were flashing as she told him, "One day, when I find the guy I'm supposed to be with, I'm not going to be afraid to love big. And I'm *definitely* not going to stop myself from loving with everything I am. Our parents might have misused love to destroy each other, but as far as I'm concerned, that just means the four of us all know better. Better than to throw away real love when it comes just because of mistakes *they* made." She looked at his paintings again, before turning back and pinning him with an unwavering gaze. "And definitely to be brave enough to risk our hearts when love comes walking through our door, even if we're not expecting it. Even," she added in a softer voice, "if that love looks like the one thing we've always thought we shouldn't have."

Oscar's howl from the corner was the perfect punctuation to his sister's words, an exclamation point at the end of Suz's heartfelt wisdom that Drake couldn't possibly ignore.

No more than he could ignore the way he felt about Rosa...whether he should or not.

CHAPTER ELEVEN

Rosa had just got out of the shower and wrapped a towel around herself when she heard a knock on her motel room door.

Oh God, they'd found her.

Whether it was her family or the paparazzi barely mattered. All that mattered was that the little cocoon of safety she'd sewn herself into for the past twenty-four hours was about to be ripped apart.

She hadn't yet made any big decisions, but at least she had started to feel as if every stitch she put on the tourist clothes she'd picked up at the general store was helping to stitch *her* back together, little by little. Of course she wasn't planning to sit in this motel room forever, but after five crazy years, was it really too much to ask for a handful of days of peace and quiet? A few moments to actually sit down and plan how she was going to deal with what had happened?

As the knocking came again, even more insistently, she realized she was standing frozen in place on the threshold between the bathroom and bedroom. Maybe she should be looking for an escape route. Maybe she should be checking to see if she could fit through the window above the shower. But as panic rapidly bore down on her at the thought of walking right back into her reality-star life, she couldn't figure out how to make herself unfreeze.

"It's me."

The world's biggest dose of relief flooded her as she recognized that voice. The only one she actually wanted to hear right now.

"Rosa, are you in there? It's Drake."

Just like that, her feet came unstuck. She didn't think as she headed across the bedroom, couldn't have stopped herself from opening the door even if she had been able to think clearly. And *ohhh*, was he ever a gorgeous sight to behold as he stood in the rain on her room's second-floor landing.

"Rosa."

All he said was one perfect, sweet word, drenched in need—and then his mouth was on hers before she could take her next breath.

His kiss was utterly unexpected. Took her completely by surprise.

And was *glorious*.

She'd never wanted a kiss this badly. Never wanted anyone's arms around her so much. Never been so desperate to know another's taste and to share hers.

Somewhere in her haze of pleasure, she felt him move them both far enough into the room to slam the door behind him, but then all she could feel was *Drake*.

His mouth was as hot as his wet clothes were cold against her skin, bared completely now because the towel had fallen down around her feet while they kissed. Somehow, though his hands were also wet, they were warm and so wonderfully big and strong as they moved down her back from shoulder to hip, then down even further to cup her bottom so that she could wrap her legs around him as they both tried to erase any space between them.

He answered her gasps of pleasure with a low groan of desire, and it was hands down the sexiest sound she'd ever heard in her life. She wanted to fall into the bed with him and never leave it. Wanted to drown in his touch, in his kisses, and never resurface back to "real" life where she couldn't ever let herself fall in love with a sweet and sexy painter.

Unfortunately, that one thought about real life was all it took to drag her back into it.

No. *No*. Not now. Not yet. Why did she have to start thinking?

Why did she have to remember that she couldn't do this with him?

Why couldn't she have stayed in a blissful haze long enough to make love with him?

Why couldn't she let herself have at least one good thing come out of all this pain?

But she knew why—knew the answer to every single question.

She couldn't hurt him. Couldn't drag him into her mess. She'd seen enough of his talent to be certain that he was a well-respected artist. But if they hooked up and anyone ever found out? If she let herself have this taste of him and then wasn't strong enough to let go afterward?

Just like that, his reputation would go down the drain.

All because Rosa was the world's biggest reality TV joke...and he was a good man who should never have made the mistake of getting involved with her.

Somehow, she made herself draw back from his mouth. At least, she almost did—she couldn't resist swooping in to lick over his lips one last time. One last taste of heaven before she made herself untangle her arms and legs from his, pick up her towel from the floor, wrap it tightly around herself, and steel herself to say the four most difficult words in the world.

"We can't do this."

"We can."

He followed up his statement by dragging her close for another kiss that felt just as inevitable as their first, but that didn't mean she could let it spiral any further. Somehow, some way, she needed to stop this glorious, all-consuming madness—even if it was the very last thing she wanted.

She tore her mouth from his, still gripping her towel for dear life. "Drake."

The desire in his dark eyes stole what was left of her breath. "Rosa."

God, she loved hearing him say her name. Loved

it as much as she loved the hard press of his muscles all along her body as he held her so tight that it felt like he would never let her fall.

But none of this—none of *him*—was meant for her. He was too good. Too sweet. Too real.

Whereas nothing about her life was good or sweet or real. Only the too-short time she'd spent with Drake had been any of those things.

"I meant it when I said that I can't do this." No lie had ever been bigger, considering she so easily *could.* But calling on his sense of honor was the only way she could think of to stop them from taking things so far that he'd regret it.

He didn't kiss her again, but he didn't let go of her either. Instead, he surprised her yet again by saying, "I won't hurt you."

But I'll hurt you. And I'll never be able to forgive myself for it.

"I know you won't." Though she barely knew him, she didn't doubt the truth of it. "But I still can't be with you."

"I know things are crazy for you right now. I'll wait."

"Don't."

The sure knowledge that she could never erase her past—and that she wouldn't risk sending his life careening as off track as hers was right now—made her strong enough to finally let go of him.

Every part of her that had been so warm while pressed against him immediately chilled as she forced herself to put some space between them and made herself say, "You should go."

Though she was wearing only a towel, he never looked away from her face. "Come with me. Sit for me again. I'll feed you pie."

He made it sound as if there wasn't one single reason why she shouldn't go back to his cabin and sit on the chair in the corner with his big dog in her lap while he painted her. As if they both didn't know darn well that if she went with him, she'd also end up in his bed.

Dangerous.

Drake was so dangerous for her.

It wasn't just his intensity that was dangerous. Wasn't only his big heart as he'd looked out for a stranger.

No, it was his belief that this connection between them was worth taking a risk for, that suddenly seemed the most dangerous of all.

Rosa had learned early on in Hollywood that if she didn't keep the walls around her heart tall and thick, she wouldn't be able to survive it. But she'd never been tested like this. Never wanted to drop all her walls so that she could let someone else in.

"Drake—" Every inch of her ached to be back in his arms. But she needed to be stronger than that, needed to force herself to close the door behind him for good this time. "I can't go with you." She held up her hand before he could come closer. "And you can't kiss me again to try to convince me either."

"You're right, I can't if you don't want me to. But *you* can kiss *me* again anytime you want. And when you do?" His eyes grew even darker. Even hungrier. And were so sexy that she nearly melted into a puddle of goo as he said, "All bets are off."

She shook her head, hoping that might clear it. When it didn't, she decided to try another approach. "We shouldn't even be having this conversation right now. I don't have any clothes on."

His mouth curved up, but he still didn't drop his gaze from her face. "Then put some on and come back with me."

Clearly, he wasn't the kind of man who was used to taking no for an answer. "I still don't understand why you want to paint me so badly."

"You make me remember why I love it." It was the most beautiful, heartfelt thing anyone had ever said to her, and she was still reeling from it when he grinned and added, "And you make me remember why I love kissing too."

She shouldn't have laughed. Shouldn't have encouraged him, especially when she was still nearly naked. But how could she stop herself from laughing when he was so gorgeous and persistent and *wonderful*?

The laughter felt strange in her chest, her throat. And not just because she had barely even smiled in the past two days. It was more that she hadn't really laughed in years. She frowned, wondering if that could be true.

Had she really not laughed in that long?

She looked up into his eyes when she felt his fingers lightly stroking her cheek. "Come to my cabin. Sit on the leather chair with Oscar. Let me paint you. We don't have to make it any more complicated than that right now."

He wasn't lying—she already knew that Drake

Sullivan simply wasn't capable of it. And yet she also knew *not complicated* couldn't possibly be true. She needed to be brave enough to lay out the consequences for him in black and white.

"I want you, Drake. There's no point in pretending I don't. So if I come back to your cabin, we both know where it's going to go. Where *we're* going to go. And I can't let us go there when I'm not—" She couldn't look into his eyes. "When I'm not good enough for you."

She both felt and saw the frustration that fueled the light pressure he put on her jaw so that she had to meet his gaze again. "Like hell you aren't."

"I know you don't watch reality TV," she shot back, "but if you knew more about me and my world, you'd get why people would judge you if they found out you and I even *know* each other."

"And if you knew more about me and my world," he echoed back, "you'd get why I don't give a damn what other people think. Especially when I know they're all dead wrong—and that the only thing that matters is what *I* think. What *you* think."

Every argument she made, he came right back at her with his own. She hated herself for even considering saying something about his parents—but she had to do whatever it took to save him, didn't she?

"What about your father? What about how you said he was obsessed with painting your mother? What about what happened to him after she left?" Every word tasted sour on her tongue, and her stomach clenched so tightly she felt sick from poking him right where they both knew he hurt.

A muscle jumped in his jaw, but he didn't back down. Didn't back away. "Maybe—" His jaw tightened even further for a moment. "Maybe being with her was worth it."

Rosa's eyes went wide. "But...you said...I thought..."

She couldn't even think a straight thought right now, let alone speak one aloud.

"I'm not going to pretend I have all the answers, Rosa. Hell, I'm not going to pretend that I've got any answers at all right now. All I know is that I've suddenly started to see things differently. Black used to be black and white used to be white. But as soon as you showed up on my cliffs?" He stroked her cheek, a feather-light touch that rocked her all the way down to her core. Rocked her in ways she hadn't known a man could. "You started to change everything."

"But what if it's a bad change?" The words spilled from her lips as if from a faucet on full blast. One propelled by all the fear she'd been trying to keep at bay for so long—a soul-deep fear of making changes in her life that might end up being the wrong ones.

His slow grin warmed her like a beam of sunshine. "I don't need to know where things will end up to be sure that I don't want to go back to how things used to be."

"I don't want to go back either." It was the only thing she was sure of, the only thing that hadn't wavered in the past seventy-two hours. No, the second thing. Because she'd been drawn to Drake from the first, and she couldn't even imagine that changing.

Yesterday, she'd told him she wasn't a victim.

But if she never took another risk, then she'd be proving herself a liar, wouldn't she? Yes, Drake was dangerous. Shockingly so, considering how much she wanted him— and not just his body or his hands on her. Because if she was being totally honest with herself, it was his heart that she wanted most.

Right now he wanted to paint her, wanted to kiss her. But what if that was as far as it ever went? What if she let herself fall...and he didn't fall with her? And what if she not only had to crawl back to her family and the TV show, but also had to do it with a broken heart? What would be the point of putting her walls up then, when behind them she was already destroyed?

"Oscar misses you."

Drake's words yanked her from her infinite worries spiral. "Oscar?"

"He's been a mopey mess since you left, just keeps staring at the door wishing you'd walk through it."

Though her worries were still spiraling around and around, sunshine began to break through anyway. Just the way that lone beam of light had fallen on her in the middle of the storm on the cliffs two days ago.

"Are you playing your dog card to get me to come back with you?"

"I am," he said with another gorgeous grin. "But only because the apple pie didn't work."

This time when she laughed again, it didn't feel quite as rusty.

Maybe he was right—maybe everything didn't have to be quite as complicated as she was making it out to be.

And even if it did turn out to be the most complicated, messy thing she'd ever done?

Maybe, just maybe, he was also right that it would still have been worth it.

"If you wouldn't mind waiting outside," she said, suddenly feeling shy about her near nudity even though she'd been wearing only a towel the entire time they'd been talking—on top of already having been wrapped naked around him, "I'll put my clothes on and go back to your cabin to see your dog and eat your pie."

When he grinned at her before turning around and heading for the door like the gentleman he'd been from the start, Rosa suddenly wished she knew how to paint.

Simply so that she could capture him forever the way he'd already captured her.

CHAPTER TWELVE

Rosa smiled shyly at Drake as she stepped out of her motel room ten minutes later. "Sorry I took so long. I was having a hard time getting the tangles out of my hair." She seemed more than a little nervous as she ran her fingers through the silky strands. The sound of a car door slamming out in the parking lot made her jump and reach into her bag for her big sunglasses. "We should go."

He hated how she felt like she needed to hide from the world, all because some asshole had taken and sold those pictures of her. But considering how hard it had been to convince her to come back to his cabin, he didn't want to risk his luck by pushing her on it right now.

But he wouldn't stop himself from putting his hand on the small of her back as they headed across the second-floor landing to the stairs. Now that he'd touched her, kissed her, he couldn't stop wanting to do it again. And again. And again.

Lord, the way she tasted.

Just thinking about how sweet she'd been, how eagerly she'd wrapped herself around him, how soft her skin had been, made Drake call upon every ounce of control he possessed to keep from spinning her around against the motel wall so that he could devour her.

He'd promised not to kiss her again—and he meant it, even if it killed him to keep that promise. He hadn't planned on jumping her when she'd opened her door, but as soon as he'd looked into her eyes, primal need had taken over. He hadn't been thinking, hadn't even realized what he'd done until she was in his arms, kissing him back with just as much hunger. Just as much need.

But this thing between them was bigger than a kiss. Because Rosa wasn't just a woman he desired. She made him want to take risks. Big ones. Even if it meant taking a hard look at his long-held beliefs about what had happened between his parents.

Drake had always assumed that if his father had it to do all over, he would never have let his mother become his all-consuming muse. But had Drake assumed wrong? Neither Drake nor any of his siblings had ever asked their father that loaded question. Hell, the five of them had hardly even said Lynn Sullivan's name aloud during the past thirty years. No one in the extended family did either, as if they all knew that simply talking about her was as good as handing their father a match for a loaded powder keg.

But now there was this whole mystery of why his father suddenly wanted to give his paintings of their mother to each of them. What could have changed?

Drake got into the driver's seat beside Rosa, and when she smiled at him, he was glad to have a reason to push thoughts of his father to the back burner. For now, he only wanted to concentrate on her. And as he let himself really drink her in, he suddenly noticed what she was wearing.

Yesterday, she had shown up at his cabin in sweats. Today, though, she was wearing the same Montauk tourist gear. It looked completely different. Closer to couture than five-and-dime.

"What did you do to your clothes?"

She ran her finger over an intricately stitched blue and green pattern along the hem. "I made a few modifications."

"A few modifications? You've turned that sweatshirt into a piece of wearable art." He knew some damn good fiber artists in the city and was certain they'd be just as impressed. No wonder she'd had the spools of thread and package of needles in her grocery bag. "How long have you been doing this?"

She shrugged, clearly uncomfortable with his question. "A while. Although I don't normally repurpose clothes. I didn't have any canvases to work on yesterday, and I needed my hands to be busy to keep from losing it."

Mentally filing away that piece of information of just how important creating art was for her, he asked,

"You stitch straight onto canvas?"

She nodded. "But it's just a hobby. No one knows I do it. Just my family...and now you."

When she didn't meet his eyes, he reached over to tip her chin up the same way he had in the motel room. "Why doesn't the whole world know how talented you are? That you're an artist?"

Instead of answering him, she licked her lips, and he couldn't resist brushing his thumb over the damp flesh. As long as he didn't kiss her, he wasn't breaking his promise. But when she shivered and her eyes darkened with desire while her gaze shifted to his mouth, he was hard-pressed not to drag her closer and kiss her breathless.

"Rosa?"

She lifted her eyes back to his. "What did you ask me?"

He nearly groaned from the sexual tension sparking like a live wire between them. He'd never wanted anyone like this. Never had to hold himself back either. "You're on TV every week, and I assume your family sells certain products to your viewers, right? So why are you keeping your art a secret?"

"It's not art," she said first, and then, "You ask too many questions."

On the contrary, he was starting to see that he hadn't asked nearly enough. Not just of his father and Rosa—but of himself too. That didn't mean she needed him to hammer on her right this second, though, so he simply said, "Did you bring your needle and thread? You could use one of my canvases while you sit for me."

"They're in my bag, although I'm not sure I want to make anything in front of a real artist."

He looked down at the hem of her shirt, then back up into her eyes. "You told me not to be modest yesterday, so I'll say the same to you now. I'd like to paint you while you work, if you'll let me."

She bit her lip as she thought about it. Finally, she said, "Okay. But the rules are still the same—you can't show it to anyone."

"I won't."

He needed to tell her about his sister seeing the paintings, but he didn't want to risk her changing her mind about coming back to his cabin. Working to justify his decision by telling himself he'd divulge it to her soon, he gently stroked her chin with his paint-covered fingertips one more time, then finally started the engine.

* * *

"Did you paint all night long?" Rosa stood in his doorway with her mouth hanging open. Oscar had given a bark of joy when he spotted her and was now leaning heavily against her thigh while she stroked his head.

Drake hadn't thought about how this would look, hadn't been thinking about anything other than praying that she hadn't yet left town and getting to the motel before she could. There was no point in pretending he wasn't consumed by painting her. Not when the proof was right in front of her.

"I've been painting since you left yesterday." And now that she was here again in the flesh, he was itching to get at his brushes and canvases again. "Wherever you want to sit, or stand, or lie down—it's all good for me."

He was reaching for a brush when he noticed her looking at him with concern in her eyes. "Wait, are you saying you haven't slept since *yesterday*?"

"I didn't need to."

She frowned. "Have you eaten?"

"I'm good." The only two things he was hungry for were Rosa—and the chance to paint her.

"No, you're not." She headed into the kitchen with Oscar close on her heels. "I'm not a great cook like you are, but I can make sure you don't starve, at least." She opened the fridge and pulled out cold cuts, cheese, pickles, and mustard. She found a loaf of bread on the counter and grabbed a plate from the open shelf above the sink.

Even watching her make a sandwich fueled Drake. Both as an artist, as he worked to capture her making a sandwich in his kitchen—and as a man, when she popped a piece of turkey into her mouth, then licked off her fingers.

Lord, did he ever want to slide his tongue along her skin.

"Come eat," she said a few minutes later, pushing the plate and a soda toward him on the small, tiled kitchen counter.

But he didn't want to waste one single second of this chance to paint her live and in the flesh. "Thanks, I'll grab it in a bit."

She rolled her eyes. "I'm going to have to force-feed you, aren't I?"

He didn't bother answering, not when he was utterly focused on capturing her expression—the slight tilt of her mouth as she scolded him, along with the light flush in her cheeks that had remained in the wake of their kiss.

"Open up."

Drake was taken unawares by the sandwich pressed to his mouth. But though he did as she asked—ordered, actually—he was barely aware of what he was tasting. All he could focus on was how close she was standing between him and his canvas, and how good it was to have her nearly flush against his body.

"I'm going to stand right here until you finish this."

He took another bite, then washed it down with the soda in her other hand. "It's good," he said as he finally registered the taste. "Really good."

Her smile came fast and beautiful, one dimple flashing. "Thanks." He wished she'd take his compliments about her artistic skills as easily as she took one about a sandwich.

After he took another bite, she took one out of the other side. "Mmm," she said around her mouthful, "it is good."

Funny how much more intimate it felt to share a sandwich with her in his cabin than any five-star dinner with white tablecloths and dim lights ever had. Intimate enough that he couldn't wait any longer to tell her, "My sister dropped by unexpectedly this morning. She saw the paintings, but she's promised not to tell anyone."

About to feed him another bite, Rosa lowered the

sandwich. "She will."

"Suz is a master secret keeper. It's what she does for a living—she makes sure that companies can keep their computer systems totally secure."

But Rosa was shaking her head. "These paintings were just supposed to be between you and me. Not you, me, and your sister."

"Other than an oath signed in blood, I don't know how I'm going to get you to trust me when I say that she's not out to hurt you."

"What did you tell her about me?"

"Only that we'd just met and I wanted to paint you."

"Was she horrified?" Rosa didn't wait for him to answer. "Of course she was. No one would want their brother to get mixed up with some reality TV trash in a nude photo scandal."

He put his hands on her shoulders. "If you're trying to piss me off by insulting both yourself and my family all at the same time, it's working." Her eyes widened. "The only thing she's horrified by is what happened to you. She told me she wished she could write a program that would erase the pictures off the Internet forever—that she'd been thinking about ways to protect people from cyber harassment for a while now."

"She really said that?" When he nodded, Rosa said, "I didn't mean to insult her. It's just really hard for me to trust people right now."

"You have every right to be cynical. If my sister were going to be a problem, I wouldn't hide it from you. But," he warned her, "if you ever call yourself trash again, you're going to find out just how dangerous I can really be."

CHAPTER THIRTEEN

Rosa was almost positive Drake hadn't meant to say what he'd just said in a sexy way...but her body didn't seem to get it.

It was just that she'd never met a man like him before. Not only breathtakingly gorgeous on the outside, but on the inside too. He looked amazing whether clean-shaven or covered in facial hair, well rested or sleep deprived, even wearing paint-spattered jeans with smudges of color all over his hands and hair.

But it was the way he'd repeatedly defended her—even from her own harsh words about herself—that rocked her to the core. And when she was standing this close to him, especially after zinging so many heated words back and forth, it was all she could do not to frame his gorgeous face in her hands and kiss him the same way he'd kissed her in the motel room. With ravenous, desperate passion.

She wanted to rip off his clothes and learn every inch of his body with her hands, her mouth.

She wanted to wrap herself around him again and beg him to take her.

She wanted to lose herself in his intensity, his desire.

And, most of all, she wanted to believe that he was right about her...and that she wasn't trash.

Only Oscar stealing the sandwich from her hand in a deft move that defied his general air of laziness stopped her. "Your dog is eating your sandwich." Her words were heavy with unquenched desire. "I'll make you another."

Her heart was pounding a rough beat in her chest as she headed back to the kitchen and tried to regain at least a tiny bit of composure.

For the past five years, she'd learned so many tricks for how to change the mood in a room, whether at a press conference or at a party, but being with Drake wasn't like being with anyone else. Mostly because he didn't see her the same way the rest of the world did, as nothing more than a vacuous sex symbol who'd "lucked" into a fortune on TV. But was he right? Was she more than that? Had she always been more?

In any case, she badly needed to find some way to drop the intensity level between them. Otherwise, she was very much afraid she wouldn't be able to stop herself from giving in to the desire that only ratcheted up every time they went deep.

Fortunately, the smacking sounds Oscar was

making as he licked the rest of the sandwich from his muzzle helped her pull focus. "Tell me more about your sister," she said as she took food out of the fridge for another sandwich. "You said she writes computer programs?"

"Suzanne founded her own company when she was twenty. She can do pretty much anything when it comes to writing software, but digital security is her specialty. Her company is based in Manhattan."

"She sounds brilliant."

"She is. But I worry about her sometimes, that she doesn't get out enough or see enough of the real world outside her rooms full of computers."

"Does she have a boyfriend?"

"Nope. Like I said, she spends most of her time with her computers."

"Would she tell you if she did have one?"

"Sure, why wouldn't she?"

"Because as soon as I said the word *boyfriend*, you got this protective-warrior look on your face." And her heart had melted even further at how much he obviously cared for his sister. "Is she pretty?"

"Very." He nodded to the hallway. "There's a picture of all of us on the wall."

Rosa put down the mustard bottle and went to take a look. There were lots of family pictures on his walls, and she made a mental note to go back and look at the rest of them later, but for now she homed in on the first one with Drake's immediate family in it. "Wow, you're not the only one with killer genes, are you?"

First off, his sister was miles beyond *pretty*. Tall

and elegant, yet curvy at the same time, she could have walked any runway in the world if she'd wanted to. Rosa loved that she'd chosen what was in her head instead of her looks to guide her career.

As for Drake's brothers? There was no way any woman alive stood a chance against tumbling half into love with a Sullivan, simply from setting eyes on any one of them.

"Alec is the one with the cocky grin." He said it with affection, and she easily guessed exactly which brother he was talking about. "He builds jets, mostly private, just outside of the city. Harrison is a history professor at Columbia. Everyone thinks he's the quiet one, at least until they get to know him."

The brains, looks, and talent in Drake's family made her head spin. "Is this your father with you?"

"That's him." The four siblings stood as one tight unit, but their father was slightly off to one side, almost as though he felt he didn't quite belong in the family photo. "We all happened to be up at his cabin in the Adirondacks at the same time, which doesn't happen that often, so Suz made us set up a camera to get a shot."

"Is that where your father lives?"

"He started building a house in the Adirondacks thirty years ago." After his mother had gone, she thought with a sharp pang in the center of her chest. "We'd all head there during school breaks, but once we were old enough to be left alone, he sold his place in the city and moved there full time."

It wasn't hard for Rosa to put two and two together—not only had his father stopped painting when

Drake's mother passed away, but he'd also retreated from the city.

"I've never been to the Adirondacks. Is it nice?"

"With big blue lakes and green mountains that seem to go on forever, most people tend to think so. It's pretty darn remote, though."

"More remote than this?"

"We're in the Hamptons," he reminded her, his brush never once slowing as they talked.

"Do you see your father much?"

Finally, the brush stopped, hovering just over the canvas. "Not recently. He doesn't get out to the city much."

"And you don't go to the Adirondacks to see him?"

"Not as often as I should." Drake suddenly looked tired, as if his all-nighter had just caught up with him. "That's why Suz came—to see if I wanted to drive out there with her." He paused as if he was trying to decide whether to say more. Finally, he said, "He says he's got some paintings of our mother to give to each of us if we want them."

The last thing Rosa wanted was to hurt Drake. But something told her he needed to talk to someone about what was going on with his family without risking judgment. And if anyone knew about weird family dynamics, she did. Lord knew she was certainly in no position to judge.

Which was why, instead of backing off, she decided to step closer to the fire she could see burning inside of him. "Do you want the paintings?"

"My father is a true master painter, and collectors consider the paintings to be priceless, but—" He put down his brush and ran a paint-smeared hand over his hair, leaving it standing on end. "When she left us, she left him so broken that he left us too. The paintings have always felt like a brutal reminder of how having me must have pushed them both over the edge."

Rosa didn't think, just crossed the room and put her arms around him. "They were wrong. Both of them were so damned wrong to hurt you." He'd been angry with her mother, and now she was just as furious with his parents. She held him tighter as she said, "It doesn't matter how much the paintings are worth. If you decide not to take them, it's entirely on your mother and father, not their innocent kid who got caught in the crossfire."

"How can you see my innocence so clearly," he said as he drew back to cup her face in his hands, "but not your own?"

"If you have an Internet connection here, I'll show you why. It will take me less than five seconds to find dozens of pictures I've posed for where I'm wearing next to nothing. Where I'm deliberately flaunting my body."

"You have every right to flaunt whatever you want to. And you have every goddamned right to strip off your clothes in front of the entire world if it makes you happy. But just like I didn't ask my mother to walk out on me and my family, you sure as hell didn't ask some creep to take those pictures of you."

He'd been passionate and intense before, but this was a whole other level. One where it felt like he'd go to the ends of the earth if that's what he needed to do to make her believe that what he was saying was true.

"You're not only innocent, Rosa, but I don't need to see any pictures of you on the Internet to know that you don't have one single thing to be ashamed of in your past."

Again, Rosa didn't think through her next move, couldn't possibly do anything but feel how full her heart was. She simply went to her tippy-toes, pressed her mouth to his.

And finally gave him the kiss they'd both been waiting for.

CHAPTER FOURTEEN

Drake didn't lose control as Rosa kissed him. Because how could he lose something he'd never had when it came to the woman in his arms?

In the span of a heartbeat, her sweet kiss went deep. Wild. And so hot that he wouldn't be surprised if his cabin caught fire right where they were standing.

"Love me," she whispered against his lips. "Please love me, Drake. Here. Now."

"Anything you want," he promised her. "Anything you need. It's yours."

All night long, as he'd painted her from memory, he'd drifted in and out of a semi-dream state where reality and imagination overlapped, blending until he could barely see their edges. Now, as Rosa's heart hammered out a fast beat against his, those edges blurred again—the real world outside his cabin disappearing until it was only the two of them and the new reality they were creating together.

One where desire ruled...and any cries were those of soul-deep pleasure.

He wound her hair in his fist and tugged her head back so that he could feast on the feather-soft skin at her neck, laving her throbbing pulse point with his tongue before nipping at the curve of her shoulder so that she shuddered and thrill bumps rose across her skin. He'd never wanted to love anyone so much, or so well—had never known what it was to truly lose himself in another's pleasure. Not until Rosa had walked out on his cliffs in the rain and changed absolutely everything.

From the corner, Oscar let out a long, low howl. And when Rosa stilled in his arms, Drake worried that the spell would be broken the same way it was in the motel when she'd stopped and told him she was making a mistake.

But all she said was, "I think we're scandalizing him."

"That's his happy sound," Drake told her as he scooped her up in his arms. She instinctively wound hers around his neck as he added, "He loves having you here." They both did. "But we don't need an audience. And I want you in my bed." Hell, he wanted her everywhere, but the bed would be a good place to start.

"I want it too." She played with the ends of his hair against his neck, almost shy as she said, "More than I've ever wanted anything else."

They were halfway to his bedroom when he had to stop to devour the mouth that was driving him crazy.

Heat spiked even higher as he took her lower lip between his teeth and her moan reverberated through them both.

A split second from taking her right there in the hall, he forced himself to walk the final dozen feet to his bedroom. Kicking the door open, then shut behind them, he all but threw her down on the bed.

"I should be gentle with you." He hoped saying the words aloud would make it possible. "I need to be careful our first time."

"No," she said as she reached for him and pulled him down on top of her, "I don't want gentle. I don't want careful." Her eyes were so big, so honest. "I want *dangerous*."

The floodgates of desire had already been yanked open by her kisses. But now?

Now the last wall of the dam exploded as he slid his hands beneath her sweatshirt so that he could take greedy fistfuls of her. But even then it wasn't enough just to touch—he needed to see, needed to taste.

Thank God she was already tearing off the thick cotton sweatshirt and her bra, baring herself to his gaze and his mouth as he licked out against the swell of one gorgeously aroused breast, then the other. But this back and forth still wasn't enough—he needed all of her at once, needed to cup her in his rough hands so that he could suckle both breasts at the same time.

"God, that's so good." She thrust her hands into his hair and urged him closer as he pressed her breasts together and let his hunger for her take over. "More," she urged him, "take more of me."

He felt her arousal climb higher and higher as

he used tongue, teeth, and hands all at once, her hips bucking up into his as he ground himself against her. Lust clawed at his insides, driving him half mad as he yanked off her sweatpants and panties, then threw them across the room. He pressed his lips to her belly, then thrust his hand between her legs to find her gloriously wet and ready for him.

Rosa's scent, the feel of her soft skin beneath his hands, her passionate response—every part of her intoxicated him. But it was the way she looked lying in his bed with her long hair wild on his pillow, her head thrown back in ecstasy, and her eyes closed, her breasts wet from his tongue and slightly abraded from his whiskers, that made time actually stop.

All his life, Drake had seen beyond the actual, then sought to capture his hyper-vision on canvas. But he'd never, not once in his entire life, seen anything as beautiful as the woman in his bed.

"Drake?" Her eyes were open again now, sparkling with so much life and heat and passion that he knew he could paint her a million times and never manage to show it all. Never even come close. "Don't stop." She licked her lips, and he had to taste them too. "Please, I'm—" She suddenly looked shy again as she whispered, "I'm so close."

"Good." He pressed his mouth to the hollow of her neck as he slipped his fingers from her wet heat to skim them over her sex instead. "Close is good." He licked her collarbone, then lightly sank his teeth into the sweet curve of her shoulder. "I love knowing you're nearly there. That I've taken you right to the edge." He circled the wet flesh between her thighs. "Just think how it's going to feel when you finally fall all the way over." With his other hand, he lightly rolled her nipple against his thumb. "So much better than *good* you're not going to believe it."

Her breath was coming in hard pants now, her pupils dilated so wide her eyes were nearly black. "It already feels like that," she said at the exact moment he found her breasts again with his tongue and teeth. "Better than anything has ever been."

He had to lift his mouth back to hers, needed her to know that it was the same for him. But soon, he was running his free hand and his mouth back over her breasts, and then farther down, over her stomach, pressing kisses to the tops of her thighs before putting his hands on them so that he could marvel all over again at just how beautiful she was. And so aroused that even blowing lightly over her sex was almost enough to send her tumbling into climax.

Drake wanted to savor this moment, wanted to draw out every single second with her so that it never ended.

But how could he resist the need to taste her?

Only, when he finally covered her with his mouth, he needed a hell of a lot more than just a taste. He needed to devour her. Needed to plunge deep with his tongue as arousal spilled. Needed to plunge his fingers back into her to feel her clench tight around him, his name on her lips as her orgasm peaked, then ripped through her.

Something snapped in him—and *dangerous* was the only way to describe the way he shoved off his clothes, put on protection, and leapt back over her on the bed.

Her eyes were wide as he grabbed her wrists in his hands and pushed them over her head. Not with fear, but with an arousal that matched his own.

"Yes," she panted, pleaded. "Take me. All of me. Don't hold back."

But he was already there, dropping one hand from her wrists to reach down and push one leg up and open for him, then reaching around to grip her hip in his hand. He stopped only long enough to take a mental snapshot of her aroused perfection before he thrust home.

One hard, perfect charge forward into heaven.

A gasp of pleasure sounded from her throat as she bucked against him, using his grip at her wrists and thigh for leverage to get closer, to take more of him.

"Oh God. It's so good. *You* feel so good."

Though her eyelids fluttered as bliss washed through her, she never looked away. And neither did he, unable to stand the thought of missing even one second of loving Rosa.

The sight of her flushed skin, the sexy sound of her moans of pleasure, the scent of her arousal—he'd never forget any of it. Would never be able to find anything, or anyone, to rival it. Sex had never been like this before, had never felt this intense. This mind-blowing.

This *meant* to be.

He crushed her mouth beneath his as he let go of her wrists so that he could pull her even tighter, while she wrapped her arms and legs around him as if she wanted him just as close. The way they fit together, inside and out, he swore she was made only for him.

"Mine." He left her lips only long enough to tell her the one thing he now knew for sure. "You're mine."

He didn't leave her breath to reply, but he didn't need to. Not when the press of her damp skin, the passion with which she urged his kisses and his thrusting hips deeper—and the staggering pleasure that took them higher and higher before finally sending them flying out over the edge together—told him that she felt the same.

CHAPTER FIFTEEN

He'd nearly killed her with pleasure.

But even if he had, it would have been the perfect way to go. Nothing in her life had ever been so extraordinary, so all-consuming. Especially not sex.

After playing the sex symbol for so many years, everyone thought she was so sexy. They assumed she ate men for lunch and spit out their bones before dinner. But they couldn't have been more wrong, couldn't have known just how uncomfortable and fake sex had always felt for her. In large part because the men she'd slept with had always wanted—and expected—her to be as glossy and camera-ready in the sack as she was while filming with makeup artists and hairstylists standing by.

Rosa had been a virgin until after they'd signed on to do the show, so she'd never had sex without that pressure right alongside it. Which meant that she'd never really been able to enjoy it.

Right now, however, she was anything but glossy. Miles from camera-ready. She was sticky and sweaty, and her hair was knotted from where Drake's hands had tangled in it, a thick fog of sensual bliss lingering while she worked to get some oxygen back into her lungs.

In his arms, she'd temporarily forgotten to be afraid. Passion, desire, and pleasure had taken over every cell, inside and out. But now that she was starting to overthink everything again, the fear that he wouldn't be able to appreciate her like this came rushing back.

She knew just when he sensed her shift from languid to stiff by the way he drew back to lever himself over her, then gazed down at her with obvious concern. "Something's wrong."

Knowing she was only making things worse by getting all weird right after they'd just had amazing sex, she made herself say, "How could anything be wrong after that?"

"I don't know," he said in a gentle voice. Even when they'd been totally swept up in passion with her wrists in his hands as he took her deliciously hard and fast, he'd been gentle at his core. "But something clearly is."

For so many years, she'd been able to bank her true thoughts and reactions. But with Drake, she couldn't seem to hold herself back. She kept telling him too much—feeling too much around him. Which meant that when whatever they were doing together came to its inevitable end, her heart would not only rupture into a million little pieces, but it would never grow back whole again.

"Why can't you just be a clueless guy like the rest of them? Why do you have to notice every little thing?"

"I don't notice with everyone, Rosa."

She'd felt appreciated—treasured—in his arms. But while she could easily have chalked that up to endorphins, she couldn't deny that his words could mean only one thing: She was important to him.

And it scared her. So much that she blurted, "I'm tired of feeling scared."

"I was too rough." He reached for her wrists, ran his fingertips over them as if to check for bruises. "You asked for dangerous, but I took it too far."

"No, the way you took me...that's not what scared me. You were perfect. You are perfect." A rough breath shook through her. "I'm the one who isn't. Not even close. Men always expect me to be, especially in bed. But no matter how hard I try, I can't do it. I just can't."

"That's why you're scared?" He looked as though he not only couldn't believe what she'd just said, but that it wouldn't compute inside his brain. "Because you think I expect you to be perfect?"

"For five years, I've had one job: to look pretty and polished all the time. It didn't matter if I'd just woken up or was coming out of the gym." She sat up, needing a little space to try to make sense so that he'd understand where she was coming from. "So even though I know I haven't looked great since we met, I've never looked like this. All knotted up and sticky. I don't want you to think—" She swallowed hard. "To think that you've made a mistake sleeping with me."

Even as she said it, Rosa knew that *she* was making a huge mistake by letting herself get closer to him like this. A mistake for which she was soon going to pay dearly. Because when she had to force herself to leave him before he was ruined by being linked to her—romantically or otherwise—it was going to rip her heart in two.

"Jesus, Rosa." He pulled himself into a sitting position too. "The only mistake is if you think the reason people all over the world are mesmerized by you is because of what you look like. There are plenty of beautiful women out there, but no one wants to follow their every move. Do you know why that is?"

Her throat tight from the realization that their lovemaking hadn't changed anything in the long term and that the clock was already running out on how long she could stay here with him, she could barely get the words out. "Because they don't understand how Hollywood works like my family and I do."

"You're wrong. So damned wrong." He pulled her onto his lap, clearly not giving a damn that she was still sticky with sweat. "The real reason people can't get enough of you is because you're smart. You're funny. You're talented. It's because you're soft and you're strong, all at the same time."

Her throat grew even tighter as it swelled with yet more emotion. "Only you see me this way." And oh, how she wished she could stay with him. How she wished that she could love him the way he deserved to be loved. Not in the shadows, but for the whole world to see. And with a whole heart, rather than one that had been shredded to pieces one too many times.

"Everyone sees you that way, Rosa." He pressed the words against her lips in a sweet, soft kiss that made her want so many more, especially if they could actually erase the dark clouds that had been hovering over her for so long. "You're the only one who doesn't." His lips whispered against hers. "How many paintings am I going to have to make of you until you see the truth?"

"I—" She shook her head, let out a frustrated breath, one that came from way down deep in her soul. She wanted so much right now, wanted all the things she knew she could never have because of a decision she'd made to film a TV show when she was eighteen years old. "I don't know if that's even possible."

"It is." He spoke with perfect certainty. "But maybe it's not seeing that will help you believe." He tangled his hands in her hair to pull her closer. "Maybe it's feeling. Feeling so much that you can't deny it anymore." He took her lips in a deep, passionate kiss, one that had her head spinning and her body tingling all over. "I'm going to make that my purpose from now on—to make sure you're *feeling* all the time. Starting right now."

She knew he wasn't saying the words as a warning, but so that she could anticipate. So that she could pant with renewed need as he ran his big hands over her naked skin, cupping and stroking until she was actually writhing on his lap.

And even though she knew better, even though she knew this perfect idyll in Drake's secret cabin in the woods couldn't last forever, no matter how much she wished it could, she was here with him now. So she would make the most of every precious second.

"Please."

He made her so needy that she couldn't help but beg. And maybe with anyone else it would have felt like giving away her own power. But though she wasn't sure she'd ever be able to believe in her own strength or talent the way he did, she already knew for certain that he would never try to gain his power through her the way so many other men had since she'd become famous.

"Tell me," he urged, "tell me what you want."

She hadn't exactly been shy during their lovemaking—how could she be, when his kisses and caresses felt like they'd stripped away everything that didn't matter? But she hadn't taken the lead either. She knew what she wanted, of course. What she'd wanted from the start, but hadn't let herself have.

"You." She put her hands on his jaw and let herself take a long, heady look at the incredible man holding her as though he'd never let her go, never let her fall. "I want you."

His grin was spiked with heat. So much heat that it took her breath away. "Then take me."

She grinned back, no longer worried about feeling shy or ashamed. At least not now. Not when she and Drake were alone in their private cocoon of pleasure.

Drawing back just enough on his lap so that there was space to put her hands on his chest, she closed her eyes and drank in the feel of him, so solid and warm and alive against her palms. Where he obviously favored the visual, she always saw best through her hands.

Slowly, sensually, she worked her way down over his broad and muscular shoulders, tracing his biceps and triceps, and then the sinews on his forearms. First with her hands, and then with her lips, over every inch. All the while, she could feel his arousal grow beneath her hips. Instinct had her teasing with a slow slide here, a wiggle there.

She was glad he let her play as long as he did, but at the same time she loved it when he hit his limit and took her mouth in a rough, perfect kiss. She never wanted this moment to end, but now that she knew the exquisite pleasure of Drake's body heavy over hers, inside of hers, she didn't think she could wait another second to get there.

Fortunately, he must have been thinking the exact same way, because the next thing she knew he had donned protection again and was tumbling her back onto the bed, his weight levered over hers.

"Rosa."

He said only her name as he moved into her, but it felt like so much more. Felt like everything she'd ever wanted but hadn't thought she could have. She'd never felt this good before, never believed it was possible.

She felt appreciated. Adored. Consumed. Devoured. And...right on the verge of overwhelmed.

But just when she hit the point where fear might have been able to come creeping back in, Drake kissed her.

And made her forget everything but sweet, spiraling ecstasy.

CHAPTER SIXTEEN

"Before the sun sets, I need to paint you again."

Drake tugged her from the warm, cozy bed where she could easily have stayed the rest of the afternoon. Especially if he was in it too.

"Maybe you could bring your easel in here so that I can stay in bed," she said with a shiver as her bare feet hit the cool wood planks.

"Later," he said as he dragged her against him for a hot, too-quick kiss. "Right now I want to paint you in the light coming in through the living room windows."

"It isn't easy being a muse," she murmured as she turned to find her clothes.

He surprised her by putting his hands on her shoulders and spinning her around to face him. "Promise me you won't ever sit for me if you don't want to."

She blinked at him, trying to figure out what

she'd said wrong. "I was just teasing," she said, but she instantly realized why he wouldn't find her offhand comment at all funny. "I'm sorry, I shouldn't have said it."

"If it's what you're feeling—"

She put her hand on his jaw, desire rising at even that one small touch. "I love that you're inspired by me in any way at all. I'm happy to sit for you until you get tired of having me here."

"Never." His eyes went so dark when he grew serious like this. "It won't ever happen. But that doesn't mean I have the right to imprison you in my painting cave."

"Do you think that's what your dad did?" She didn't want to hurt him with her question, but she didn't think either of them could skirt around it now either. "Do you think he made your mom his unwilling muse?"

His jaw jumped beneath her palm, and she wanted so badly to soothe him. "I don't know." She ran her hand down from his face to place it over his chest, his heart beating fast as he told her, "None of us know much at all about what happened between them."

"What about the paintings? Wouldn't you be able to tell from looking at her expression? From what you see in her eyes?"

"Maybe." His frown deepened. "Unless my father only painted what he wanted to see—or my mother only showed him what she thought she was supposed to as his muse."

Rosa wished Drake's family was perfect, wished he didn't have to deal with such a complicated situation.

But maybe that was part of what had drawn them to each other from the start. And maybe that was also why they weren't afraid to dig beneath the surface.

Right now, however, she wanted to see the light, the inspiration, in his eyes again. So instead of continuing to dig, she smiled and said, "You promised me pie and a dog on my lap." It took another few moments for his eyes to clear, but when his mouth found hers again, she breathed a sigh of relief against his lips. "After the sun sets," she whispered as she made herself draw back, "we'll continue that thought."

She felt his eyes on her—hot and hungry—as she pulled on her sweatshirt and panties and headed out to the kitchen. Oscar stretched lazily before padding over to her. "Do you have any treats for him?"

"He'll happily take a slice of pie," Drake said, already at his easel, "but there are dog bones in the corner cupboard."

She fished a bone the size of her fist out of the container. "Sit." Oscar plunked his big butt down. She held out her hand, and with the utmost care, he licked the bone into his mouth. "You really are adorable. One day I want a dog just like you."

"You don't have one?"

"I travel too much, plus my little brother is allergic."

"Tell me about your siblings."

"I have two brothers, actually pretty similar to yours, from what you've told me. Aaron is the cocky one. Sporty. Smart. A bit of a player, if I'm being honest." She gave Oscar another bone, then washed her hands and reached for the pie on the counter. "I really do love him, though, even if he can be pretty insufferable sometimes. Lincoln is quieter. Just as charming when he wants to be, but usually happier in his head—just like my dad was." Trying to keep from getting emotional again when she'd intended to keep things light, she said, "Lincoln can't believe he has so many fans on the show. But there's just something appealing about that strong, silent type."

"No sisters?"

She shook her head. "I always wished I had one, but after what happened to me—" Damn it, she was doing a terrible job of keeping things light. "I'm just glad there wasn't another girl in the family to take pictures of, and that my mom wasn't filming that trip with us either."

Thankfully, Oscar's loud snuffling at the edge of the counter where the pie sat helped her shake off the darkness that threatened. She turned the oven on and put the pie in, figuring it would be ready to eat by the time the sun set. "Come on, big boy, let's go pose for the painter."

It was like crossing the room with a lion at her side—while another one held a paintbrush, his dark gaze both intense and protective. She knew she shouldn't let herself become too dependent on Drake, but unlike pretty much everyone else in her world, she couldn't imagine him ever attaching strings to anything.

As soon as she sat in the leather lounger, Oscar got up in her lap, then turned his muzzle so that he could rest it on her shoulder like a baby. She laughed as she stroked him. "I love you too."

"Lucky furball."

Drake's brush didn't stop moving the way it did whenever things got really serious, but his soft comment still hit her smack dab in the center of her chest.

Did he really mean it? Would he actually want her to love him? And if she did, was there a chance that he would ever love her back? Truly love her, mistakes and all?

Just like that, her fears came rushing back. So many fears. Too many. She truly was sick of being scared.

And yet, she thought as she looked around the room at the paintings propped up against the walls, the woman on Drake's canvases didn't look scared. Pensive. Sensual. Confused. Wild. But not scared. Above all, it was bravery and strength that shone through.

She'd meant it when she told him that she didn't understand how he saw so much, even the things she could barely see in herself. Rosa wanted to be brave, wanted to be strong like the woman in his paintings.

The only problem was that she didn't know if being strong meant staying here with him...or walking away without letting him get any closer to her and her messes.

Only her body had clear answers right now, with the pleasure he'd given her—the pleasure they'd given each other—nowhere near close to fading. Turning to stare at him now instead of the paintings, she was filled with such longing to kiss him, to touch him, to love him with everything she had during whatever time they still had together. He was so intuitive. Did he know that the only time in a very long while that she'd truly felt strong, brave—*good*—had been in his arms? Almost as though his bravery, his strength, had been pouring through his skin to hers.

There was nothing she wanted more than to be right back there in his arms again. But since Drake wanted to paint until sunset and she refused to do anything that would distract him from his calling, she decided she needed to do something to keep her hands busy and off of him. Something more than just being pinned in place by his huge sweetheart of a dog.

As if he could read her mind, Oscar climbed off her lap and back onto his bed so that she could grab a small blank canvas from Drake's stash. "Can I use this?"

It took him long enough to answer that she knew he must have already gone deep. "Use anything."

She loved that feeling, when she got so lost in something she was making that everything else fell away. She was glad that after months of being blocked, he had finally found his way back into the groove.

Grabbing her needles and thread from her bag, she took the canvas back to the leather chair and began to stitch. She'd never again take for granted this wonderful feeling of being warm and sated, with a dog snoring at her side and the sun setting out over the ocean. But best of all was knowing that Drake was there, creating alongside her.

Her knight in shining armor, who had already given her so much more than any fairy-tale prince could have.

CHAPTER SEVENTEEN

Long after the sun had set and the timer on the oven had dinged for the apple pie, Rosa remained utterly absorbed in the project on her lap. Oscar was sprawled beside her on the floor, belly up, as peaceful and happy as Drake had ever seen his big lump of a dog.

Drake hadn't minded being two bachelors—one human, one canine—rattling around his cabin and New York City penthouse. But when Rosa was with them, his space became warmer. Brighter. So much more alive. Even as she worked quietly with great concentration, she was all those things.

At last, she looked up at him. "Oh no!" She jumped up, dropping the canvas on the chair. "I forgot the pie."

"I got it."

Halfway across the room, she was close enough

for Drake to pull her in for a kiss. She immediately melted against him, her arms circling his neck as she kissed him back. He was a beat from carrying her into the bedroom again when he heard her stomach rumble.

"You're hungry. Come share my pie."

"Is that slang for something dirty?"

He laughed so loudly that Oscar lifted his head to see what all the fuss was about. Drake's cabin was so small that he was easily able to put his hands on her waist and spin her around to sit on his kitchen countertop. "Stay there while I get a fork."

She raised an eyebrow. "You're kind of bossy," she teased as she dipped a finger into the pie and brought it to her lips. "*Come back to my cabin*," she said in a low voice that was supposed to sound like his. "*Go pose for me. Sit on the kitchen counter and don't move.*" She licked warm apple filling from her fingertip, her eyes closing for a moment of bliss before she opened them to say, "It's pretty sexy, actually."

Hell, she was the one who was both sexy and sweet, sitting on his counter in nothing but a pair of panties and a Montauk sweatshirt, with tangled sex-hair and apple pie on her lips. He nearly slammed the cutlery drawer shut on his hand as a powerful realization hit him right there in the middle of the kitchen.

Rosa was it for him.

This had happened to so many of Drake's cousins that he didn't try to fight it, even if other bachelors his age might have gone to battle, with everything they had, against falling in love.

Or maybe the reason he didn't need to fight it was

simply because from the first moment he'd set eyes on Rosa until this very moment in his kitchen, he'd found endless reasons to love her.

The way she was filled with light, inside and out, even when darkness would have surrounded anyone else in her position.

How much it had obviously hurt her to hear about the loss of his mother and his father's relentless pain.

The fact that she still deeply loved her own mother even if her heart had been torn apart by the way her mother was dealing with the photos.

Rosa was so much stronger than she knew, and he wouldn't stop looking for ways to make her see it too. Yes, he knew that her life was anything but simple right now, but Drake was finally starting to see that keeping things simple didn't always mean they were better. And he sure as hell wasn't afraid to take on her demons, not when he wished he could have gone to battle for her by doing more than just calling Smith for help.

She was, he knew now, worth any risk.

Even the risk of repeating his parents' mistakes.

He wanted to say, *I'm falling in love with you.* But he knew better than to do that just yet. He didn't want her to claim it was hot sex talking. Or to say that he only loved painting her. Or that he hadn't had any sleep last night and would feel differently after he had.

Besides, given that her life was complicated enough already, it definitely seemed smarter to focus on the simple things—food, laughter, pleasure—to give her a chance to learn to trust again.

Soon, however, he'd put on the full-court press

to make sure she knew that he wasn't going anywhere... and that she shouldn't either, because he didn't need her to protect him from anyone or anything. No, what he needed was *Rosa*, messes and all.

Drake pushed the fork into the pie, then lifted it to her mouth. "Open up."

"See?" she said with a little smile. "Bossy." But she happily took the bite he offered and then the next before she'd even finished the first. "Mmm, I need more."

"Never thought I'd be jealous of an apple pie," he grumbled as he answered her request with a third bite that was all apple.

"It is really good," she said when she'd finished it. "But I'm thinking we can make it even better. How do you feel about being each other's plate?"

Drake couldn't get his shirt—or her top—off fast enough.

"I take it," she said through her laughter, "that's a yes?"

"It's a *hell* yes. You first."

For as hard as his blood was pumping and as fast as his heart was racing, he was amazed by how gentle he was able to be as he laid her down on the counter, wearing only her panties now. He wanted to feast on her, and it was damned tempting to forget about the pie altogether. But since he also hoped that this sexy game was her way of opening up to him a little bit more, he didn't want to screw things up by changing the rules. Not when she'd had way too many rules changed on her already.

Dipping his finger into the pie, he lifted it to

her breasts and circled one nipple with the warm, sweet filling. Her eyelids fluttered to half-mast as he bent to lick it off. It was hard to go slowly, to savor, when all he wanted was to devour—especially when her hands had tangled in his hair to bring him closer. But he wouldn't rush giving her pleasure as he licked every inch of her left breast, then started all over by painting apple pie around her right nipple and giving it the same hungry treatment with his tongue.

"My turn now," she panted when he lifted his mouth from her skin.

"I'm not even close to having my fill yet." He scooped up an apple chunk, and when he dropped it into her belly button, her slightly breathless laughter was easily the sweetest thing he'd ever heard. Quickly, however, humor shifted to an aroused moan as he purposefully nipped at her skin while biting into the apple. One more bite—one more sexy moan—and the piece of apple was gone.

"Drake," she said as she tried to sit up, "I want to do the same to you now."

But he had already hooked his fingers into the sides of her panties and was pulling them down her legs. "I need one more taste first."

Tossing the cotton aside a moment later, he lowered his mouth to her sex. And she was so much sweeter than pie as she shattered against his lips, his tongue, his fingers, that he already knew he'd never get his fill of her.

* * *

Up on the counter, Rosa was at the perfect height for Drake's lazy exploration back up her torso with his lips and tongue while she slowly resurfaced from yet another mind-blowing orgasm. "As soon as I can figure out how to move again," she said, "you're in for it."

He grinned against her soft skin. "Don't rush on my account. If you hadn't noticed, I'm having a mighty good time already."

"Me too." She could hear the surprise in her own voice. She could still hardly believe that she could feel so relaxed—or have so much fun with anyone. She pushed herself into a sitting position, then hopped off. "No need for you to get on the counter," she said as reached for the button of his jeans, then unzipped them and pushed them to the floor. "Wow." His erection was so big and hard and beautiful that she almost dropped to her knees to worship it, before she remembered she was supposed to do this with pie.

"Rosa." She was just swiping some pie with one finger and dropping down when he put a hand beneath her chin and tipped her face up. "You don't have to—"

"I *want* to," she said, bringing his hand between her thighs. "Can't you feel how much I want you like this?"

Heat flared in his eyes as he told her, "I love how much you want me. Just as much as I want you." Without missing a beat, he thrust his fingers into her so erotically that she had to reach for his shoulders to hold on. "Come for me again, Rosa. Just like this."

He didn't give her time to think, just covered

her mouth with his and thrust his tongue against hers in the same perfect rhythm in which his hand was moving between her thighs. Within seconds, he'd stoked her to blazing hot again, everywhere he touched aching for more, more, *more*.

Her knees buckled from her release when it came sudden and fierce, but he held her so steady with his free hand that she didn't need to think, didn't need to worry, didn't need to do anything but let herself drown in an ecstasy that felt like it would never end.

"God, I love that," he murmured against her lips between kisses.

"You're going to love this too."

She made sure to take him by surprise this time, not only with the layer of pie she spread over his shaft, but by how quickly she got on her knees to lick it off. He throbbed hard against her tongue, every last inch of him so delicious that she wanted to eat him up in one greedy gulp. But he'd taken such care with her again and again that she took her reckless desires in hand and made herself go even slower on her second pass with her tongue over his rock-hard length.

"*Rosa.*" Her name falling from his lips was somewhere between a growl and a prayer. "It's so damned good. Too good." He tangled his hands in her hair, and she swore she could feel him warring with himself over remaining gentle when it was clear that he was barely holding back *dangerous*.

She loved that she could make him feel like this, so aroused that he *nearly* forgot to be careful. But nearly wasn't good enough. She wanted every ounce of his passion with nothing held back—just the way he made her feel every time he kissed or touched her.

Before he could attempt to regain control, she took him deep. His thigh muscles clenched against her hands, his fingers tightened in her hair, and when his hips moved, she moved with him. Took him again and again until the only sounds in the room were his groans and her gasping breaths.

She was so lost to the pleasure of loving him this way that she was taken utterly unawares when he pulled back so that he could pull her up off her knees and lift her back onto the counter. Her mind was too fuzzy with arousal to be able to do anything but watch as he quickly pulled a condom from the pocket of his jeans, jammed it on over his erection, and yanked her hips to the edge.

"Wrap your legs around me."

But she was already there, already moving to take him inside when he slammed into her. Both of them held on for dear life as they took from, and gave to, each other again and again and again, her fears, her shame, her worries all falling away. Because in this moment, as he loved her with everything he had—and she loved him right back—there wasn't room for anything but *him*.

* * *

Drake put a big slice of apple pie on the floor for Oscar before they went to take a bath to clean the sugar off. Getting into the tub with Drake and slipping and sliding against all his sexy muscles made her burn for him all over again. But before she could make a move, the warm water lulled her half to sleep.

Dimly, she could feel him running a soapy washcloth over her. The next thing she knew, she was wrapped in a towel and he was carrying her over to the bed.

"I didn't mean to fall asleep," she whispered. "I was going to seduce you."

"I'm going to hold you to that rain check," he said as he pulled back the covers and laid her down. "But for now, I think we could both use some sleep."

Drake got in beside her and put his arm around her waist. And as he pulled her close, the last thing she remembered before sleep took her all the way under was—finally—feeling *safe*.

CHAPTER EIGHTEEN

Rosa woke up sprawled across Drake as though his body were her personal mattress, his chest her pillow.

Last night, she'd been too exhausted to seduce him the way he'd continually seduced her. Heck, it barely took one of his smiles and the lightest brush of his fingertips over her cheek for her to end up completely lost in him. She'd promised herself she wouldn't use him to drown her sorrows, but she'd simply been unable to keep herself from kissing him—and then showing him on an even more intimate level just how good he made her feel. Inside and out.

And now here she was, in his bed, his arms wrapped around her, his heart beating against hers. She'd never slept all night with a man. Not when there were always cameras waiting to catch her every move, and any "morning after" activity would be especially notable.

But though cameras might not be waiting right outside his cabin, she knew the world was still waiting for her to emerge. Just as that familiar tightening started to twist up her stomach, Drake shifted slightly beneath her and she realized he was waking up too.

Maybe it was crazy, but even with the same threats hanging over her, in the new light of morning she wanted nothing more than to fully appreciate these hours of peace and pleasure in Drake's arms by making good on her seduction rain check.

Deliberately letting the feel of his big, warm, muscular body beneath hers take over everything else, she pressed a soft kiss to the pulse point on his neck. Just that quickly, she felt his heartbeat jump beneath her smiling lips.

Slowly, she ran kisses over his face—his jaw, his cheekbones, his still-closed eyelids—holding out on touching her lips to his until she simply couldn't take it anymore. On a soft moan, as his tongue met hers, she had to press her naked body closer to his.

One of his kisses was all it had ever taken to rev up her arousal into the stratosphere. It would be so easy to let that arousal steamroll her slow seduction, but this morning her need to savor, to discover, to treasure every single second with Drake was even greater.

From the way his breathing had changed and his muscles moved beneath hers, she knew he had come fully awake. Fortunately, he still let her show him with her lips, her hands, and her body all the things she didn't know how to say with words. All the things she didn't think she *could* say.

Here in his bed, there was no shame, no fears left that he wouldn't like what he saw when she was less than camera-ready. Nothing to stop her from giving him all of herself, at least for a few precious moments while birds sang outside his bedroom window and the surf crashed against the cliffs.

Rosa was teasingly running her fingertips over the deep grooves of Drake's abdomen when he finally opened his eyes. So much heat blazed in them that her breath actually whooshed out.

"Come here and kiss me again."

He didn't wait for her to say she would, simply lifted her right where he wanted her, so that her breasts pressed against his chest, her hips were over his, and his hands were tangled in her hair as they dove at each other.

Somehow she managed to drag her mouth from his to say, "Grab the rails of the headboard."

He raised an eyebrow. "You sure that's where you want my hands?"

A shiver ran through her at the thought of *all* the other places she'd much rather have his hands. Seeing it, his gorgeous mouth quirked up at the corner. Which sent yet another shiver through her, of course.

"It's time for me to make good on my rain check," she finally managed to reply in a very breathless voice. "I can't do that if you're touching me." *And driving me absolutely crazy.*

Slowly, as if he knew precisely how much she liked it when he teased her, he untangled his hands from her hair and lifted them to the headboard. "Not much time left on the clock," he warned her in pretty much the sexiest voice ever.

Oh God, knowing that he was quickly approaching the end of his patience with letting her play sent sizzles all the way to her core.

"Then I'd better make the most of every single second."

The muscles and tendons of his shoulders, arms, and torso flexed as she pressed her palms flat over his chest. For a handful of precious moments, she closed her eyes and just let herself feel his heart beating.

When she opened her eyes, she nearly gasped at the way he was looking at her. Not just with desire, but with something that looked like *love*.

She couldn't move, couldn't breathe, couldn't think.

Could only yearn for a love like his.

How could she do anything but kiss him again and wrap herself all around him and wish that she never, ever had to let go? It had never been this easy, this good, with anyone else. So good that she wanted to freeze-frame right here in this moment, forever.

The next thing Rosa knew, she was beneath Drake, his strong limbs pressed over hers.

"I know I should have some control by now," he said as he ran sweet, hot kisses all over her body, sending her spinning around and around and around, from head to heart, body to soul, by the time he spoke again. "But when it comes to you..."

He was inside her before she could take her next breath. Somewhere along the way he must have slipped on protection, but she'd only barely been able to hang on to her senses when he was kissing her, touching her, thrilling her.

As they moved together as though they'd been made only for each other, Rosa finally gave up trying to control the magic. For this one perfect morning, she simply let herself be utterly bewitched. Enthralled. Possessed.

And when she felt herself falling, she not only trusted Drake enough to let herself go, but for a few wonderful moments in his arms as pleasure peaked higher than ever, she trusted herself too.

* * *

Working together in the kitchen a little while later, they devoured huge helpings of bacon, eggs, and toast. Oscar did his fair share, licking their plates so clean that washing them almost seemed like a waste of time and water. But since Rosa was eating Drake's food and sleeping in his bed, she washed while he dried. They were just finishing up when Oscar nudged the back of her leg with his leash in his mouth.

Rosa laughed as she washed off the soap bubbles and dried her hands. "Time for a walk, is it?"

"You don't want to see him when he misses it," Drake teased. "Grouch city."

She couldn't imagine it. "Actually, I wouldn't mind stretching my legs a little before I get back into serious posing mode on your leather chair."

"My sister left a pair of mud boots here last time she visited, if you want to try them on."

Sleeping in his arms, making breakfast together, walking his dog in his sister's borrowed boots—if she let herself, it would be so easy to believe this was something more than a temporary break from her life. Especially if she let herself stay much longer.

It was going to be hard enough to finally face the public, the TV producers, and her family. But leaving Drake was suddenly looming even larger than all of that. Because once she left him, she could not only never come back—she could never speak of their time at all. Not if she wanted to keep him clean.

"Rosa?" His big, sexy hands were on her face, and he was gently stroking her cheeks with his thumbs. "I lost you there for a minute, didn't I?"

There was no point trying to deny it. "I was thinking about the show." *And how much I hate the thought of leaving you soon.* She tried to smile as if her stomach wasn't in knots. "Do you have a jacket to go with your sister's boots?"

Serious eyes held hers for a few more moments, before he nodded. "Out on the mud porch."

Once jackets and boots were on, the three of them headed out into the woods. The sun was out, but the morning air was cool enough that she was glad for the jacket over her sweatshirt. For the past five years, she'd worn custom and couture, but she wasn't sure she'd ever been quite as comfortable as she was in a faded red raincoat, yellow mud boots, and her Montauk sweatpants. She felt surprisingly sexy too, which mostly had to do with the fact that this morning after they'd made love, she'd washed her bra and panties in the bathroom sink and left them hanging to dry, so she was currently going completely commando beneath her sweats.

She could practically hear Drake's brain working, knew he wasn't going to let her comment about the show go that easily.

One obvious way to distract him would be to mention what she wasn't wearing beneath her clothes. They were both so hot for each other that it was a minor miracle their clothes had stayed on this long. But it wouldn't sit right if she manipulated him like that. Regardless of the things she'd done during the past five years in the name of fame and reality TV, playing Drake in any way would make it so that she'd never again be able to look herself in the eye in any mirror, ever.

"Go ahead." She squeezed his hand to try to ground herself in his steady strength. "I'm ready for whatever you want to say."

His deep blue gaze locked with hers. "Do you want to go back to your show? And before you answer, you should know that I'm on your side whether it's yes or no."

Rosa was completely thrown off by his acceptance of a possible yes. As he'd said before, it was tempting to try to assign black or white to everything, but the truth was that nothing was really all good or all bad, was it?

Except for Drake Sullivan, who was one thousand percent good.

"It was fun at first," she admitted. It would be a lie to say it wasn't, and lying to Drake wasn't okay. "Being famous was part of the fun. Limos. First class. Luxury hotels. Designers making clothes just for me.

Everyone was so interested in the music I was listening to, the TV shows I loved, what I wore—it was really flattering. Gave me a big head for a while, if I'm being honest. I was eighteen when we started filming, and I thought I was so grown up already. I didn't realize that I'd be growing up in front of the world, that my screw-ups and crushes and fights with my mom wouldn't be over in a day or a week like they were before the show, but would stay around forever on screen."

"I can't imagine most people would have thought of that before signing on. And I'm guessing the producers sold you on the fun parts most of all."

"They did, but it's not their fault that no one takes me seriously. If only I'd been more aware of the reputation I was building—"

"You were a kid, Rosa. It doesn't sound like you acted differently than anyone else does at eighteen or nineteen. Besides, you're easily resilient enough to withstand a few public screw-ups."

"If I wasn't, I would have quit the first week," she agreed. "Even the bad stuff that came along with becoming famous, like losing some privacy and reading the mean things people said about me online and in the press, didn't feel so bad. But then one day I saw myself on TV. And I was shocked...because I didn't recognize her. I didn't recognize *me*. Not just because of all the makeup, the hair, the clothes." She paused, hoping he'd understand. "My laugh didn't sound real. And I couldn't think of the last book I'd read. The last hike I'd been on. The last friend I'd spent time with—not celebrity friends, but the real ones I'd known since kindergarten."

She was surprised to look back over her shoulder and realize they'd walked far enough that Drake's cabin was no longer in sight. "That was the first time I thought about getting off the ride. But it was already going so fast, I couldn't see how. And it just kept going faster and faster after that."

"You're off now."

"Only because I freaked out about the pictures and ran."

"You call it running—I call it knowing you needed to take yourself out of the situation so that you could heal some first before carefully thinking through your next move."

She stopped in a ray of sunlight, another one that seemed to be aiming straight for her as she thought about what he'd said—and how different a perspective it was. One made of strength and intelligence rather than blind fear and foolishness.

"When I saw the pictures for the first time—" She took a breath, one that helped her push past the stomach twisting that happened every time she thought about it. "I didn't think I could ever get over it. Not when I know that no matter where I go or what I do for the rest of my life, the pictures will always be out there." She looked up into Drake's face, staggering in both its handsomeness *and* its kindness. "But I hadn't counted on meeting someone like you, someone so convinced that I can heal."

"More now than ever, Rosa." He smiled down at her. "You'll not only heal, you'll kick ass while you're at it."

"Maybe I *will* kick ass at the healing part," she found herself agreeing, "but that's just step one, and I'm still drawing blanks on the steps after that. Not only going after the guy who took the pictures, but also dealing with my family." A huge lump rose in her throat as she said, "I have no idea how my mom and brothers are going to react if I tell them I don't want to do the show anymore. The producers told me last year that if I quit, the show would be canceled. It hurt so much to lose my dad. I can't risk losing them too."

Drake didn't give her false platitudes, didn't say, *You won't*. He simply pulled her into his arms and held her.

CHAPTER NINETEEN

Frustration ate at Drake as they walked back through the trees to his cabin. He wanted to do more than provide Rosa a temporary refuge from the media. He wanted to hunt down the creep who had taken the pictures—and every single person involved in buying and running those pictures both online and in print—and tear them all to shreds with his bare hands. He wanted to find a way to scrub the Internet of any pictures she hadn't authorized.

And he wanted to make damned sure that Rosa's family didn't turn their backs on her for wanting out of the show.

"It's so peaceful here. So quiet and full of trees."

He lifted her hand to his lips, brushed a kiss over her knuckles. "If you think this is quiet, you should see my father's place in the Adirondacks. Makes Montauk seem like Times Square."

"It sounds as though you like it a lot. Did you ever consider getting a cabin in the Adirondacks instead of the Hamptons?"

"The Adirondacks are his place."

"No reason it couldn't have been yours too."

"It's always seemed like he wanted his space."

"Maybe from bad memories, but I can't imagine he'd want it from his kids. Especially not a son like you. That would be crazy."

"And I think it would be crazy for your mom to even think of turning away from a daughter like you."

Neither of them said anything more about it as they took off their coats and boots and headed inside. Drake gave Oscar a good rubdown with a towel, and once free, the dog did a frisky circle run around the living room, knocking the small canvas off the leather chair.

"It looks like a kindergarten project," Rosa said as she hurried over to pick it up. "I hope you don't mind my wasting one of your canvases."

He'd wanted to ask more than once if he could look at what she'd been working on the day before, but he kept getting distracted by taking off her clothes and loving her. "Can I see it?"

"It's just a hobby," she prevaricated, but at least she handed him the canvas instead of continuing to hide it.

She'd stitched an ocean of blues and greens into the small canvas, but instead of simply echoing the view out his front door, she'd approached it in the way he imagined Picasso would have during his Cubist period, if the artist had used thread instead of paint.

He was about to tell her how talented she was when she said, "Now you know why I don't share my stuff on the show. I see things in a weird way—not like other people do. Stitching on clothes is one thing, but the other stuff I come up with?" She shook her head. "It's not what anyone wants to see from me."

"How do you know that?"

She looked at him as though he were several brain cells short of a full set. "The stuff I make is weird. Everyone at the network agrees. The producers. The PR team."

"If they all agree, then none of them know a damn thing about art." He moved closer. "Or is that really the reason you don't share your art with anyone? Because you're seriously talented."

"You're sleeping with me. That colors your opinion."

"Bullshit." He moved closer again, close enough that her canvas was now pinned between them. "I'm sleeping with you. You have a brilliant gift. Those are two totally separate things. People need to see this, Rosa, see what you can do. See things in a new way—*your* way."

"No!" Her cheeks were flushed, her eyes wild as she pushed away from him, dropping the canvas so that he had to catch it before it hit the floor. "Everything else in my life is public. Open. Exposed. I need one thing, one private thing that I don't have to share. What I do with my hands, with my brain, behind closed doors, is mine." Her mouth wobbled a little as she added, "I thought closed doors meant it was mine, anyway."

The fury that rose in Drake whenever he thought about the pictures that had been taken without her consent was familiar now, but not at all dulled by repetition. On the contrary, he got angrier every single time. And now, he hated that she felt she needed to hide her art. He couldn't imagine not being able to share his creations, instead hoarding them in attics and locked closets. It would be like strangling the core of what made him who he was.

"I want to help." He made himself un-fist his hands, tried to calm down so that he wouldn't feed her tension with his. "Tell me how I can help."

"You already have. You helped with my car and got me to the motel and have fed me more than once. You're the friend I needed more than anything right now, but never thought I'd find."

"I didn't know I needed one either," he told her, "but then you showed up in the middle of a rainstorm, and it turned out I did." He paused before adding, "Friends let friends help, especially with the tough stuff."

"Thank you," she said in a soft voice. "I know you mean well, but I can't see that there's anything you, or anyone else, can do at this point to erase what's out there."

"Like I said before, my family is really well connected."

"Who could be connected enough to help get rid of the pictures?"

"My cousin is Smith Sullivan."

"Smith Sullivan? The movie star?" Her eyes

widened in a way that was almost comical, she was that shocked. "You're one of *those* Sullivans?"

He nodded. "My brother Alec is really well connected too, since he sells half his planes to people in TV and movies. And I've got another cousin, Ian, who's a billionaire. He's got to know someone who might be able to help."

"Wow. I had no idea. None at all. Although," she said as she looked back toward the pictures hanging in his hallway, "I probably should have seen the family resemblance. Still," she said with a shake of her head, "even if one of them was willing to get involved—and I definitely wouldn't want to drag any of them into my mess—I already know there's no way to erase the pictures."

Ignoring the part about dragging his family into her mess for the moment, he said, "Maybe erasing them isn't an option—not unless my sister can come up with some new software. But what if there's a way to make sure no site or magazine ever runs them again?"

"How?"

"Someone like my cousin has got to have some power over the media. I'm thinking if he takes a stance against what happened to you, the major players aren't going to want to piss him off."

"Smith is easily one of the most powerful people in Hollywood, and I'm sure no one wants to get on his bad side," she agreed. "But why would he do that for me? For someone he's never even met, especially someone from reality TV, which is about as far south of his Oscar-winning movies as it gets."

"Because he's a good guy, for one. And because family supports family."

"Of course he should support you. But I'm not family."

"You're with me, so you are."

"No one is supposed to know I'm here, or even that we've met." He watched panic bloom as she added, "You agreed."

"I did, but things aren't that simple anymore." He put down her artwork and reached to pull her close again. "You're not a stranger now, Rosa."

He weighed letting out the word *love*. Wanted more than anything to tell her just how deep his feelings for her ran. But he knew she wasn't ready to hear it yet, not when she was still trying to keep to an agreement that had been made before they'd come to know each other.

Still, he needed her to know, "I'm falling for you. My sister saw it in my paintings, saw what I feel for you, saw that I was already falling that first day."

She swallowed hard, shook her head again. "You can't."

"I am. And I know I should have told you this before now, but that first day, after I took you to the motel, I called Smith."

"You did *what*?" She yanked herself out of his arms, and he made himself let her go so that she could let the steam out. "How could you? You promised me you wouldn't tell anyone we'd met."

"I kept my promise, Rosa, but I also asked him if there was anything he could do to help you. I told him I couldn't say more, just that it mattered to me."

"He's not stupid. He must have put two and two together."

"Good."

"I've already told you why that isn't good. People will think you've lost your mind if you're with me. They'll look at your paintings differently. You'll lose their respect."

"If this is what losing my mind feels like, I'm all for it. And I learned early on that people's reactions to my paintings don't have a damn thing to do with me, but everything to do with them. As for respect? As long as I can look myself in the mirror every day, I'm good."

"You don't know how mean, how horrible people can be."

He could see in her expression just how much vitriol she'd had to deal with over the years, and it only infuriated him further. It wasn't just her mom and the creep photographer from whom he needed to defend her—it was millions of strangers who didn't know the first thing about her, even if they thought they did.

"I don't want you to end up hurt because of what people think of me." Oscar got up to lean against her side, and she looked down at him. "You either."

"No, damn it," he said, his intention to tread carefully flying out the window when every word she said was taking them closer and closer to good-bye. "You think staying is what will hurt me—and I'm not just talking about staying in Montauk. Staying with me wherever we are, wherever we go. But it's exactly the opposite. The only way you can hurt me is to run."

She didn't say anything in response to that,

simply stared at him with big, sad eyes. She wanted to believe him, he could see that. And it was impossible to deny the depth of their physical connection. But after being burned so badly, she obviously still needed time.

Time that was running out way too fast.

"I understand that you're wary about getting into a relationship while everything in your life is in flux. But I'm pretty sure we don't get to pick and choose when the right person comes along." His chest clenched as he pulled her tightly against him. "And I sure as hell don't intend to lose you now that I've finally found you."

CHAPTER TWENTY

Never in a million years would Rosa have imagined she'd meet a man like Drake during the darkest hours of her life. But she had. Only, where anyone else would have been reveling in being with someone so wonderful, she was doing everything she possibly could to remind him—and herself—why it could never work. Especially not right now, when everything in her life was such a total, freaking mess.

But what if Drake was right about not getting to pick and choose when the right person walked into your life? And what if she finally let herself stop worrying about hurting him and allowed herself to fall head over heels in love with him instead?

Oh God.

Love.

She was falling in love with him.

If Oscar hadn't been sitting against her side keeping her steady, she might have toppled over from the shock of realizing just how deep her feelings ran.

She'd already told Drake how scared she was of losing her family. Now, with the shock of her realization still vibrating through her, she had to tell him, "I don't want to lose you either."

Yet again, his arms came around her. But this time he followed with a kiss that felt like the other half of his vow. "You won't," he promised.

Rosa was so afraid to trust again. But Drake had been nothing but honest with her from the start. If he said Smith would want to help, and wouldn't be put off by talking with a reality TV star, she needed to stop doubting him.

Plus, ever since she'd seen the short clip of the entertainment "news" program playing on the TV in her motel room, Rosa kept returning to the word the lawyer had used: *cyber-attack*. She hadn't been able to see past the shock, and the shame, at first. And she'd always assumed that online bullying came with the celebrity territory. She'd tried her best to minimize its effect on her life by making sure her PR team blocked the worst of them from her social media feeds.

But as she thought more about what the lawyer had said, she began to see that this wasn't just someone saying mean things about the way she looked or how empty they thought her brain was. So even though her mother had said they were going to sic their best legal team on the guy who'd taken the pictures, was there more that could be done?

"Actually," she said, her heart jumping fast in her chest, "I'd appreciate it if you'd talk to Smith again. But if he doesn't want to get involved—"

"He will." Drake's smile warmed her all over. "Although I think you should speak directly to him this time."

Her heart jumped even faster. But she knew Drake was right. She couldn't ask someone to be brave for her if she wasn't willing to do the same. "I just hope I don't come off like a geeky superfan."

Drake grinned even wider, obviously pleased that she'd agreed. "Knowing him, he'll eat it up. I'll text to see when he's available."

When he walked out of the kitchen to get his cell phone, Rosa dropped to the floor and put her arms around Oscar, glad for his warm, furry body against hers. "You really are a sweetheart, aren't you?" she whispered. She had always loved dogs, but with her travel schedule, there was no way she could have one. Maybe if she started over...

Her head immediately hurt just thinking about it. Especially if starting over would mean leaving everything she knew behind, including her family. Although if she imagined a future with Drake at her side, suddenly things didn't seem quite so bad, or so scary.

Was she crazy to let herself think this way? To dream about actually having a future with him? Should she be working harder to guard her heart, to keep her walls up, so that if they couldn't make it work, it wouldn't hurt so bad?

"Smith is free now."

Before she could change her mind, Drake put the phone in video mode and dialed and got down on the floor with Rosa and Oscar so that she could see Smith on screen.

"Hey, cuz. Good to hear from you again."

"Same here. I'd like to introduce you to my good friend Rosa."

Smith smiled, the million-watt movie-star smile she'd seen a dozen times over the years at the theater. "Great to meet you."

She opened her mouth to reply, but nothing came out. She'd met plenty of famous people over the past few years, but Smith had her star struck. "I'm such a big fan." Ugh, she had promised herself she wasn't going to be a goof, but she couldn't help it. She couldn't believe she'd ever thought Drake's family was *normal*. Movie stars and billionaires and pro athletes were about as far from normal as it got.

"Valentina and I feel the same way about you."

She was stunned. "How can that be?"

Smith laughed, a warm sound that reminded her of Drake's laugh. Drake's was sexier, of course, but boy, did the two men have a lot of overlap. "We've both watched your show over the years. When I'm out on the road and missing my own family, I enjoy living vicariously through yours for a little while."

Rosa was beyond shocked. Not only that he'd watched her show, but that he'd actually enjoyed it. Her heart squeezed knowing that her family had touched him in some way.

"Thank you for saying that, and for even taking

this call when I know how busy you are. I hate the thought of asking you for help—"

"Don't be." His expression shifted straight from friendly to intense. "What happened to you is just plain wrong. If any of the women I love were violated that way..." He scowled. "I want to help, Rosa. Valentina and I have been thinking about how we can. I was actually just about to get in touch with Drake to run our idea past him. It's better to run it directly by you, though."

Rosa felt so surrounded by unexpected kindness that she nearly dissolved into a big puddle of tears right there on the cabin floor with Drake flanking her on one side, Oscar on the other. "I'm sure anything you do would be really great."

"I'm aiming for a whole lot better than great."

Rosa had never acted or even wanted to, but she could see what a thrill it would be to work with Smith in any capacity. Like Drake, he was just so solid. So steady and confident, but without even the slightest cocky edge.

"I'd like to release a public statement stating that I won't work with any press—both online and in print—that continues to print the pictures. I'll follow it up, of course, with a personal call or note to the biggest, so that there can be no question about where I stand on the issue."

"That would be—" Her throat had such a big lump in it that there was no way she could have spoken past it if Drake hadn't been beside her holding her hand. "Absolutely amazing. But what about the movies you're promoting? I'd hate for your stance on my behalf to put your business at risk."

"I'm not worried about my business, Rosa. But I am worried about the daughter I hope to have one day. We've got to make this world safer for her. This is just one small step, but hopefully it will move us in the right direction."

The lump in her throat finally won, tears spilling down her cheeks as she said, "Thank you."

"I wish I could do more." And she believed he truly did. "I'll call you if I feel I need to check in again before making the statement, okay?"

She nodded, knowing better than to try to speak. After thanking his cousin, Drake disconnected, then focused on gently brushing her cheeks dry. When she had herself under slightly better control, she asked, "Is everyone in your family like Smith?"

"We're all human and can have our bad days, but yeah, Sullivans tend to be pretty great all around."

"He's doing so much for me, going out on such a limb—it makes me realize that I need to start doing that too." She was silent for a few moments as the realization of what her next step should be suddenly became clear. Her heart was pounding, but it wasn't fear driving her pulse for once. "Instead of turning off your phone, do you mind if I use it? I'd like to do some research on cyber-attacks."

His smile made her heart race even faster for an entirely different reason. Rosa knew that what she was going to find online wasn't going to be fun, but if Drake was her reward at the end of the tunnel?

Well, then, she was starting to think she might be able to deal with just about anything that came her way.

* * *

An hour later, Drake took the phone from her and shut it down.

"Why did you do that?"

"Your expression has gotten grimmer and grimmer every five minutes. I can't stand to see the light go out in your eyes."

"There's just so much bad stuff that happens. Cyber-stalking, hacking, private pictures people post out of revenge after a breakup..."

"Come here." Drake took her hand and walked outside with her so that they were gazing at the ocean. He hoped she saw the way the light sparkled off the water, that she noticed the gulls swooping down to play in the surf and the squirrels chasing each other up and down tree trunks.

"There's good stuff too," she murmured. "Thanks for reminding me."

"More good than bad, I hope."

She wasn't looking at the view anymore as she said, "So much good that I keep pinching myself to check that it's real. To see if *you* can possibly be real."

The fact that she had started to think of what had happened to her as a crime rather than as her fault—and that she'd just trusted his family not to screw her over when it was damned hard to trust anyone at all after what she'd been through—felt to Drake like big steps in the right direction.

One where she stayed with him and Oscar,

making their lives warmer, brighter, and a hell of a lot more full of life.

Drake framed her face in his hands and let himself take a good, long visual drink of her beauty before he lowered his mouth to hers and drank from her lips. The sparks that were always simmering just beneath the surface instantly flared, hot and wild.

"You always know," she breathed against his lips. "Always know exactly what I need to make everything feel so much better."

He had already begun to strip her clothes away when he felt a faint shiver move through her. Scooping her up, he took her back inside the cabin, telling Oscar to go lie down in the bedroom as he kicked the front door shut. He took her to the leather chair, then sat with her straddling his lap.

"So do you, Rosa. So do you."

He took her mouth again before finally stripping away her sweatshirt, finding her bare and so beautiful it nearly stopped his heart just to look at her. He had to put his hands on her, his mouth following barely a beat behind as she arched closer so that he could lave both breasts at once with his tongue.

"You're so damned soft. Everywhere I touch." The way she rocked into his hips hardened him to near bursting beneath the zipper of his jeans. "Everywhere I taste."

"Touch more," she urged. "Taste more."

Every time, he promised himself he'd go slowly, be gentle with her. But it was the one promise he could never manage to keep, especially when he yanked her sweats down and found her bare.

"Rosa." He groaned her name into her mouth as he found her wet and hot at her center. "Come for me." He stroked over her, plunged into her with his fingers. "Let go for me."

Her eyes went wide, her pupils so dark he swore he could see inside her soul for a split second before she shuddered through the orgasm beginning to whip through her. Hard and fast and, judging by her moans, damned good.

"I can't get enough of you," she panted before she'd even come down all the way from her release. "Every time I think it can't get any better, it does."

She was the one tearing at his clothes now, and he paused only long enough to grab a condom from his pocket before helping her get his shirt and jeans off. The second that protection was in place, she was lowering herself onto him, his heart hammering harder and harder with every inch he slid. Until they were finally, completely, perfectly connected.

Emotion rippled from every part of her as she stared into his eyes. "If I could stay here forever with you..."

Instead of finishing her sentence, she pressed her mouth to his and gave him a kiss so sweet that the three little words he'd been trying to hold back awhile longer nearly slipped out. But Drake knew there was only so much she could be expected to handle in one day. So even if he wanted much more—even if he wanted *everything*—it was enough for today that she'd at least agreed to talk to Smith. And that she'd done it with Drake at her side, rather than continuing to believe their relationship needed to stay hidden forever from everyone.

Still, if he couldn't yet say the words aloud, he needed to say them any other way he could. And he would make damned sure Rosa knew what she meant to him in every single moment—especially this one, where they were two halves of a whole.

He reached up to put his hands on her cheeks, and their kiss spiraled hotter and hotter. Sweeter too, even as she held on to his shoulders for leverage as she rode him.

His brain went dark enough to see stars as she took him deeper with each stroke. Moving his hands to her hips, he gripped tightly and thrust high, then again, and again, until she was sobbing his name against his mouth and spinning them both off into endless, perfect pleasure.

* * *

They were both still panting and holding tightly to each other when she asked, "Do you still want to paint me?"

"Always." He was surprised she even had to ask when he'd never held back just how much she inspired him.

"Then paint me like this. Just the way I am now."

He couldn't be hearing her right. He forced himself to pull back enough to say, "I meant it when I said I don't want you to sit for me if you don't want to."

"Maybe it doesn't make any sense, but if you

paint me without my clothes on, what you see will replace the other pictures I have in my head. The ones I'm so damned tired of seeing every time I close my eyes."

Of course he understood why she would want to reclaim her nudity—to make her body her own again. And he was dying to paint her like this, her smooth, soft skin flushed from their lovemaking.

"I'll burn them," he told her, even though earlier he'd told her he wouldn't even consider it. "After you've taken the mental pictures you need. So that you don't have to doubt that anyone else will ever see them."

"Don't you dare." She looked over her shoulder at the paintings all around the room. "Your art deserves to live on forever, not to turn to ashes because I'm afraid someone might see them one day. I'm not even sure you should hide them anymore."

"Getting to paint you at all is already more than I could have hoped for." He wanted to leap at everything she was offering him, but he also didn't want her to regret anything she did or said during this roller coaster of a week. At the same time, his fingers were literally itching to paint her. *Just like this.*

"Go," she said as she moved to let him up and off the chair, then repositioned herself so that her legs were tucked up beneath her bare hips and her head was tilted against the back of the seat. "Start painting before you burst."

He pulled on his jeans, and as he picked up his brush, he realized the best part of painting her like this wasn't having her gorgeous curves on full display. It was the sated, happy smile on her face as she looked into his eyes.

A smile that he wanted to see every day for the rest of his life.

CHAPTER TWENTY-ONE

A scratching sound woke Rosa the next morning. She was surprised to realize daylight was coming in through the drapes in Drake's bedroom. Between his painting, her stitching, and all the crazy hot sex, she wasn't sure what time it had been when they'd finally dropped into bed and slept.

But just because they were living on a crazy non-schedule didn't mean that Oscar was. And as the scratching continued, she realized the dog obviously needed to take care of business outside.

Not wanting to wake Drake—he'd never made up any of that sleep he'd lost during his twenty-four-hour painting frenzy, and Lord knew he'd expended plenty of energy making her come again and again and again— she silently slipped from his arms. Pulling on his flannel shirt that was flecked with a rainbow of paint splatters, she buried her nose in it and smiled at having his scent all over her as she headed into the living room to let Oscar out.

The big furball was waiting by the front door, his tail thumping as she walked toward him. "Aren't you a patient boy," she praised in a soft voice, giving him a quick stroke over his back before letting him out.

For the first time in what felt like forever, the sun was out and shining, and though she was barefoot, she followed Oscar through the trees toward a patch of warmth. As she closed her eyes and lifted her face toward it while the surf crashed onto the rocks just beyond the forest, she felt good. Really good.

Less than a week ago, she hadn't thought this kind of happiness could ever be hers.

She'd come to Montauk for a respite from her life and to figure out her next step. She'd expected things to stay rocky, but the more time she spent with Drake— one of the calmest, most confident, yet humble people she'd ever met—the more she thought that maybe she *was* strong enough to deal with the fallout both from the nude pictures and from her desire to leave the show.

Yes, her new strength still felt more than a little tentative and shaky, but she figured it was a start. Just as she was starting to believe that maybe she and Drake could find a way to make things work beyond their cabin refuge. After all, Smith had not only been really nice to her on the call yesterday, she also hadn't sensed any judgment of Drake for hooking up with her.

Just then, however, a cloud blew in front of the sun. And where she'd felt so warm just moments before, the cold suddenly seeped in beneath the flannel shirt and made her shiver.

"Oscar," she called out, "time to go back in."

But it was a woman who appeared from between the trees, instead of Oscar. A pretty blonde who was probably a couple of years older than Rosa. She was carrying a pie.

"Hi, Oscar," the woman said as he came over to say a quick hello to the newcomer. He thumped his tail against the woman's leg a couple of times before loping off to chase a squirrel in his lazy way. The woman smiled after Oscar as she said, "I didn't realize anyone was here with Drake. My grandmother hasn't seen him in the store for a couple of days, so she thought it might be nice if I dropped by with this pie before they're all gone. You must be his sister."

If only Rosa could get away with saying she was Drake's sister, she thought, as the scene played out in what felt like slow motion. But there was no way she could hide her face, no way she could run from the scene barefoot, wearing only Drake's shirt and nothing else. She could hear the clock ticking down on the horrible situation with each and every hard thud of her heart.

Ten.

Nine.

Eight.

Seven.

Si—

"Oh my God." The woman's eyes went wide with shock. "You're Rosalind Bouchard. What are you doing here?"

Rosa needed to say something. Anything to try to fix this. But both her brain and her tongue were so tied up with blooming panic that she couldn't figure out how to get a proper thought through either one.

For the past few days, Drake's property had felt like a perfect, private cocoon. But she'd known it couldn't last forever, hadn't she? Stupid Rosa, to think that she could be the one to decide when it was time to go. Even stupider to believe that her tentative, fragile happiness could withstand being faced with her past as *Rosalind Bouchard,* reality TV's bad girl.

"I thought you were in Miami with your family, dealing with the nude photo scandal. Especially now that all those new pictures have come out."

"*New pictures?*" Rosa finally came unstuck, if only to echo the two horrible words. Bile rose in her throat at the thought of new pictures circulating.

All those new pictures.

Her knees wanted to buckle. She wanted to sink right into the leaves and let them bury her.

Only, as she watched the stranger take in her knotted sex-hair, kiss-bruised lips, and Drake's half-buttoned flannel shirt, Rosa knew she didn't have the luxury of falling apart. Not yet.

Not when there was so much damage control to be done first on Drake's behalf.

No doubt, if Rosa left things like this, the stranger would get on her phone and social media apps the second she turned around and walked away. And if she came inside and saw the paintings—especially now that there were several of Rosa in the nude—she wouldn't have a chance of persuading the woman that she and Drake weren't an item. But if there was even the barest chance that she could pull this off, she had to try.

"I'm just a family friend," she said, trying with all her might to sound normal, though it wasn't easy with blood rushing like a flash flood into her head. "I was in the neighborhood, so I thought I'd drop in to say hello." Her legs felt as shaky as a newborn deer's as she walked toward the stranger. "It's really nice of you to bring pie. So Mona is your grandmother?"

"You know her name?"

Rosa hoped her smile didn't look as pasted on as it felt. "She's a lovely woman." Rosa took the pie from the woman's hands, somehow managing to keep her own from shaking. "Really sweet. And wow, this smells great."

Keep talking, she silently coached herself. *Use what you've learned from all the interviews you've done over the years to turn things where you need them to go.*

"I'm sure Drake is going to love eating this pie when he gets back. I'll be sure to leave a note for him so that he knows it's from you."

"Where did he go?"

Rosa shook her head as if she had no idea. "Probably out painting some incredible vista."

She crossed a million mental fingers that he wouldn't wake up and walk outside right then. Rosa hated lying, but she would do whatever it took to keep him as safe as he'd made her feel.

"He's always been like a brother to me." The lies tasted like sawdust on Rosa's tongue, especially when she had to deliver them in such an easy tone. No man had ever been less like a brother. "Thanks again for bringing the pie. Oscar, time to head back in now to get your breakfast!"

Thank God, he trotted right up to her as if he'd merely been biding his time playing around with squirrels while he waited for her to call him.

"I'm sorry," Rosa said to the woman, giving her another smile, "I didn't get your name."

"I'm Trinity. And I still can't believe you're standing right here in front of me when I've been watching you on TV for years."

So far, Rosa had managed not to answer any questions. Knowing her luck wouldn't hold out forever, she headed for the quick close. "It's been really great to meet you, Trinity. And thanks for watching the show." She put her hand on Oscar's ruff and, brilliant dog that he was, he started to lead her back to the house. "Have a great day." She gave the woman one last smile over her shoulder, then opened the cabin door and walked inside.

Closing it behind her, she leaned against it and looked around the room at Drake's easels and paintings. He was so brilliant. So sweet. So good.

"Rosa, there you are."

As he came out of the bedroom with a big, sexy grin on and nothing else, her heart skipped a beat in her chest.

She wouldn't cry. Wouldn't let herself fall apart again the way she had the first time out on his cliffs. She thought, *I'm falling in love with you, and the very last thing in the world I want is to leave you.*

But what she made herself say was, "It's time for me to go."

CHAPTER TWENTY-TWO

No.

It was the only word Drake could think. The only thing he knew to be true.

If Rosa truly didn't want to be with him any longer, he would never hold her here against her will. But if she was leaving for any other reason—and he figured there could be dozens of possible options to choose from right about now—he wouldn't let her run again.

Not without him at her side.

He didn't trust himself to say anything at first, simply put his hands on her face and kissed her. And when he finally made himself draw back, he said, "I love you."

Joy flickered in her eyes, but a split second later, that joy was gone. "You can't." She tried to push him away. "You don't."

"I can." He lowered his mouth to hers again. "I do."

Right here, right now, whether she liked it or not, he was making his vows to her. Vows that he wouldn't let her feel hopeless, afraid, or alone ever again.

"What happened while I was sleeping? What's brought the panic back into your eyes?"

"Oscar needed to go out and it was so sunny and bright. I felt..." She closed her eyes. "I felt hopeful. Like maybe I could get through this. Maybe I could figure things out." When she opened her eyes, they were bleak. And full of the cynicism he hated to see. "There was a woman outside. A pretty one, with pie. Mona's granddaughter."

At last, the scene began to take shape for Drake. "She recognized you."

"Of course she did. And there I was, wearing nothing but your shirt. She had to know what we'd been doing even though I lied. I told her we were just family friends. That you're like a brother to me."

He laughed. He couldn't help it, when nothing had ever been more preposterous.

"It's not funny."

He brushed a lock of hair from her eyes. "She's going to find out the truth of what we are to each other soon enough, Rosa. Everyone will." Because he wasn't going to let her run from him like she'd tried to run from everyone and everything else.

"There are more pictures! New ones!" She finally managed to duck out from beneath his arm. "You can't be with me."

Rage at hearing of more pictures hitting the Internet rose so fast it choked him, but he needed to hold it at bay. For now. "I'm with you now. And we'll deal with the pictures together."

"I can't drag you into this with me. Not like this. Not when the scandal has just got even bigger. I need to leave right away. Before Trinity thinks of a reason to come back and finds us here together. Before she sees me on all these canvases, and pictures of your paintings end up on the Internet too." With every word, he could hear and feel her panic growing more and more out of control. "I should never have come here. I should have found somewhere more remote, looked for a better place to hide out."

There were so many things he wanted to say to her, but only one truly mattered right now. "I love you," he said again, wanting to make sure she didn't ever forget it.

For the past few days, he'd watched her begin to believe more and more in her strength. Yesterday had seemed like such a big turning point on so many levels.

Now, however, her belief seemed to have been stripped away again.

He knew it was the shock of learning about more pictures—and being surprised by a fan in the woods when she thought she was safely hidden from that world—that had done it. But he also knew Rosa was more than strong enough to deal with all of it.

Right at this moment, however, it was clear that he wouldn't have a prayer of convincing her of any of that. So instead of trying, he said, "If you want to hide, really hide, I have just the place for you."

She looked at him as if that were the very last thing she expected him to say. "You do?"

"I do."

Looked like he was going to be paying a visit to his father's cabin at Summer Lake in the Adirondacks, after all.

But he wouldn't let them leave without a reminder of how far they'd come in his little Montauk cabin. He swooped her up into his arms and carried her toward his bedroom.

"Drake, put me down. Didn't you hear anything I just said? We need to leave." She shook her head. "I mean, *I* need to leave. You should stay here. You should forget about me."

"We'll be leaving together," he informed her, deciding to simply ignore her urging him to forget her since it was so ridiculous. "But it's a long drive to the Adirondacks, and we'll feel better if we clean up first." Better still by reconnecting in the most elemental way possible.

He carried her past the bed and into his bathroom. Already naked himself, he didn't bother stripping her out of his flannel shirt before walking into the shower and turning it on. He could feel how cold she was, and not just because she'd been outside with barely anything on. He might not be able to warm her up all the way just yet, but between his body against hers and the warm water, he could sure as hell try.

Turning her so that her back was to the tiled shower wall, he set her on her feet, then reached for the front of his shirt and ripped it open. A couple of buttons pinged against the wall and floor as she gaped at him in shock.

"Now? You actually want to do this now?"

He threaded his hands into her wet hair and lowered his mouth to hers. "Always."

Her lips were too cold against his, but only until she began to kiss him. "This is crazy," she murmured as he ran his hands over her curves, shoulders to hips, then back up along her belly and waist until he was cupping her breasts. She moaned, "Crazy," again as he played with the tips of her breasts first with his fingertips, and then with his tongue.

He couldn't argue with her about *crazy*, given how consumed he'd been since the moment he'd first set eyes on her. All his life, he'd tried to keep crazy out, thinking it would protect him from sharing his father's fate.

But Drake was no longer convinced that crazy was a bad thing.

As he rained kisses down her body, he lowered himself to his knees until he could center his kisses over the sweet, addictively soft flesh between her thighs. Her hands bunched in his hair as she let him reposition her legs so that one was propped up on the built-in tiled seat.

"You make me lose control," she said as she looked down at him through long, wet lashes. "You make me forget why we shouldn't do this. Why I shouldn't let you be with me."

"Good."

His response, raw with possession, continued to

reverberate in the shower as he found her again with his tongue, his control as far gone as hers. For the moment, at least, she was no longer fighting him—trying to fight what had always been between them—as she rocked her pelvis into him, truly the most sensual creature alive.

He needed more. Needed to be closer. Needed to be completely connected with her when she let herself fall.

Thank God, when he stood again he found one more condom left on the shower ledge. He wasn't sure he would have been able to stop even without it. Not when making love with Rosa—and becoming one with her—had become as deep a necessity as breathing.

Seconds later, he had on protection and reached for her hips to lift her so that she could put her legs around his waist. In one gorgeous movement, she sank down onto him, taking him so deep that his vision actually went black for a moment.

He'd initially been the one kissing her after she'd come in from the cold, but now she was devouring his mouth, nipping over his jaw, sucking at his neck. They rode hard and fast against each other, but even in the midst of *crazy* he made sure to cradle her head and hips against the tile. Made sure to keep her safe, always.

"*Drake.*"

When she gasped his name into his mouth, he knew she was close. But it wasn't enough just to make her come, just to give her pleasure. Not this time. He needed to make sure the physical was completely entwined with the emotional so that she couldn't forget so easily what was between them.

He drew back so that he could look into her eyes. Her cheeks were flushed, and her lips were full from his kisses.

"I." He thrust hard and deep on the word, and her lids fluttered half closed with pleasure.

"Love." He took them both higher again, felt her inner muscles grip him so tightly he could barely hold on as she exploded around him and sent them flying together.

"You."

CHAPTER TWENTY-THREE

Drake's SUV had a big backseat, but Oscar insisted on sitting in Rosa's lap. The entire car smelled like dog, and his panting steamed up the windows, but with every mile they drove, Rosa welcomed his warmth more and more. Especially when he periodically lifted his head to lick her cheek as if to say, *Everything's going to be okay. You've got us.*

Drake hadn't said much during the six hours they'd been driving, only checking in a couple of times to see if she was hungry or thirsty. Not because he didn't care. On the contrary, she now knew *exactly* how much he cared.

I love you.

Three little words that kept playing over and over inside her head.

I'm with you now. And we'll deal with the pictures

together.

Just like always, he'd stood by his words, not only by working to break her out of her panicked state by taking her into the shower and loving her brainless— but also by barely taking the time to stack his canvases in the back of his car before he checked her out of the motel and set off for his father's house in the Adirondacks. And, just like always, he knew she needed some time to process the most recent twists to her scandalous week. Not only that there were new pictures...but also that he loved her and was clearly planning to stand by her, no matter what. Even if it meant changing her hiding place to a different forest six hours away.

At the same time, this road trip wasn't merely about finding a new refuge so that the paparazzi wouldn't swoop in before she was ready for them. It was also about Drake going to see his father.

He was so close to his siblings, his cousins. Only with his father was there a fracture. One she would give anything to help patch up.

It seemed telling—in a positive way—that the first safe place he'd thought to go had been his father's house. No matter what else happened—and even if her own relationship with her mother remained a mess—she vowed to help him.

Thankfully, with every mile they covered, she felt more of that strength she'd started to build coming back. Panic had been her first instinct outside the cabin when she'd heard about the new pictures, but with Drake as steady as ever beside her, she was able to remember that panic wasn't her only option.

No, she was game for plenty of other emotions now, including fury that the creep who had taken the pictures of her had held some back so that he could get even more money for the second round.

"I'm going to take him down."

Drake didn't seem surprised that this was the first thing she'd said to him in hours. He simply smiled and said, "I know you are."

Rosa leaned over to give him a kiss, then bent to give Oscar one too. "Can I have your cell phone again?"

Though Drake immediately handed it to her, he said, "You don't need to see the new pictures, Rosa."

"I do." She willed her hands not to shake as she pulled up a browser and typed her name into the search box. "I need to know exactly what I'm up against instead of continuing to bury my head in the sand."

But, strangely, none of the sites that had run the first set of pictures had anything new up. In fact, as far as she could see, none of the previous pictures were still running either.

"What are you seeing?" A muscle jumped in his jaw, and his hands tightened on the steering wheel as he waited for her answer.

"They're not here. I mean, there's a story that says there are new pictures, but—" She couldn't believe what she was reading. "But no one is running them."

Drake turned from the road to look into her eyes for a split second. "Smith."

Thinking the same thing, she scrolled back to the search box and typed in Smith Sullivan's name alongside hers, then read aloud from the first story that popped up.

Smith Sullivan has taken a major stand this morning against cyber-attacks and the exploitation of women as he weighed in on the Rosalind Bouchard nude photo scandal. "If this happened to your sister or girlfriend or daughter, would you run the pictures and call it news? No, you'd do everything in your power to get them taken down and convict the person who took and sold them." Sullivan has made it clear that he will no longer work with any media outlets that continue to run the photos.

Rosa clicked on a follow-up link and told Drake, "Evidently, the pictures were pulled from every major site within the hour. No one dares defy him, even for click bait like these pictures."

"He always was a good guy. Fame and Academy Awards haven't changed him one bit."

She'd swung in so many emotional directions today. Waking up joyful, then slamming into deep, dark panic. And now, utter gratitude.

But as she read on, some of the panic rose again. "It also says they've been trying to reach me and my family for comment with no luck so far, but that they've heard a rumor that I'm vacationing in the Hamptons." The trees had been getting thicker and thicker since they'd crossed into Adirondack Park, thick enough now that before she could read too much more, the phone lost its signal entirely. Relieved to be able to turn it off, she had to tell him the final thing she'd read before the phone had gone dead. "My connection to the Sullivan family also seems to be a big question right now. It doesn't look like Mona's granddaughter named you in any of her tweets, but they're not going to have to look far to realize you've got a place in the Hamptons."

"Good. Everyone should know you're mine. Ours," he amended as Oscar licked her cheek in a nonverbal echo of his owner's statement. Before she could respond, he said, "We're here."

The driveway to his father's house was long, at least a quarter mile, and Rosa gasped when they got to the end. "It's so beautiful." She'd never seen water so blue or that looked so pure and soothing as it lapped against the golden sand. A couple of ducks swam near the shore.

Drake turned off the engine, but stayed behind the wheel. "It is."

She reached for his hand, sensing the tension thrumming through those two little words—and knowing that this time it stemmed from his wariness over seeing his father. "I think you're right."

"About what?" he asked.

"Do you remember asking me why I thought starting over had to be hard?"

She was glad when his mouth quirked up a little at the corner, even though he obviously knew she was talking about him and his father.

"Turns out it's a hell of a lot easier to dish out advice than to take it," he said.

It felt good to laugh. Felt even better to pull him in for a kiss. "Thank you for bringing me here, Drake, and for being so great during my freak-out this morning.

In fact, I think I'd probably better thank you in advance for my next one. I have a feeling things may keep being messy and complicated for a while."

"I love you." He kissed her again. "It's as simple as that."

* * *

"It's so great to meet you!" Suzanne Sullivan threw her arms around Rosa the moment they walked through the door.

Drake's sister had looked beautiful in the photograph hanging in his cabin, but in person it was like staring straight into the sun. Suzanne's eyes were so bright and intelligent and full of laughter that Rosa promptly fell in love with her second Sullivan. Third, actually, since she was head over heels for Smith after the way he'd gone out on a limb for her.

Drake pulled his sister in for a hug, then asked, "Is Dad here?"

"He had to go take care of a foundation problem at one of the properties he and Jean are working on."

Drake took Rosa's hand and brought her close, tucking her safely beneath his arm. Suzanne beamed at them as he explained, "After Dad built this house and moved permanently from the city, he started working with a couple of local builders—Jean and her son Henry."

As Rosa took a few moments to appreciate the contemporary yet rustic-style house, she wasn't surprised by the career he'd switched to. "This house is incredible. And it fits so well with the natural surroundings."

The proportions of the home were big all the way around, with ceilings that she figured must vault up at least sixteen feet, and plenty of space. Room enough to hold four kids easily. Which, to her way of thinking, meant that Drake's father had planned—hoped—that his children would one day come and feel welcome. Whether he'd actually done a good job of expressing that to his kids was another question entirely, but it made Rosa feel more hopeful for Drake than ever.

Suzanne spent a good minute or so giving Oscar some love before standing and saying, "I've got coffee on if either of you wants some."

Rosa's coffee need roared to the surface. "You're a lifesaver." Just like Suzanne's brother.

With Drake still holding her hand, Rosa followed Suzanne into the kitchen—a perfect rustic kitchen built entirely of knotty pine, with green granite counters—where a steaming mug was soon pressed into her free hand. She barely kept herself from taking a too-greedy gulp of it and scalding off the top layer of her tongue.

"I'll take our bags into the bedroom I usually use." He kissed her before leaving the room.

Unable to stand letting the thousand-pound elephant in the room crush everyone, Rosa decided to be as direct as possible. "I know you're probably really worried about your brother being with me."

"I'm not."

These Sullivans kept flooring her with how steady, how strong-willed and confident they were. Then again, she remembered being confident like this once. Before she'd let the show change her. Then the horrible pictures had been released, and shame had taken over absolutely everything.

It was that very shame, in fact, that had her saying, "You should be."

"Why? He's happy. Happier than I can ever remember him being. Both as a man and a painter, judging by the paintings he did of you. And even though I know none of this can be easy for you, it seems like he's making you happy too."

"He is." Rosa couldn't hold back from his sister what she felt. "I never thought I'd find anyone like Drake. He's been amazing. The calm in the storm. The light in the dark. But..." She needed his sister to understand. "That doesn't mean there isn't still a huge mess to deal with. It doesn't mean *I'm* not still a huge mess. This morning, when I found out there were more pictures, I kind of lost it. I wanted to run again, needed a better hiding place than the Hamptons. So here we are."

Suzanne moved closer and reached out to take Rosa's hand. "Who wouldn't have lost it? Who wouldn't have wanted to run and hide, at least for a little while? Drake was right to bring you here, to bring you home."

Rosa was struck by the way his sister said the word *home*—and how, after only a few minutes here, it resonated with her too.

"Have you seen this?" Suzanne picked up the paper on the counter and handed it to Rosa. It had Smith's face on it, and a quick scan confirmed it was what she'd read on Drake's phone in the car.

"I'll never be able to thank Smith enough for this. He doesn't even know me."

Drake's sister grinned. "You've got us on your team now. In fact, I wanted you to know that I've been thinking more and more about your situation. Especially about the fact that it isn't just your situation. So many women, and men, are finding themselves in a similar position, with pictures being stolen or taken against their wishes and ending up on the Internet."

"I did some research," Rosa said. "It made me sick to realize how much this kind of thing happens."

"Not usually on your scale, but yeah, it's happening a lot. I don't know if Drake told you, but Internet security is my specialty."

"He did. He's your biggest fan. And I can see why."

Suzanne grinned again. "It goes both ways. I'm really lucky to have such great brothers. But anyway, what I was going to say is that I've been looking for a new challenge, and I'm thinking this is it. Take your situation, for example. Smith has convinced most of the major media outlets to take down the pictures and not run them anymore. But most people won't have Smith on their side, and there's still a need for software that can actually erase them—or block them—completely, or you'd still be able to search on the pictures and find them pretty easily."

When Rosa cringed at the reminder, Suzanne said, "Sorry, Rosa, I'm just thinking out loud. I didn't mean to upset you. Sometimes I say more than I mean to. Especially when I get all up in my head about something."

"Actually, it's nice to be so straightforward about it all." Rosa was surprised to find that it really was, especially with another woman. "Drake and I have talked about the pictures, but he always gets so upset."

"It's because he loves you and he hates that you're being hurt."

Rosa couldn't stop her eyes from growing huge. "Did he actually say that to you?"

Suzanne cocked her head. "Of course he doesn't want you to be hurt. Oh, wait—you mean the part where he loves you." She smiled. "I could see it in his paintings, see exactly what he feels for you."

Rosa was still speechless, her mouth likely hanging open in surprise, when Drake walked back into the kitchen. Maybe he could see that she was out of her depth—yet again—because he crossed straight to her, put his hands on either side of her face, and kissed her. His kisses had always been the one surefire way to ground her. And, she thought as she kissed him back, to send her flying.

"What's going on here?"

Rosa pulled away from Drake at the sound of the deep male voice, her heart hammering as if she'd been caught doing something wrong. But he wouldn't let her go too far, keeping her hand in his tightly enough that she couldn't possibly slip away.

She recognized the two men who walked in as his brothers, Alec and Harrison. Alec was flat-out gorgeous—tall and broad-chested, with tanned skin and well-groomed dark hair. He was the kind of guy women gravitated to in droves. Polished and obviously wealthy, but still all man. She could easily imagine just how charismatic he could be when he felt like turning it on.

Harrison was as good-looking as his brothers—just as tall and broad and masculine—but that wasn't what hit first. Rosa was struck, instead, by his academic air. The impression that he was currently working through some complicated puzzle in his head. His dark-framed glasses might have been geeky on anyone else, but on him they only seemed to up the sexiness quotient.

Of course, to her eyes, neither man held a candle to Drake. Then again, she wasn't exactly objective where he was concerned, was she?

She should have thought this might happen, that everyone in his family would have been summoned to his father's home to collect the paintings of their mother. But she hadn't been able to think beyond running from discovery in Montauk—and also hoping Drake could patch things up with his father.

Suzanne had been immediately welcoming, but since she'd seen the paintings in Drake's cabin, she hadn't been blindsided by their relationship. His brothers, on the other hand, clearly hadn't heard word one about her. And, judging by Alec's expression at least, weren't necessarily impressed with their brother's choice of women.

"Alec, Harry, this is Rosa."

She couldn't miss the *you'd better be nice to her or else* tone of his introduction. It was clear, however, that Harry didn't have the first clue who she was as he walked over to shake her hand. The only surprise seemed to be that Drake had a woman with him at all.

"Great to meet you, Rosa."

"It's nice to meet you too, Harry."

All the while, she could feel Alec's eyes on her. Judging. Weighing. And then deciding she came up short. Way short. Suzanne might not be worried about her brother's new girlfriend, but Alec clearly had a problem with her.

She could feel Drake stiffening beside her and desperately wished she could defuse the situation. Unfortunately, since she couldn't change who she was or what she'd done, the only thing she had in her arsenal was to smile and say, "It's nice to meet you, Alec." Before he could respond, she turned to Drake. "Why don't I take Oscar for a walk so that you all can catch up?"

She swore Oscar could understand English, because he immediately trotted over to her side with a leash in his mouth. Where he'd found the leash she had no idea, but she didn't care. All she wanted was to get out of the tension and let the brothers settle things. And if Alec really didn't want her there...well, she'd figure out something. Because there was no way she was going to get between Drake and his siblings on top of all the other messes she was already dragging him into.

She'd barely left the kitchen when Drake came up behind her and put a hand over hers to make her turn and face him. "Don't go. My brother is an idiot. I'll make him apologize for the way he just acted. He doesn't know you yet, but once he does—"

She put a finger over his lips. "He's not an idiot. We both know it's got to be a heck of a shock to see me standing there kissing you. Even without the pictures, it would have been weird. And now that he's probably seen me naked..." She fought back a shudder. "All I'm saying is that he didn't do anything wrong by reacting the way he did. Not when it's obvious that he loves you and wants to protect you." She made herself smile. "It's exactly what I'd hope your siblings would do."

"I brought you here so you could feel safe. Don't run again, Rosa. Not from me."

This morning she'd freaked out and talked about leaving, but she knew deep within herself that she wouldn't have gone very far before running right back into his arms.

"It will go easier for you guys to talk about the situation with your father and the paintings without me here, at least at first. And I could do with some fresh air and a little quiet." When it looked like he was going to argue with her, she put her hands on his bristly jaw and went on her tippy-toes to kiss him again. "All the good things you want for me with my mother, I want for you with your father. Maybe spending a little time talking things through with your brothers and sister will help get you closer to clearing them up."

With that, she kissed him again, then headed outside with Oscar into the crisp, cool forest.

CHAPTER TWENTY-FOUR

"What the hell are you doing with *her*?"

Drake sprang at his brother. "One more word and you're going to leave here looking a hell of a lot worse than when you walked in."

Just as Alec opened his mouth again to reply, Harry stepped between his brothers and caught Drake's fist halfway to Alec's face. Harry might spend plenty of hours poring over dusty tomes, but he'd managed to fit in martial arts training too.

"Cool down. Both of you." Harry had stopped Drake's punch from landing, but he knew better than to let him go just yet. "Someone had better fill me in fast."

"I'm in love with Rosa." Drake would shout it from the rooftops if he could. "She's been through hell this week and just got slapped with a fresh round this morning. I'm itching to tear someone apart." He snarled at Alec, "Perfectly happy if it's you, bro."

Suzanne stepped into the fray next, putting a hand on Drake's arm. "That's awesome that you're in love," she said first, and then to Harry, "Rosa is a reality TV star. I know you live in a box of dusty books, Harry, but you've got to have heard of the Bouchards."

He thought about it for a few seconds. "Their name sounds familiar."

"I swear, it sometimes seems like you actually live in medieval times, instead of just studying them," she said with a roll of her eyes. "Anyway, Rosa's family has been on TV for the past five or so years, and they're really, really popular. Especially her. If you ask me, it's not just because she's so pretty, but because when you watch, you wish she was your sister."

"You've got to tell her that," Drake urged. "She's let too many people online and in the press convince her that she's been making trash, but even Smith and Valentina told her they like to watch her show."

Alec snorted. "You've got to be kidding me."

By then Harry had loosened his hold on Drake's arm enough that when he lunged again, Drake nearly landed his punch.

"Alec, shut up for once, so I can finish giving Harry the deets," Suz said before turning back to Harry. "This week, some naked pictures of Rosa hit the press. Pictures she didn't authorize."

"Someone hacked her accounts?"

"Wow, so you do actually know something about modern technology. But no, it was even worse than that. One of the film crew snuck a camera into her hotel while they were filming and took pictures of her changing and getting in and out of the bath. She had no idea she'd been attacked like this until the pictures were sold and literally splattered everywhere, print and digital."

Harry looked utterly disgusted. "That's terrible."

"She doesn't deserve any of this," Drake bit out. "Especially not the shame of feeling like the pictures were her fault. She thinks she needs to hide out forever because the world will just heap more crap on her if she resurfaces."

"That's bullshit." Drake was surprised both by Alec's comment and by how disgusted he looked. "Just because your girlfriend has made some questionable career choices, there is no way those pictures are her fault."

"*Questionable career choices*." Suz put air quotes around the words. "You're so full of it, Alec. We all know the reason you immediately recognized Rosa is because you secretly mainline reality TV in your spare time."

Alec was the one snarling this time. "Her face is everywhere. You'd have to live under a rock not to know who she is."

"I'll take that as an affirmative on your viewing habits," Suz said with a snort of her own. "You're just jealous that Drake found someone as amazing as Rosa first."

"Stop winding him up, Suz," Harry said in the voice of mediation that he'd been using with them for over thirty years.

"Look," Alec said in what Drake knew was

intended to be a more reasonable tone, "the last thing I expected was to walk in and see the woman who's been all over the news this week standing in my brother's arms. When the hell did you even start dating her? And if you're an item, how come you aren't coming up in any of the endless news clips about her?"

"You can let me go now," Drake told Harry. "I'm not going to tear him apart just yet."

Harry looked between his brothers to confirm intent on both sides before stepping away.

Drake poured himself a cup of coffee and gulped it down so that the caffeine could hit his system before he started answering his sibling's questions. "I met her a week ago when she showed up out of the blue on my cliffs in Montauk. I was trying to paint and hadn't been paying any attention to the news, hadn't turned on my phone or checked the Internet, so I didn't have a clue what the stranger on my cliffs was crying over. Then when I ran into her at the general store later that day and it was clear she was running, hiding, I still didn't know who she was or what she was running from until I saw the headlines on the newsstand." His hands fisted at his sides. "That day I helped her with her broken-down car, but I wished I could do more."

"We all do," Suz said. "I've already started sketching out the architecture for software that could erase pictures like these off the Internet."

Alec raised an eyebrow. "You can do that?"

"I can sure as heck try."

"With you there is no try, there is only do. Internet creeps aren't going to know what hit them once you and your soon-to-be-written software get hold of them."

Suz grinned at Alec's vote of confidence, then turned back to Drake. "You're not done telling your story yet."

Drake knew there was no point in trying to hide the truth from his brothers. "I'm painting her."

Harry's eyebrows went up. "Say that again."

"The first time I set eyes on her..." None of his siblings was an artist, but they all knew what passion was. Suz for her computers. Harry for history. Alec for his planes. "I couldn't stop myself from painting her. Even knowing better, even knowing the risks of falling too hard and caring too much. Rosa's the muse I didn't know I was looking for." He shook his head. "More than a muse." He looked each of his siblings in the eye, one at a time. "She's it for me."

"What about her?" Alec asked. "Does she feel the same about you?"

Drake ran a hand through his hair. "She's been screwed over pretty bad. It's been hard for her to trust."

"She trusts you." There was perfect certainty in Suz's words. "She wouldn't be here with you, with all of us, if she didn't."

"I hope so." But Drake wanted so much more than Rosa's trust. He wanted her heart. Wanted to know that he was as deep in her soul as she already was in his. "She's got some big battles to fight. I'm hoping she'll let me fight them with her, but I know there are some that are going to have to be all hers." He went to the sink and rinsed out his mug. "Anything else she wants you to know, she'll tell you herself."

His siblings were silent for a few moments, each of them digesting what he'd said. Finally, Alec spoke. "When people see the paintings you've done of her, the art world is going to lose it. You know that, right?"

"Those paintings are private. All of them."

Suzanne made a frustrated sound. "I know both of you have your reasons to keep your paintings of Rosa out of the public eye, but I swear I haven't been able to stop thinking about them." To Harry and Alec, she explained, "I saw them when I dropped in on Drake in Montauk to see if he wanted to ride here with me. They're brilliant. Beyond, actually. And since I know you guys are thinking it, I'll tell you they're nothing at all like Dad's paintings of Mom. They feel totally different—light and bright and joyous, instead of obsessive and codependent."

"Speaking of obsessed and codependent," Alec said, "what has Dad told you about why he suddenly wants to pass on his paintings to us?"

None of them heard the sound of boots on the wide-planked wood floor until it was too late...and their father was standing in the doorway, clearly having heard more than any of them wished he had.

"Dad." Suz jumped up. "We didn't hear you coming in."

Drake had spent thirty years wary of being rejected by his father. But if he didn't want Rosa to keep hiding out, he needed to stop hiding too. He'd told her she had it in her to start fresh, insisted that the status quo wasn't necessarily the easier, safer way. Looked like it was time to stand by his words.

Which was why, despite the equally wary look

on William Sullivan's face, Drake walked over and gave him a hug. "It's good to see you, Dad."

His father's surprise was palpable. So was that of Alec, Harry, and Suz, for that matter, as they gaped at father and son from across the room. The thing was, Drake had done enough thinking about Rosa's messy situation with her mother that turning the mirror on himself had been unavoidable. He couldn't expect Rosa to try to work things out with her mother if he wasn't willing to do the same.

"I didn't expect you all to come at the same time."

Drake could easily hear the subtext—his father hadn't really expected *any* of them to come except for Suz and maybe Harry. The five of them hadn't been together in the Adirondacks for years. Probably because it always felt like there was a ghost hanging over them all, the paintings of their mother that were stored in the cottage a short distance behind the house a heavy weight none of them really knew how to carry.

"You want to tell us what's going on?" Alec stood with his arms folded, looking like he wished he was anywhere but here. And clearly, putting his foot in it twice in the past half hour, first with Rosa and then with their father, hadn't put him in an apologetic mood. If anything, it had made him more blunt.

Out of the corner of his eye, Drake could see that his sister was about to dive into the fray to try to save their father from this uncomfortable situation. But even though Alec was lacking a hell of a lot of finesse today, he was asking the question they all wanted—and needed—an answer to.

Drake caught his sister's eye and shook his head. *You can't save him this time, Suz.*

He could see how hard it was for her to wait out their father's uncomfortable silence. *I know I can't*, her eyes seemed to say, *but why does it have to be this hard?*

Drake had given up wishing things could be different with his dad a long time ago. But now, he wondered if he'd given up too soon without ever actually learning the whole story of what had happened between his mother and father.

"A reporter called," his father finally replied. "When I didn't call her back, she came here and waited until I came home from a job site. She told me she was writing a story about the thirtieth anniversary of my last painting." His father headed for the coffee now and poured himself a cup, but set it down before drinking it. "I need something stronger than this." He reached into an upper cupboard for a bottle of whiskey. "Anyone else?"

"I'll take one." Alec uncrossed his arms and finally moved toward their dad. Suz shook her head, as did Harry. Drake figured it might help loosen things up a little, so together the three of them knocked the shots back, then set the glasses on the counter.

"Thirty years." William looked at Drake first, then Suz, then Harry, then Alec. Youngest to oldest. "How the hell did thirty years pass?"

"Did you do the interview?" Harry asked.

"No. I kicked her the hell off my property and told her to come back at her own risk. But it got me thinking. Thinking about how three decades is long enough to keep holding on to a ghost." He poured himself another shot.

"And more than long enough to screw things up with all of you." He looked at each of them, looked more deeply than Drake could ever remember. "I hope you'll all stay, at least for the night, all of us around the same table at the same time—" He rubbed a hand over his face. "But I understand if you're too busy, if you need to get back to the city."

"We'd love to stay, Dad." Suz looked at her brothers. "Right, guys?"

"Sounds good," Harry said.

Alec poured himself another shot before saying, "I can wait until tomorrow to get back."

"Drake?"

"I was planning to stay. But you should know that I brought someone with me. Her name is Rosa. I've been painting her." Anticipating his father's surprise, he added, "I had to, even though she only agreed to sit for me as long as I never show the paintings to anyone."

"I know I have no right to tell you what to do," his father said in a grave voice that matched his expression, "but if she's that uncomfortable with people seeing her on canvas, even if you make her all the promises in the world about keeping them for your eyes only, you're still setting yourself up for trouble."

"She's already in trouble. That's how she found me. How I found her."

"What kind of trouble?"

"She's on TV. A reality show. She's famous. Really famous. Someone took pictures of her without her consent and sold them to the press. Nude pictures." Suzanne made an angry sound in the background. "She's spent the past week trying to find her footing again. Trying to decide exactly how she wants to deal with the situation."

His father's frown furrowed deep. "This morning on the job site, the radio was on. I'm pretty sure I heard about your Rosa, about the pictures. The newscasters were saying that no one in the press has heard from her since the day they hit, that she's disappeared. Her mother was on, and she was obviously worried. More than worried. Terrified about what her daughter might have done because of the pictures. She was begging anyone with information to come forward."

"Rosa's been safe with me the whole time," Drake told his father. "Actually, she's with Oscar right now, taking him for a walk. But I hope when she gets back that she'll be welcome here."

"Good. I'm glad she's safe, and of course she's welcome here. But why doesn't her family know where she is? Why couldn't she at least tell them that she needed time to think about everything?"

"She would have done that if she could. But her situation—the show, the pictures, and her relationship with her mother—it's all far more complicated than that." And if anyone could understand *complicated*, Drake figured it was his father.

Just then, William's phone buzzed in a jarring ring tone that couldn't be ignored. "Damn it, I've got to get back to the job site. But I'll be back as soon as I can to make dinner. And then—" He looked pained. "We can talk about the paintings."

CHAPTER TWENTY-FIVE

The Adirondacks felt like the polar opposite of Miami. Yes, there was sand and water, but that was where the similarities ended. Rosa had spent her whole life in the sun—but this cool air, and all the green, felt so right. Montauk had been a good temporary refuge, but somehow this was like coming home. Especially with Oscar loping along beside her, a big bear of a dog who always looked after her.

Just like his owner.

Rosa really hoped everything was going okay with Drake and his brother Alec. While it hurt to be judged so quickly—and so negatively—she knew all too well that it came with the reality TV territory. So even if she still felt the sting in the disparaging way Alec had looked at her, it wasn't anything she hadn't felt before.

And maybe, she told herself, it wasn't a terrible

thing for Drake to see what it would be like to go public with dating her. That it wouldn't just be strangers judging his choices, but his closest flesh and blood. He'd worked hard to persuade her that he didn't care what strangers thought, but she knew family was everything to him. She'd never forgive herself if she came between Drake and his family.

She'd hoped the walk would untwist her insides, but her concerns about how things were going between Drake and his brother gnawed at her gut. As if he could sense her mood, Oscar nudged her hand. She found a smile for him, especially when a duck swam to the edge of the lake and sent him barking and running toward it. Laughing as she let him tug her through the trees toward the shore, she was surprised to realize that they'd walked all the way to the edge of town.

It was straight out of a picture postcard—the bright blue sky, the lake sparkling in the sunlight, a pretty white gazebo at a waterfront park. During the past five years, Rosa had filmed all over the world and was lucky to have seen incredible beauty on nearly every continent. But nothing affected her the way this small main street on the lake did.

Summer Lake looked like the kind of place where everyone knew one another—and had one another's backs too. Where kids grew up together jumping off the dock in summer, building snowmen in winter, and high school sweethearts became husband and wife in a sweet ceremony on the beach with everyone in town celebrating their love.

Longing settled deep as Rosa imagined what it

would be like to live here. She couldn't stop herself from spinning off into a fantasy of living in one of the lakefront cottages, stitching art in an upstairs studio at a gallery on Main Street, chatting on the sidewalk with friendly faces. Drake was in every frame of her daydream, of course. Waking up in his arms every morning. Creating with him. Dancing on the beach as the sun set. Skinny-dipping at midnight beneath the stars and making love in the lake.

Oscar shook himself, splattering her with enough water and sand to bring her back to reality. One where she was an infamous star who still needed to deal with an endless stream of naked pictures, not to mention her fractured relationship with her mother.

But even as she tried to remind herself of all the reasons her daydream could never become a reality, she couldn't silence a voice inside her head that was saying, *Why not?*

All along Drake had believed she could make a change, that she was strong enough to do whatever she truly wanted. Slowly, during this week with him and Oscar, she'd started to believe too. At least, until she'd stumbled into a fresh freak-out this morning.

But she was still standing, wasn't she? She hadn't fallen completely apart again.

Oscar tugged her forward into town, taking her close enough to be able to read the *LAKESIDE STITCH & KNIT* sign on the awning of one of the stores. Suddenly, all she wanted was to lose herself in beautiful yarn and thread. She still had a few twenty-dollar bills in her pocket and would love to add some reds and oranges to the blue and green threads she'd been playing with all week.

But she didn't have her big sunglasses on, or with her. And even if she did, Oscar was a massive enough presence that they weren't exactly going to go unnoticed. The odds of someone on the pretty main street discovering her were fairly high.

Yesterday, she would have turned around. Wouldn't have dared set foot in a small-town street, let alone a yarn store. But once upon a time she'd been a strong, confident person, hadn't she? And even if at eighteen she hadn't truly understood the ramifications of her career choice, she'd chosen it. No one had pushed her into it, and she wouldn't lay that blame on her mother or the network. Staying on TV for five years had also been her choice.

Only a few days ago, she hadn't recognized the strength Drake portrayed in his paintings—had even doubted his vision of her. But as she peeled back the layers of shame about the pictures, with Drake supporting and loving her through every single step, she finally saw that her strength was still here.

She was still here.

And she was finally ready to reclaim her life. Every last piece of it, from career to family to love.

She'd start, Rosa decided, by walking into Lakeside Stitch & Knit with her head high and getting her hands on some pretty new thread. Thread that she was going to make art with. Art that she was going to stop belittling by calling it a hobby.

Funny how things could feel so unclear for so

long. Until suddenly they weren't anymore.

Rosa had hidden long enough. Not only during the past week, but by hiding who she *really* was all these years.

The walk she and Oscar had been taking through the woods had been slow and meandering. Now, purpose underlay her every step. Her heart was pounding hard, and she couldn't lie and say she wasn't scared. But she was going to push through that fear for once, rather than letting it continue to control her.

"Be a good boy while I go into this store," she said to Oscar as she tied his leash to a lamppost right outside the store. She could have sworn he nodded at her before lapping at a bowl full of water that some nice dog lover had put outside. She gave him a pat on the head. "I won't be too long."

She wouldn't have said she was cool as she walked into the store, but she wasn't on the verge of passing out either. The moment she crossed this threshold was her fresh start. No more running. Not from strangers. Not from the press. Not from her family.

And especially not from herself.

Surrounded by shelves, bins, and baskets of yarn, a lovely gray-haired woman sat in the middle of the room on one of the very comfortable-looking chairs, knitting what looked like a cable sweater in a seafoam green yarn.

"Welcome to Lakeside Stitch and Knit. I'm Olive. Can I help you find anything?"

For a moment, Rosa couldn't find her voice. She took a deep breath and smiled at the woman. "Everything looks so beautiful. I just wanted to look around, if that's okay."

"More than okay." Rosa was struck by how beautiful the woman was when she smiled. "The embroidery on your sweatshirt is exquisite. Did you do it?"

"I did, but it's just a hob—" Rosa caught herself a split second before she downplayed her talent the way she'd just told herself she wouldn't. "Thank you. I love to stitch. I usually work on canvas, but this was all I had."

"May I take a closer look?" Warmth, and something that felt an awful lot like happiness, filled Rosa's chest as the woman got up and moved closer. "You created all this with only two colors?" Olive was clearly impressed as she called out to a middle-aged woman who had just emerged from the back. "Denise, come take a look at this stunning embroidery done by—"

"Rosa." She refused to let her voice shake. "My name is Rosa."

"It truly is a pleasure to meet you, Rosa."

If the other woman recognized her, she didn't give any sign of it as she came forward with a smile and an outstretched hand. "It's lovely to meet you, Rosa. I'm Denise." Her eyes widened as she looked down at the embroidery on the hem of the sweatshirt. "What beautiful artistry."

There was that word again—*artist*. When Drake had said it to her, Rosa hadn't let herself believe he could actually mean it. Now, however, she wouldn't let disbelief win again.

"Thank you." Graciously accepting the

compliment felt a little easier the second time. "Your store is wonderful."

"My mother and I love it. We're glad to hear that you do too."

Rosa's heart tugged at the perfect picture Denise and Olive seemed to make as mother and daughter co-owning such a beautiful store. Had they ever fought? Ever felt so fractured that they wondered if they'd be able to repair their relationship? Or had things always been perfect between them?

"I work with my mom too," she found herself saying. "At least, I used to."

She was saying too much, but thankfully, another customer walked in to save her from herself, from sitting in one of the comfortable chairs with Olive and spilling her guts about absolutely everything while she stitched.

"Christie," Olive called, "come see this gorgeous embroidery our new friend Rosa has done on her top."

When a pretty woman with long, golden-brown hair and startlingly green eyes turned toward Rosa, she couldn't hide her shock. "Oh! Hi!" She quickly turned her attention to Rosa's sweatshirt. "Wow, this is incredible. I'd love to learn how to do something like that." She looked up at Rosa. "I'm sure it's way too hard for me, though, considering I'm still fairly new to knitting."

"I can't knit at all," Rosa told her, trying with all she had not to worry that Christie had obviously recognized her. "Once you learn how to make and space the stitches, it's really just practice more than anything."

"What about coming up with the design? How do you do that?"

"I just try to take the vision I have in my head and bring it to life with the thread."

"You make it sound so easy, but I'm sure if I tried it I'd be all thumbs."

"Honestly, I could get you started in five minutes. Once you felt confident in the rhythm, the feel, of the stitches, you'd be well on your way."

It wasn't until she said the words aloud that she realized just how true they were—not only for embroidery, but for everything in her life as well. Getting started with something new was always the scariest part. The rest was just confidence and practice. Just like Drake had said during that first meal they'd shared together on the card table, when he'd asked, *Are you sure it has to be hard?*

Olive leaned out to look through the front windows to where Oscar was relaxing in a patch of sun on the sidewalk. "Is that Drake Sullivan's big dog with you?"

Rosa felt herself flushing. "We were taking a walk through the woods and couldn't resist coming into your store."

"I don't mean to pry, honey," Olive said, obviously noticing her discomfort. "Although Drake would sure be lucky to be with a woman as lovely as you. I've always thought what a handsome young man he is, with a heart as big as his talent." She waved her hand in the air as if to push the tangential comments aside before continuing. "In any case, I was thinking if you were going to be in town for a little while longer, perhaps we could convince you to teach an art embroidery class."

"Me?" Instantly, the familiar panic bubbled up. "Teach a class?"

"I can tell you for a fact that Christie isn't the only one who would like to learn about your techniques. I would too. And if we posted a picture of your work on our website and in the local paper, it would be a packed house in here, no question."

"I don't—" Rosa shook her head. "I'm not sure..."

"My mother doesn't mean to pressure you," Denise said. "Why don't you take some time to think about it and let us know if you feel comfortable setting something up?"

Rosa appreciated that Denise was giving her a way out, but she'd just spent the past week *taking time* and *thinking about it*. Just minutes before walking into the store, she'd decided she was done running. Done hiding. Done worrying about how difficult it would be to make a fresh start—and just make one already.

This was her chance. So even if she was scared, she needed to take it.

"I'd love to teach a class." She could feel Christie's surprise, even as the other woman tried to hide it. "But before we schedule it, you should know a few things about me, because I'd hate for your customers to get upset about your being connected with me."

"What could they possibly have to be upset about?" Olive asked, her brow furrowed in confusion.

"Nothing." Denise's fierce tone took them all by surprise. "Not one damned thing. I'm very sorry for what that creep did to you, Rosa."

Tears jumped into Rosa's eyes before she could

stop them. She wiped them away with her fingertips. "I am too. But I'm done hiding now. Done feeling like it's my fault."

Denise's arms drew her in, held her tight. "We're all on your side."

Christie nodded vigorously. "We were high-fiving each other over at the inn when we saw what Smith Sullivan said to the press—about how he'd never work with any of them again if they ran any more stolen pictures of you."

"You're all so kind." The strength of the women around Rosa helped feed her own strength. She turned to Olive. "I have a few big things to deal with before I can be certain of my schedule, but I can tell you that even though I've only been in town a few hours, I already know I'd like to stay at Summer Lake for as long as I possibly can."

"Wonderful. Any help you need on any front, you know where to come." Before Rosa could start blubbering again, Olive said, "Now, you take your time browsing." She put a hand on Rosa's shoulder and led her over to a display against the right wall full of sumptuous color and luxurious texture. "You might want to start with this silk floss we just brought in from Italy. Nothing better to work your way through the ups and downs of life, if you ask me. And I should know..."

With a firm squeeze of her shoulder, Olive left Rosa to marvel at her luck in finding so much support everywhere she went from women she'd never met before, like Suzanne and these three wonderful women in the knitting store. And most of all, she marveled over finding Drake.

The man she loved.

CHAPTER TWENTY-SIX

Rosa felt a million times lighter as she and Oscar walked back through the woods to Drake's father's house. As she'd said to the lovely women in the yarn store, she still had plenty to deal with. But even if her load hadn't yet changed, her perspective on it had. She was ready. Finally ready to face it all head on, no matter how difficult it might be.

But first, she needed to talk to Drake. She needed to tell him how much he'd meant to her from the moment he'd found her drenched and scared on the side of the road in the middle of a rainstorm. She needed him to know just how much she loved him. And she needed him to know that she was finally brave enough to trust that their love could last through any firestorms that might come her way in the future.

Oscar seemed just as happy as he lazily splashed

through puddles and loped after squirrels and birds. Every few minutes, he'd saunter back to her side and nuzzle her hand.

"You feel it too, don't you? It's home."

She knew he couldn't really understand her—and certainly couldn't answer—but yet again, it felt like he did when he licked the palm of her hand, then gave her a big doggy grin.

"You're such a big part of it," she told him. "You and Drake."

The beauty of the Adirondacks, the incredibly kind welcome of the women in the yarn store, the silence broken only by the chirp of a bird and the croak of a frog—those were all big things. But the man she still couldn't believe she'd found, and his big sweet dog, were what completed her. Truly and deeply, in a way she'd never thought possible.

Her heartbeat jumped when the house came into view in the curve of a cove. She hoped things had gone okay between Drake and his brother after she'd left, that they'd found a way to work things out.

But even if they hadn't, she wouldn't let that scare her away. No, she'd simply pull up her big-girl pants and convince Alec to come around. She'd show him she wasn't some empty-headed girl from a reality TV show, but someone worthy of his brother's love.

Same went for Drake's father. When she finally met him—soon, hopefully—she wouldn't let any negative first impressions win.

"Rosa."

She gave a little yelp when Alec appeared

suddenly from out of the trees.

"Whoa," he said, "I didn't mean to scare you."

"I'm okay." She would be, anyway, once some of the adrenaline coursing through her drained away. "I didn't hear you coming."

"When we were kids, the four of us used to play a game where we tried to sneak up on each other. I was always good at it." It struck Rosa how much nicer—and slightly less cocky—Alec was when talking about his family. "I want to talk with you before you go in."

"I want to talk with you too." She'd let enough people insult her. Starting now, she wouldn't let anyone else roll over her. Letting the steam rise rather than bottling it up the way she always had before, she said, "I know you think you might know me from TV, but you don't know the first thing about me."

"You're right, I don't," he said, surprising the heck out of her for a second time in a matter of seconds. "I was an ass when Drake introduced us. There's no excuse for my behavior, but I hope you'll accept my apology."

"That's a pretty fast about-face." Even if she didn't want to, she couldn't help but be wary. "Especially when you still don't know me, still haven't talked to me for more than thirty seconds."

His eyebrows went up as if she'd surprised him by not automatically accepting his apology. Surprised *and* impressed him, actually. "My brother wouldn't tell all of us he's in love with you if you weren't worth falling for."

"He told the three of you that?" She'd never met anyone like Drake—so open, so unafraid, so willing to stand up for what—and who—he believed in.

"Nearly rearranged my face while he was at it." Alec ran a hand over his jaw as if to make sure the very well-aligned bones were still intact. "Will you accept my apology?"

Still reeling from the fact that Drake had told all of his siblings he loved her while she was gone, she nodded. "You were an ass, but I'm willing to forget about it and start over if you're willing to forget what you've seen on TV and take me as I am now."

But Alec was obviously wary too, because instead of simply agreeing, he said, "Whoever you are now, I sure as hell hope you're in love with him too. None of us want to see the same thing happen to Drake that happened to our father."

"It wouldn't." She was certain of it. "He's too strong. Too solid. And he has all of you."

"You're right that we'll always have his back, no matter what. And we'll also do whatever we need to protect him." Alec looked her hard in the eyes. "But right now I need to know—are you going to stay or go?"

"I want to stay." It was the second time today she'd made that statement. And each time it had felt right. Scary too, but that seemed to be par for every single course she was on right now. "I've got a lot to take care of, though."

"Drake is already on your side. Now the rest of us are too." His grin was probably irresistible to every woman on the planet. But not her. Because her heart was already taken. "Whatever you need, just ask."

Was it really that easy?

Before today she would have doubted, would have been cynical. But she was tired of second-guessing every single thing, so she decided to push her bravery another step forward by taking Alec's statement at face value.

"Okay. Thank you." She was glad they'd cleared the air, but she was now more desperate than ever to talk to Drake so that she could tell him everything she was thinking, feeling. So that he would know just how much she loved him right back.

As if she had conjured him out of sheer desire, Drake emerged a moment later through a grove of trees. "There you are."

Joy blasted through her, head to toe, just looking at his smiling face. And when he grabbed her and kissed her as if she'd been gone two years instead of only two hours, she was surprised that her heart didn't simply explode out of her chest in an array of multicolored fireworks.

When he finally let her up for air, her knees were wobbly enough that she needed to hold him so she didn't simply melt to the ground in a puddle.

"That's one hell of a greeting," Alec mused in a voice laced with humor.

"The best anyone has ever given me." Rosa's voice was breathless, her lips still tingling, and she couldn't stop staring at Drake. Couldn't stop being amazed that she'd actually found him. And that he'd found her. "I'm actually wondering if I should leave again now just so I can come back to that."

Drake's mouth was on hers again so fast that

she didn't even have time to take her next breath. And it wasn't only her knees that went weak and her lips that tingled from his kiss. Every last cell in her body vibrated with *want*.

"That's what you get when you stay." She was still spinning, still trying to get her breath back, when he pulled her even closer and turned to his brother. "Were you being an ass again?"

"Don't worry," Alec said. "I apologized."

"And I accepted," she told Drake.

"We may even like each other now," Alec drawled.

"Baby steps," she teased with a laugh. "Seriously, though, we've agreed to get to know each other better before we make any more snap judgments."

She could see how relieved Drake was that she and his brother weren't at each other's throats. And how happy he was to tell her, "My father is back from his job site, and he's making dinner for all of us. He's surprised that we're all here, but I think he's pretty happy about it."

"Of course he is." Her heart swelled with hope that Drake and his father would soon grow closer. "I can't wait to meet him."

Now that she'd finally made the big decision to move forward with her life, rather than keep hiding, she had so much to do. Contact that lawyer who had come to her defense on that TV talk show so that she could begin her own personal proceedings against the creep who had taken and sold the pictures. Call the network to let them know she no longer planned to be on the show. And, of course, finally talk to her mom face to face about it all.

But after nearly a week in hiding, she could wait one more night to set the wheels of the next big changes in her life into motion.

Tonight, it was Drake's turn.

* * *

"My father—" Drake paused, obviously weighing his words carefully. Alec had gone inside ahead of them, and they were now standing alone on the steps just outside the door. "I've never brought a woman home before. None of us have, so this is a pretty big deal. And when I told him I was painting you—"

"He wasn't exactly thrilled about it?"

A muscle jumped in Drake's jaw. "I won't let him hurt you."

"He won't." She smiled to let him know she meant it. "Whether his reaction came from my reputation or his worries that you and I are repeating his history with your mother—I'm not going to fall apart. And I'm not going to run into hiding again either." She put her hand on his jaw, loving the scratch of stubble against her palm. "I'm done with that." She pressed a kiss to his lips—a promise of many more to come. "I have so much to tell you, but right now, let's enjoy dinner with your family."

Despite the questions in his eyes, he let her lead them in the door. "Mmm," Rosa said, pausing to inhale the delicious aroma of roasting tomatoes and peppers. "It smells great." At the same time, thinking of her mother and brothers making and sitting down to dinner without her made her chest ache.

A man with salt-and-pepper hair looked up from the island where he was chopping peppers. Drake's father. He didn't smile at her the way Suz and Harry had upon meeting her, but he didn't scowl like Alec had either. Instead, he simply stared. Stared in a way that reminded her of the way Drake sometimes looked at her—with a painter's eyes that saw far beyond those of the layman.

"Dad, this is Rosa. Rosa, this is my father, William."

She heard that note of warning in Drake's voice again, and though she loved him for wanting to protect her, she didn't need him to slay her dragons anymore. She squeezed his hand to let him know she was okay, then slipped hers free to go meet his father properly.

Drake's dad hadn't moved from the island, hadn't even put down the knife, but she didn't let that deter her. The first test of her fresh start had been walking into the yarn store with her head held high. The second had been standing her ground with Alec, and then agreeing to start fresh after he'd apologized. She refused to fail this third test, even if William Sullivan didn't look like he was planning to make things easier for her.

"It's so nice to meet you." When he still didn't reply, knowing Drake was about to pounce—and that each of his siblings was watching with no small measure of concern—she turned on the faucet at the kitchen sink, washed her hands, and made herself ask in an easy voice, "Are you making Enchiladas Suizas?" Again, she didn't wait for his reply before she slid another knife out of the wood block on the counter along with another cutting board and began to chop the onions. "My mom taught me how to make enchiladas when I was still so small that I needed to stand on a stool to reach the counter. It's been a while since I made them, so I hope you don't mind if my knife skills are a little rusty."

The only sound for a few long moments was the steady beat of the steel blade landing against the wood board. Everyone's gaze lay on her, but none was more intense than that of Drake's father. This moment, she knew, could go either way. Silently, she prayed for the good one, even with the tension currently thick enough to cut with the knife in her hand.

"I'd appreciate the help, Rosa." William looked up at Drake. "Margaritas are in the blender if you two want one. I could use a top-up." He turned back to Rosa. "And I want you to know that if I could run that asshole who took those pictures of you down the middle of my table saw, I would do it in a heartbeat."

Rosa's knife was the one falling still this time as she looked up from the onions to give Drake's father a huge smile. She now knew where Drake had learned his knight-in-shining-armor skills. "I'll let you know if I need to borrow it."

And just like that, the freeze-frame that had been holding everyone captive disappeared. Suz and Harry laughed over Oscar rolling over and begging to get his belly rubbed, Alec walked out of the kitchen to take a call, and Drake headed for the blender while Rosa barely held in a huge sigh of relief.

She wasn't much of a drinker, but it had been one heck of a day, so when Drake handed her the filled-to-the-brim margarita, she welcomed the cool bite of the lime, the warmth of the tequila. But while the alcohol went straight into her bloodstream, it was the kiss Drake gave her after her first sip that ran a million times hotter through her veins.

CHAPTER TWENTY-SEVEN

Drake had rarely seen his father this relaxed. This animated. Same went for his brothers and Suzanne. Primarily because Rosa had a way of drawing people out of themselves.

Where Drake had always been more inclined to sit back and watch, she jumped in with questions and sincere interest in every answer given, every story told. It was, he realized, the way she'd always been with him at the cabin. Even when she'd been afraid to get close to anyone, she hadn't been able to stop herself from asking him about his father and the paintings, hadn't been able to keep from caring about the man who had found her on his cliffs.

She'd always glowed bright, even on that first day when the rain had been pouring down on her as she sobbed. Tonight, however, she radiated so much light that Drake could barely contain his need to paint her. Along with the paintings out in the back of the SUV, he'd brought a stash of paints and a couple of blank canvases.

Something had happened this afternoon while she was out walking with Oscar. She'd always been strong in his eyes, but before now it had been a struggle to get her to see it. Whereas tonight, she'd come back roaring like a lioness. One who finally seemed to know her own strength. As soon as dinner was over, he needed to talk to her alone to find out what had transformed her so deeply, inside and out.

And so he could tell her, again, just how much he loved her. More now than ever as she laughed with his family over enchiladas and margaritas, Oscar snoring softly beneath the big dining table.

"Okay, let me make sure I have this straight," she was saying. "The four of you were hanging from the rafters like monkeys when you were building this house, and that was right when the inspector walked in?"

"I was doing a handstand, actually," Suz said with more than a little pride.

Rosa turned to his father. "What did you do?"

"I told Brian we were training for our family circus and got up there with them. And then I grounded them until they were teenagers."

Laughter burst from her. "I shouldn't be surprised. My brothers and I were just as nuts when we were kids."

"You think you can beat the rafters?" Alec challenged.

"As soon as we could walk, my parents had us on water skis. One day, I found that old Go-Go's video—

you know the one where they're waterskiing in pyramid formation? Even though I was only eight, I told my five- and six-year-old brothers we had to do it, and we couldn't tell my parents anything until we'd perfected the trick. We convinced one of my friend's older brothers to take us out, and when I climbed up on their shoulders, it was like flying."

"I'm impressed," Harry said. "The four of us talked about trying a water-skiing pyramid, but we always chickened out."

"Good call." Her mouth quirked up in an adorable half smile. "When we got back to the dock, I've never seen my parents so mad. We were also pretty much grounded for the rest of our lives—although they bragged about it plenty when they thought we couldn't hear them."

"As a parent, you want your kids to be fearless," Drake's father said. "You want them to believe that they can do absolutely anything. But then when they push the limits, all you can think about is how destroyed you'd be if anything ever happened to them."

He put his fork down, the entire tenor of dinner having shifted as soon as he'd said *destroyed*.

"I know I haven't said this nearly enough, but I'm so damned proud of all of you."

"We know you are, Dad," Suz said immediately, obviously intent on smoothing over the situation the way she had her whole life.

But where had smoothing things over, where had brushing things under the rug, ever gotten them, apart from an awkward, distant relationship with their father?

Earlier, Rosa had told Drake she was done running and hiding. They could all take a lesson from her.

Right here, right now.

"No." Drake looked his father straight in the eye. "We don't know it."

"Drake." Harry didn't often sound threatening. But when he did, he was big enough and good enough with his fists that you knew to take it seriously. "We don't need to do this tonight."

Drake had always believed Rosa was strong enough to risk speaking up, and resilient enough to weather making a huge change. He knew his sister and brothers were too.

The only person at the table he didn't know nearly well enough was his father. But he wanted so badly to get to know him, wanted more than anything else to bridge the gap between them before the distance grew so big that no one dared. Tonight, with Rosa by his side. Even if it meant the possibility of upsetting every member of his immediate family.

"You know why we were hanging from the rafters that day?" Thirty years of the frustration and pain that Drake had always been so careful to shove away finally rose, hot and fierce. "To try to get your attention. To try to get you to see that even though you'd lost your wife, there were four kids waiting for you." Rosa slid her hand into his beneath the table, and he let her warmth, her strength, fuel him. "We needed you. But all you've ever seemed to need are the paintings."

"That's not true." His father's deep voice vibrated with emotion.

"Then tell me," Drake said in a voice that he deliberately softened, "tell all of us something that is true."

"I didn't know what to do." His father had never sounded more defeated. "I never knew what to do, not with your mother and not with any of you after she was gone." He looked at each of his kids. "I still don't know, couldn't think of any other way to get you here than to say you had thirty days to take the paintings, or I would get rid of them." He ran a hand over his eyes, held it there as though he couldn't bear to see their expressions. "I didn't think any of you would come otherwise."

Drake needed his father to know, "I didn't come for the paintings. I came for answers."

Alec had been silent throughout the heated exchange, but now he said, "So did I."

Suz took a deep breath before adding, "Me too."

Harry had always been the hardest to read of the four of them, the one who held his thoughts and opinions the closest. But though he hadn't wanted to unlatch the cage, now that the wild animals were running free, he obviously realized there was no point in trying to get them back inside. Especially when, at his core, he was just as wild as the rest of them. "That's why I'm here too."

Though William Sullivan's hand was strong enough to easily lift a steel beam, it shook as it dropped away from his face. "I know I owe all of you answers. But I don't know where to start. I never have."

"At the beginning." Harry's entire adult life had been devoted to studying history, so it made sense that he would be the one to direct the timeline. "Start with the day you met our mother."

"You know that already," their father said, "how we met at a party my brother Ethan threw in the city. Lynn was the most beautiful woman I'd ever set eyes on—and the most challenging too."

"What do you mean, *challenging*?" Suz asked.

"Your mother almost seemed to float, as if her feet never quite touched the ground. And she was obviously overwhelmed by the people, the noise. So I asked her if she wanted to leave, to find someplace quiet." Drake could see that his father was lost in memories. "I took her hand and vowed to keep her safe. She seemed relieved. She told me she needed help to stay grounded. We fell in love that night as we searched for someplace quiet to go to get to know each other better, and I painted her for the first time the following morning. We were married soon after, and then we had you, Alec. She loved you. Loved all of you so much."

"Then why did she leave?" Drake needed to know the truth, once and for all, even if it hurt. "Was it because four kids were too many?"

The way his father's eyes went wide with shock at the question was already an answer. One that filled Drake with long overdue relief.

"The four of you were the reason she tried to stay. But—" Their father ran his hand over his eyes again, as though he wished he could hide. "It was my fault. I drove her away. With my paintings."

"How could your paintings have driven her away?" Suz asked. "You worshipped her in them."

"I more than worshipped her. Just as you said earlier when you didn't know I was in the house, I was obsessed. And that only made things worse."

Drake watched his father at war with himself, as if he wasn't sure that he should continue. "Whatever you've got to tell us, we can take it."

"I know you can. The only one I'm not sure about is myself."

"We're family," Suz reminded him in a voice drenched with tears that were clearly about to fall. "We're supposed to be here for each other. For you."

Harry nodded. "Keep going, Dad."

Only Alec didn't look completely on board with finally hearing the truth about the end of their parents' marriage. His face was stony, his eyes hard.

Regret heavy in his voice, their father finally continued. "After we were married, I found out things about Lynn's past. About how she'd often closed into herself as a teenager and tried to shut out the rest of the world, and then she did it even more as a young woman in her twenties. Noise, crowds, speed—she couldn't take any of it. But whenever she was pregnant, whenever she had a baby in her arms, she seemed at peace. Content. As close to grounded as she could be." He grimaced. "At least, until my paintings of her started to find an audience all over the world. When one of my paintings made the cover of *Time*, it was similar to having something go viral today on the Internet. And she hated the spotlight." He shook his head. "*Hated* isn't the right word for it. It was more that she worried that everyone walking down the street was looking at her. She became more and more paranoid that people were saying things about her. She stopped wanting to go out. Stopped wanting to see anyone, even family, because she swore they were all judging her. Shaming her."

"I know that feeling," Rosa said, the first thing she'd said since Drake's family had begun this difficult discussion. "I know how much easier it seems to run and hide from the world, rather than to face it."

"She wasn't strong like you are, Rosa," William said. "She could never have weathered what you're dealing with right now. Five minutes in the kitchen with you was all it took to see that you aren't going to let anyone back you into a corner and keep you there. When Drake told me he was painting a woman who didn't want anyone to see the paintings, I couldn't believe it. Couldn't stand the thought of his stepping into my shoes, desperately trying to hold on to a woman who was always meant to float away. Repeating history. But I now know that isn't going to happen, because you have a resilience that my wife never did." Grief was etched into every line on his face. "I thought that if I painted Lynn enough times, I'd finally find her hidden vein of tenacity. The fearlessness that is in each of our children. Only to realize too late that all my paintings ever did was drive her farther away. Higher up into the sky. Until one day, she simply disappeared. I'll never be able to forgive myself for driving her away."

A dark and ominously heavy cloud threatened to descend over them. But Drake was tired of his family being shrouded in darkness. As his father had said earlier, thirty years was long enough.

"It wasn't your fault."

Everyone but Rosa started in their chairs. She simply kept holding on to his hand while he fought to finally heal the wounds that had torn his family apart for his entire life.

"It is," his father insisted. "I just told you the truth. A truth I've been so ashamed of for so long. And I understand if all of you hate me."

"I hate that she left. I hate that she wasn't strong enough to withstand fame, the heat of the spotlight. I hate that she couldn't figure out a way to get some help so that she could stick around and see her kids grow up. But I don't hate *you*, Dad. I've never hated you, even when you were gone all the time and it would have been so much easier if I did."

"Are you saying—" Hope lit his father's eyes, so much hope that Drake's chest clenched tight to realize just how badly his father needed to know his kids loved him. "You actually forgive me?"

Fierce heat rose again inside Drake, but it wasn't directed at his dad anymore. Shame had made his mother so paranoid that she couldn't imagine living. Shame had made his father bottle up his feelings for thirty years. Shame had sent Rosa into hiding.

"I'm saying we should all give shame and guilt a big fat kick in the ass and start the hell over."

"A fresh start." A tear rolled down his father's face as he reached out to put a hand over Drake's. "That's what I want too."

"Me too," Suz said through her tears as she put her arms around their father and held on tight. Harry came around on their father's other side and clasped a hand on his shoulder.

Only Alec stayed apart, his face an unreadable mask as he slid his chair back from the table, then walked out of the house without a word.

* * *

Drake caught his brother in the driveway getting into his car.

"I'm happy for you," Alec said before Drake could say anything, "but I'm not going to pretend to play happy family with William now that he's suddenly ready to be a father."

Drake understood that, as the oldest, Alec's experience of their mother's leaving had been different. Of the four of them, he'd not only spent the most time with her, but he'd also been old enough to understand that she wasn't ever coming back.

Knowing he had to tread carefully, Drake said, "I know we haven't solved everything. Not even close. But tonight was a step in the right direction. To finally get honest answers to the questions none of us have ever felt we could ask."

"Mom was just like he said—she barely touched the ground. It almost seemed as if she might just float away sometimes." Alec looked toward the cottage where their father stored the paintings of their mother, then shook his head as if he didn't want to think about any of it anymore. "I need to head back to the city. Let me know if Rosa needs my help with anything. I'm happy to lend her one of my personal planes if she needs to go somewhere in stealth mode."

There was no point in reminding his brother that he'd said he'd spend the night in the Adirondacks. Not now that Alec had locked down. So instead of talking more about their father, Drake said, "Something tells me Rosa's done with stealth mode. But thanks for being on her side. Mine too." Alec was shutting his door when Drake said, "I'll hold on to your paintings until you want them."

CHAPTER TWENTY-EIGHT

Drake was still standing in the driveway watching the dust from Alec's tires settle when Rosa slid her hand into his. She didn't ask if he was okay, just let him lead them silently through the woods to a private cove. Far enough from his father's house that no one could see or hear them. And dark enough that they were barely shadows as he drew her out of the trees and toward the water.

"I need you," he said as he began to strip away her clothes. "Here. Now."

"I need you too." She put her hands on his face. "I love you."

The words of love from her lips—and the love he could feel in her kiss—sent him reeling even faster, even harder, than tonight's dinner discussion had.

"I love you so much." She rained kisses over his

face. "I should have told you before, but I was scared. I'm still scared of plenty of things, but not of what I feel for you. I'll never be scared of that again."

"*Mine*." He crushed her mouth, her body, against his. "I want you to be mine. Forever."

"Good, because I'm not going to let you go, no matter what people say. No matter what they think."

He knew exactly how strong she was—how strong she'd always been—but hearing her say the words was huge. "I love you, Rosa. That's never going to change. No matter what."

The moon was shrouded by clouds, but even in the pitch darkness, he knew her expressions, her body, by heart. He loved her little gasps of pleasure as he slowly lowered her bra straps from each shoulder and pressed kisses all along the skin he'd just bared. She gripped his shoulders as if to hold herself steady, her breath coming faster and faster the closer he got to her breasts, his tongue sliding in damp circles along the soft flesh. Finally, he found one taut tip, her breath going as he drew it between his lips and suckled.

Greed took over as he cupped her breasts to take both into his mouth at once. She rocked her hips against his as he ran his tongue over her. Threading her hands into his hair, she pulled his mouth back up to hers, kissing him with fierce passion.

"Take me, Drake." She dropped her hands to his shirt and nearly tore it off in her need to get him naked. "Here." He'd only just pulled a condom out of his back pocket when she yanked the button and zipper of his jeans open and shoved them down. "Now."

Their hands met on her waistband, both of them working to get rid of the last barrier between them. As soon as they'd slid protection on his throbbing length, he lifted her up into his arms. When she wrapped her legs around him, he cupped her luscious hips in his hands and brought her even closer.

Drake wanted to start clean with everyone and everything tonight. He'd always been drawn to water—not only painting it, but diving in, going deep, and coming up feeling renewed. Thankfully, there was enough moonlight now to safely take them down the sandy path to the hidden cove.

Holding on tight with her strong arms around his neck, Rosa nuzzled him as he carried her into the water, making him even crazier for her as she ran her nose, her lips, her tongue, over him.

"Tell me if it's too cold," he said when her feet and hips were submerged.

"Take me under, Drake. Take me all the way." Her teeth nipped at his earlobe. "A little cold water isn't going to break me. Nothing can anymore. Not now that I've found you...and you helped me find myself again."

He took her mouth in a savage kiss, one that captivated.

Enthralled.

Consumed.

All his life Drake had held a part of himself back to make sure that he wouldn't end up following in his father's footsteps. But he didn't need to hold back with Rosa. Not when he knew she wouldn't break.

And neither would he.

They were only partially submerged when he lifted her hips, then plunged her down onto him, hard and deep. She gasped into his mouth as her inner muscles gripped him in a hot, wet, perfect clasp.

"*Drake.*" Nothing had ever sounded as good as his name on her lips. Nothing but, "*I love you.*"

Wet and wild together, they tumbled in the water, their mouths fused even as they momentarily went under. They came apart just long enough to catch their footing and reach for each other again, her arms around his back, her legs around his hips as he braced himself above her, then drove deep again.

On the shore, with the water lapping over their naked bodies, they were shameless in their passion for one other. Reckless in their quest for pleasure beyond anything either of them had ever known. Utterly abandoned and unrestrained as their sounds of bliss rose in the darkness.

And as they gave each other everything, Drake knew that no matter what happened with Rosa's mother or his father or her TV show—or any other hurdles that might come up in the future—they already had everything that mattered.

Each other.

* * *

Rosa wanted to stay there forever in the lake wrapped all around Drake. Still, she knew he was right to get them out and dressed before a chill could set in. And it felt so intimate, zipping and buttoning him into his clothes, then letting him do the same with hers.

What had begun as a terrible week had ended with such beauty. And more love than she'd ever thought possible.

Rosa suddenly remembered her mother's email: *We can turn something terrible into something amazing.*

Earlier that week, when she'd read those words on the burner phone in her Montauk motel room, she'd been sickened at the thought of exploiting the nude photos—and people's pity—to make more money with their family brand or to build up her fan base.

Tonight, she saw things differently. Clearly.

"I know what I need to do." To turn *terrible* into *amazing*. "I know what to say to all the women who think they need to run and hide."

The moonlight illuminated Drake's smile as he paused while finger-combing sand from her tangled hair. "Of course you do."

"But I need to talk with my mom before I do anything else." She looked out at the lake, breathed in the fresh scent of the mountains. "I just wish I didn't have to go back to Miami so soon. I really love it here. I don't want to leave."

"You don't need to. Alec can fly her in—tomorrow, if she can come that fast. There's a private landing strip a couple of miles away. And we'll make sure the press doesn't follow her here if you don't want them to."

A *zing* of nerves hit Rosa, twisting together in the pit of her stomach. She honestly didn't know how her mother would react to anything she was planning to say.

Then again, after sitting at William's table tonight and seeing what was possible when family wasn't afraid to open up to each other, she felt hopeful that she and her mother might be able to find their way too.

Still, she needed Drake to know something. "While Alec and I talked, and he did apologize, he warned me not to hurt you. I'm not sure that means he's ready to lend me a plane for my mom."

"He's the oldest, so that's his standard speech." He brushed sand from her neck and made her shiver at how good his touch felt. Always. "Trust me, he's on your side. We'll call him to make the arrangements as soon as we get back to the house. What else do you need?"

Rosa's head was still spinning from their extraordinary lovemaking. She'd never given her entire self to anyone before, nor had she ever taken all a man had to give. Her body, her heart, were both still so full. And growing fuller by the second as Drake offered her more and more.

"I'm going to need somewhere big enough to fit a film crew."

"My father's house is big enough."

"He's a private man, and my staying with him is already potentially invasive for the quiet life he's tried to build here. I can't bring a film crew in too. Besides, you don't even know what I want to film yet."

"I don't have to know to be certain that it's going to be great."

She threw her arms around him and kissed him. "If I could feel my feet, I'd drag you back into the lake and jump you again."

"There's a cottage just beyond these trees. It's closer than the house so that we can get you warm faster. Now, tell me your plans."

"I found out that the network wants to do a special two-hour show, but I wasn't going to do it because I couldn't stand the idea of using what happened as a springboard for more money, more followers, bigger ad contracts." They were on the threshold of his father's small cottage when she said, "But I've realized that if millions of people are going to tune in, even if most of them probably think they're going to see a train wreck, I can use that time to do something good. Something that might help."

"I know the perfect place. My friend Calvin is the mayor. The city hall building is classic without being stuffy. I'm sure he wouldn't have a problem letting you film there. In fact, given that he has a ten-year-old sister he would do anything to protect, he'll probably insist on helping you."

"Always so confident." She wrapped her arms around Drake after he fished a key out from under a rock and opened the door. "Once upon a time, I would have wondered how you could be so sure. But after spending some time with everyone tonight, I see now that it runs in your family."

Rosa had expected the cottage to be a storage room, or maybe a simple guest house. But when he flipped on the lights and she saw the paintings, she couldn't hold back a gasp.

Because Drake's mother stared back at her from every single canvas.

CHAPTER TWENTY-NINE

"My father has stored the paintings here for thirty years." This cottage had been the original building on the property and was at least a hundred years old.

While Alec rarely set foot inside the cottage, Drake was never able to stay away. Not only because he couldn't resist magnificent art, but also because these paintings were his only link to his mother.

Normally, the paintings were hidden beneath dusty tarps, but tonight Drake was surprised to find them arranged on the walls in chronological order. He couldn't imagine how emotional his father must have been hanging each painting, from the first time his wife had sat for him, through the years when they'd been building a family, until the end of both their marriage and his career.

Whenever Drake had come here before, he'd

uncovered only a couple of paintings at a time. This was the first time he'd ever seen all of them together.

Love. Loss. Longing. Passion. Shame. Devotion. *Obsession.*

You couldn't help but feel every moment of joy, each sob of despair. Emotion sang from every brushstroke, every drop of color and contour.

This was why his father's paintings now sold for millions of dollars—and why people would lose their minds if they knew that more than one hundred William Sullivan originals had been growing damp and dusty in a hundred-year-old cottage in the Adirondacks.

"*My God.*" Rosa gaped at the paintings. "They're absolutely breathtaking."

He watched as she followed the painted story of his mother and father's love affair, first with solo paintings of his mother, then with babies, and then with children growing older often appearing alongside her.

Rosa tugged him over to a canvas in which his mother was looking down at Drake as a newborn. "Look how much she loved you. Whatever happened that sent your mother running, no one could look at this painting and think she didn't want you, that she didn't love you. Because she obviously did, Drake. With everything she was."

"So many times over the years," he admitted in a quiet voice, "I came and stared at this painting and wished. Wished that she really had loved me." He'd never bared so much of himself to anyone else, not even his siblings. "But every time I thought she must have, I always thought I must be wrong. Because she didn't stay."

"The things your father told you tonight about what her reasons might have been—did hearing any of it help?"

"Some. But it hurts too. Hurts to know that I might have had a mom all these years if only they'd been able to figure out a way to help her."

"I know." She wrapped her arms around him. "If it's too overwhelming to be in here right now, we can go."

"It always was before, even though I couldn't ever stay away for very long." He held Rosa tightly as he made himself look at the painting—really look deep this time, without being afraid of what he'd see. "She really does float without her feet ever quite touching the ground, doesn't she?"

"She does."

"It helps to know that she didn't leave because of me, didn't take her life because she couldn't handle another kid. I just wish my father could see that she didn't leave because of him either. Then maybe he would stop wasting his talent and start painting again."

"Do you really think he's wasted his talent all these years?"

Drake turned to Rosa in surprise. "You just said it yourself—how extraordinary his paintings are."

"They are, no one could ever question that. But he built his own house, didn't he?" When Drake nodded, she said, "It's pretty darn extraordinary. You can tell a true artisan built it. And I'll bet the houses he's built for people all over the lake are just as thoughtful, just as full of artistic touches that have his stamp on them."

"You're right that he's a brilliant artisan, but it isn't painting. And painting was his whole life."

"I don't think that's true. I think your mom, you and your siblings, were his life. I know I only just met your family, but I feel like I can so clearly see a piece of each of you in him."

"How? Where?"

"Maybe, like with Harry and his love for history, painting was your father's way of really studying the histories of the people he painted from all angles, in all lights and moods. Or he could have used painting the way Suzanne uses a computer program—to create something that would make the world a better place. Or perhaps painting was his ticket into the glamorous life, like Alec's exclusive private planes. Or it could simply be," she said as she turned away from the paintings to meet Drake's gaze, "that he's called to beauty the same way you are, so deeply, so instinctively, that he can't walk away from it without needing to try to capture it for everyone to appreciate, even after the fleeting, radiant moment has passed."

Drake was floored by her insight. He'd always thought he saw past the normal bounds, but now he realized he'd had blinders on his whole life—at least where his father was concerned. "How do you see so much?"

"I don't know if you should give me too much credit, since I could be way off base."

"You're not." Drake felt the truth of it in his bones. "Me, Suz, Harry, Alec—we *are* all connected to my father. Even if Alec still doesn't want to acknowledge that connection, that doesn't mean it isn't true. I'm not going to lie and say I don't wish my father hadn't stopped painting, but at least now I can see that he probably needed to make that change to survive."

"I obviously don't know his reasons for putting down his paintbrush," Rosa said as she turned into his arms, "but I can understand how after your mother left, he might have needed to capture beauty, to create art and study the world around him, in a different way. Maybe making a huge change that didn't make sense to anyone else was the only thing that made sense to him. And maybe it was not only a way to survive what he'd been through, but to hopefully come out better on the other side one day."

"Better." Drake pressed his mouth to hers, loving the sweet sigh of pleasure she made when their lips met. "Everything is already so much better. Because of you."

"I was planning to rip off your clothes again once we got inside here," she whispered, a sexy confession for his ears only. "But your memories of this room should be about your mother, not getting naked with a woman who can't keep her hands off you."

"The cottage is bigger than it looks." He took her through a doorway, past a small kitchen, and into the bedroom that he hadn't been in since he was a teenager looking for a private place to bring girls.

The first thing he noticed was that the old bedframe and mattress were gone. The second thing was how great the lighting was—gallery quality. The third was the lone leather swivel chair in the center of the hardwood floor. And the fourth?

Well, if Drake had thought the surprises were over for the night, he was wrong again.

"Drake." Rosa gripped his hand tighter. "These paintings aren't your father's."

"No." He still couldn't believe what he was seeing, though more than two dozen pieces of proof were staring at him from the four walls. "They're mine."

CHAPTER THIRTY

"He never told me he was collecting my work."

Rosa could see Drake's shock as he looked at his own paintings on the walls.

"He's got something from every show I've ever had."

While she wasn't sure she'd ever be able to wrap her head all the way around the size of Drake's talent, in this moment Rosa was most struck by how much he loved the Adirondacks. The paintings on these walls from his many shows over the years made it clear that he had always been deeply inspired by these mountains, lakes, and forests. By the Adirondack wildlife and the wide expanse of sky that seemed bluer and brighter than anywhere else.

There was no question that he enjoyed his cottage in Montauk. But if not for his fraught relationship with his father, would he have chosen to paint—and to live—at Summer Lake instead?

Drake did another slow scan of the walls. "Why didn't he tell me?"

"Ask him. Tonight." She took his hands. "Now that the ice is finally broken, don't let it freeze over again." It was obvious to her just how much William Sullivan loved his kids. The private gallery he'd built to honor his son's talent only reinforced it. "And when you're done talking, I'll be waiting." She moved his hands to her hips. "Waiting to make you mine, and for you to make me yours any way, every way, you want. Waiting to tell you *I love you* again."

He kissed her until she could barely remember why they weren't already naked and making love. "There are so many ways I want to love you," he said, "it could take a lifetime. The shower this morning, the beach tonight—they were only a start."

Every nerve in her body felt impossibly, wonderfully alive as she went to her tippy-toes to kiss him softly. "Let's go so that you can talk to him, one-on-one this time. Something tells me he's probably waiting up for you."

Their walk back to his father's house held different but equally wonderful sounds, smells, and sights from those she'd appreciated during her earlier walk with Oscar. Holding Drake's hand, she drank in the fresh, sweet scent of the forest, the faint splash of the lake water against the shore, the way the moonlight found its way in between branches.

As they headed for the house, fatigue finally set

in. And no wonder, given that she felt as though a million revelations had been made today.

Still, Rosa knew that tomorrow would be the biggest day yet for her. Not only because she would officially come out of hiding, but also because she so badly wanted to break through the wall of ice that should never have been allowed to freeze between mother and daughter.

Her heart beat unsteadily behind her breastbone as she made yet another silent wish that her mother would even want to come see her and talk to her at this point. Her brothers too. Because what if fleeing and shutting everyone out had done permanent damage to her relationship with the people she loved most?

No. She couldn't let herself think like that.

But as they walked back into Drake's father's house, the last thing she expected was to find William Sullivan standing with a woman she knew.

Knew better than anyone else in the world.

* * *

"Mom?" Rosa was as shocked to find her mother in William Sullivan's living room as Drake had been to see his own paintings on display in the small cottage. "What are you doing here?"

The last word was barely out of her mouth when her mother leapt across the room and threw her arms around Rosa. "Oh, honey, I'm so glad you're okay. We were all so scared." She started sobbing, her arms tightening so hard around Rosa's rib cage that she could barely breathe. All the while, Oscar stuck to her like glue, as if he knew she needed him now more than ever.

Rosa's sudden onslaught of tears made it hard to tell her mom, "I'm sorry, I shouldn't have left like that, I just didn't know what else to do. But I knew you'd be worried, which was why I emailed so you'd know I was okay."

"That was days ago." Her mother wiped away Rosa's tears, even before her own. "Anything could have happened since then. I've imagined a million horrible things. Thank God William called me."

Still beyond stunned by the fact that her mother was even here, Rosa nearly couldn't wrap her head around what she'd just said. "He called you?" She turned to look at Drake's father in confusion. "But I only just met you tonight."

"Please don't be angry with him," her mother begged. "He heard me say on the radio this morning how scared I was that something might have happened to you. And when his son Drake told him you were here together earlier today, he couldn't stop imagining how he would feel in my shoes."

"As a parent, I had to track down your mother's number," William said in his deep voice, "to let her know not only that you were okay, but also that my son was looking out for you."

"Calling was William's idea," her mother agreed, "but coming here tonight was mine. I needed to see you, honey, needed to know for sure that you're all right."

The beginning of the day, when Rosa had been surprised in Montauk by a stranger carrying a pie, seemed like a million years ago. "I was going to ask you to come tomorrow. I just needed some time first."

"We've always done everything together." Her mother gripped her hands. "Why did you feel you had to run away? Why didn't you trust your family to be there for you? Why didn't you trust *me* with what you were feeling?" Before Rosa could answer, her mother said, "I never pushed you into anything you didn't want to do, did I? I always tried to be so careful not to be one of those awful momagers. I thought you were enjoying it all. Weren't you?"

"You know I was. At first, anyway." But Rosa pulled her hands away, needing some distance again so she could say, "It's just that sometimes it was hard having our family life and business all bound up together. Especially when I felt like I couldn't talk to you about anything outside of the show. I kept waiting for the cameras to go off, but they never did. Not after the show got so big, and we were always either filming or doing photo shoots and interviews. Not even the day we found out about the pictures of me. The cameras were rolling even then." She took a deep breath before saying, "I miss you, Mom. Miss you just being my mom instead of my co-star or manager or whatever we became."

"But I've been right here, honey. Right here as your mother, no matter what else is going on."

"No, you haven't." Rosa hated to hurt her mom, but she wasn't going to run from speaking the truth this time. Not when she'd finally learned that running didn't make things any easier or better. For the first time in a long time, she was going to deal with her problems—

and her fears—head on. "I needed my mom when the pictures hit. But I got a PR spin doctor instead. It's like you completely forgot why we signed on for the show in the first place—to save our family, not to tear us apart."

"How can you say that?" Rosa had to bite the inside of her cheek to keep from taking it back as her mother's face crumpled again. "I was devastated. Absolutely devastated by what that awful man did to you."

"You told me it was nothing people hadn't seen a million times before."

"I swear, Rosa, I said that to try to help."

"How on earth could you possibly think saying that would help me?" Rosa's question was loud enough—and so forceful—that it reverberated off the vaulted ceilings in the huge living room.

Her mother didn't start crying again, just blindly reached for a couch behind her and collapsed on it. That was when Rosa finally realized how different her mother looked. Where Isobel Bouchard usually never left the house without perfect makeup, hair, and clothes—even before they'd signed on for the TV show, she'd always believed in taking special care with her appearance—tonight she seemed to have forgotten that any of those things mattered at all.

Rosa also realized that at some point, Drake and his father must have left the room. Oscar had stayed behind, still right there at her side.

"Ever since the day you were born, my biggest fear has been that someone would hurt you." Her mother's words were so soft that Rosa had to move closer to catch them. "When your dad died, that fear magnified a thousand times because you only had me to keep you safe. So when we found out about the pictures..." Her mother wiped away the tears that had started falling again. "I knew I had failed. Failed in the worst way a mother can fail her daughter." Her face was ravaged with guilt as she said, "The last thing I wanted was for you to feel like those photos diminished you in any way. All I could think was that you needed to know that you are so much stronger, so much better, than anyone who would ever try to harm you like that. And that you don't have one single thing to be ashamed of, honey."

Rosa dropped to her knees on the rug in front of her mom. "Why didn't you just say that to me?"

"Because the whole thing is my fault. You have nothing whatsoever to be ashamed of, but I do."

"You don't."

"I *do*. If we hadn't signed on to do the show, if we hadn't become famous, then you would be just another normal young woman."

But Rosa had done enough research by now to know that the same kinds of violations happened to normal women every day.

Only, before she could say as much, Isobel said, "I can see now that I left you no choice but to disappear the way you did. Will you let me apologize?" Rosa was overwhelmed by the raw emotion in her mother's voice. "Will you give me a chance to make things right between us again? Even if I don't deserve it?"

"*Mom*." She took her mother's hands in hers and found them so cold that she instinctively began to rub them. "The last thing I want is to lose you. To lose our family."

"That will *never* happen. The four of us made it through after your father passed away, and I promise you that no matter what happens now, I'm going to fight whatever battles I need to fight to make sure we keep sticking together. Through thick and *thin*." Her mother's voice cracked on thin. "I can see now that I was wrong, so terribly wrong, for the things I said to you. I should have been there for you above and beyond anything else. I shouldn't have made you think for even a single second that the show, or business, was more important to me than you. I'll never be able to forgive myself."

But Rosa now knew exactly what happened when a mother or a father couldn't forgive themselves. She'd just witnessed it with Drake and his father. Knew how bad it was when families broke apart and stayed apart.

"I'm not going to lie to you and say it doesn't still hurt," she told her mother. "Because it does. But you weren't the only one whose head was turned by the spotlights and the money and the fame."

"That doesn't excuse what I've done."

"If we were laying out excuses, Mom, I'd have more than my fair share. But we can't go back and change who we were or what we did. We can only change who we want to be now and in the future." Still holding her mother's hands, Rosa moved from the floor to sit beside her on the couch and took a deep breath before saying, "I don't want to do the show anymore."

Her mother was silent for a long moment. Finally, she nodded and said, in a very soft voice, "I can't say

I'm happy to hear that when I know the show will be canceled without you. But I do understand why you wouldn't want to do it anymore after everything that's happened."

"It's not just the show. And it's not just because of the pictures either. It's that I've finally realized I don't want to be in the business at all. I've actually been thinking about spending more time"—she felt nervous telling anyone her budding plans, even her mom—"on my embroidered canvases." She remembered how bowled over the women in the yarn store had been and made herself amend it to, "My art."

"I've always told you how talented you are, honey. But you were so shy about ever sharing your talent with anyone else."

"I still am," she admitted, "but this week showed me that I'm strong enough to survive anything that comes. Even people hating what I create, whether it's a TV show or a canvas covered in silk thread."

"Not just survive, honey. You'll thrive the way you always have in the face of a challenge."

"You're the one who taught me how to do that. How to be strong. How to be confident." Rosa's throat tightened again. "How to love."

Her mother's mouth finally shifted into a small smile. "The man you walked in with—is that Drake?"

Rosa smiled too and felt joy all the way down to her toes just from thinking about him. "I love him." Oscar nudged her hand so that the fur on his head was easy to stroke. "I love you too, Oscar."

"I'm so happy for you, honey. If Drake is anything

like his father, you've found a good one."

Rosa's eyebrows went up. She hadn't seen her mother express interest in a man in a very long time.

"I never thought I'd find a man like him," Rosa said. "As good on the inside as Dad was. The day I left Miami, he found me in the middle of a rainstorm and brought me in out of the cold."

"You just met him this week? I assumed you'd met him before at some event."

"There's so much I want to tell you, Mom. And I promise I will. I want you two to spend time getting to know each other. But right now I need you to know that I've decided I want to do what you said in that email. I want to turn something terrible into something amazing."

"If anyone can, it's you."

"I wish I could have figured some of these things out without naked pictures of me floating all over the Internet." Rosa let the now-familiar anger rise within her, before deliberately releasing it. "I refuse to say that there are any silver linings here, but if people all over the world are waiting for what I'm going to say, I'm going to make sure they hear it. Loud and clear. I want to help make a difference, any way I can."

And as she explained her plans for the two-hour special, and they brainstormed ways to make it even more powerful, the invincible mother-and-daughter team that they had once been finally began to grow strong again.

CHAPTER THIRTY-ONE

Drake had wanted to stay in the living room with Rosa to make sure her mother didn't step out of line, but William had insisted, "They need time to work things out alone."

During the past hour, Rosa and her mother had been loud enough for Drake and his father to hear them through the walls of the study more than once. Though he hadn't been able to make out their exact words, Drake could tell how upset Rosa was.

He'd gotten up and headed for the door, intent on charging back into the living room. But his father had blocked the door, saying, "I know you want to help, but this isn't the way to do it."

"She's been hurt enough already." And Drake would do anything it took, would go to the ends of the earth, to keep Rosa safe. Even from her own mother, if need be. "I won't let it happen again."

"Neither will Rosa."

Though he'd had to force himself to stop and take a deep breath, Drake knew his father was right. He didn't need to rush into the living room to save her.

Because Rosa could save herself.

So he stayed with his father and made himself ask, "Why?"

William held his gaze. "Which *why* do you want first?"

They'd made a beginning at dinner. But now, Drake wanted to understand what he'd seen tonight in the cottage. "Why have you been collecting my paintings?"

Surprise registered for a moment in his father's eyes. "You went to the cottage tonight?"

Drake nodded. "You never once let on that you were buying my work."

"I didn't want you to think I was hovering over you all the time, but I still couldn't resist buying a painting at your first show. Anonymously, of course. Each time you had another show, I would tell myself to let you be...but you're my son. And your art felt like my only lifeline to you. The only way I could follow your growth. The only way I could get inside your head, your heart."

"I had no new paintings of yours to follow," Drake pointed out. "No way to get inside *your* head or heart."

Grief washed across his father's features. "I couldn't paint anymore. I just couldn't. Couldn't really do much of anything for a long time. Not until Jean and

Henry asked me to work on building houses here with them."

Drake thought of Rosa's insight about his father likely needing to make that change in order to move forward. "Does building give you the same satisfaction painting did?"

"Painting wasn't always healthy for me. Even before your mother, the truth I didn't want to admit is that I was driven more by pressure than inspiration. More by competition than enthusiasm. When people said I was good, I felt that I needed to be great. Until great wasn't enough anymore, and I had to be the best. And then when I met Lynn, that urgency spun into obsession. You're right that building isn't the same as painting. But for me, it turns out that's not a bad thing."

Drake silently processed his father's revelations. So many things had fallen between the cracks during the past thirty years, too many to deal with in one night. But at least they were making a start.

He hoped like hell that Rosa and Isobel were too.

There was one more thing that Drake needed to know for sure tonight. "It was worth it, wasn't it? To be with Mom, even if a part of you knew that it might not be forever?"

"I would do it all again, just to have the four of you. And I promise you I would also try to do it better. So much better."

After the decades-wide chasm between them, of course it was good to hear that. But though Drake believed his father, he wanted to know what was in his heart, not as a father, but as a man who had once loved a woman beyond all reason.

"And if we'd never been born? If those years with her were all you'd ever have?"

"One second, one hour, one day, one year." His father's words were raw with unguarded emotion. "Any amount of time loving Lynn was worth all the pain that came afterward."

Before Rosa, Drake could never have understood. Now, nothing had ever made so much sense.

"I'd like to donate the paintings you're going to give me to a few museums."

The Met in New York City, of course, but also the small museum here in Summer Lake, along with the De Young in San Francisco, the Seattle Art Museum, and the Center for Maine Contemporary Art. One in each city where Sullivans lived.

"All but the painting where she's holding me as a baby." Drake would forever prize that one.

"Your mother asked me to paint it for you." His father's voice was hollowed out by the memory. "She said she wanted to make sure you could always look at that painting and remember how much she loved you."

"Almost as if she knew she was going to leave."

His father didn't look away. Didn't deny it either. "I know we can't fix everything tonight, but I'm damned glad you're here, Drake."

"I am too."

By the time they headed back into the living room, the two women's heads were bowed together, and it looked like they were taking notes on a cell phone.

Oscar saw the men first, and when the dog caught

Rosa's attention by lifting his head from her lap, the smile she gave Drake nearly blinded him in its beauty. They'd been apart only an hour, but he crossed the room with eyes only for her, breathing her in like oxygen when she met him halfway.

He brushed his fingertips over the dried tear tracks on her cheeks. "You're okay."

He didn't say it as a question. Despite the smudges of exhaustion under her eyes, he could see not only that she was okay, but also that finally talking with her mother had lifted a big part of the load she'd been carrying.

"I am." She put her hands on his chest, and he could feel his heart beating against her palms as she looked deep into his eyes. "So are y—" She lost the battle with a yawn. "You."

He kissed her again, then said, "Time for bed."

His father obviously had the same idea as he held out a hand to help Rosa's mother to her feet. "I'm going to show Isobel to the guest room."

Isobel smiled at William and said something to him in a low voice before moving toward Drake and Rosa. "Thank you, Drake." Her words were thick with emotion. "Thank you for being there for my daughter when I wasn't."

Drake was still wading through his impressions about Rosa's mother, and despite the fact that she was saying all the right things now, he wanted to get to know her better before he made up his mind. Tonight, however, one thing was perfectly clear: Isobel Bouchard loved her daughter.

Love, he knew, didn't mean you always made the right choices. Fortunately, it did go a long way toward making forgiveness—and new beginnings—possible.

"I'm glad you're here so that you can both have a chance to talk some things through."

Rosa's mother clearly understood that he would protect her daughter against any and all threats, even her. Just as he was taking the measure of her, he could see that she was doing the same with him.

"Whatever happens in the future," she told Drake as she pressed a kiss to Rosa's forehead, "I will be forever in your debt."

Rosa's eyes were nearly closed by the time they made it up the stairs and down the hall to their bedroom. "Did you ask your father about why he bought your paintings?"

"We talked and it was good." He watched her barely smother another yawn. "Looks like you and your mom worked through some things too."

"We did." She yawned again. "I want to tell you everything, want to hear more about what your dad said."

He wanted to hear the same from her, but sleep was more important right now. "Lie with me awhile first." He quickly stripped her clothes away, then laid her beneath the thick covers on the bed. Moments later, his own clothes were off, and he was sliding in beside her, pulling her into his arms.

By the time she curled up against him, her breathing was soft and even. Though Drake badly needed sleep as well, he needed this more. Needed to have Rosa warm and safe in his arms. Needed to feel her heart beating against his. Needed to breathe in her sweet scent.

And most of all, he needed to take a quiet moment in the dark to appreciate being the luckiest guy in the world.

CHAPTER THIRTY-TWO

"Cal, I'd like you to meet my girlfriend, Rosa. Rosa, the mayor and I go way back."

It was the first time Drake had used the word *girlfriend*. He liked the sound of it. Was going to like it even more when it was *fiancée*. Better still when it was *wife*.

He knew he was racing ahead. And he didn't give a damn. At long last, he understood what his cousins in San Francisco and Seattle felt for the people they'd fallen in love with. Forever wasn't just something you saw in a movie or read about in a book. It was so much more than a few pretty sentences in a Valentine's Day card.

Forever was sweet and raw, messy and beautiful, scary and strong.

Forever was *Rosa*.

"It's great to meet you," Calvin said. "I'm glad

you thought of us for your TV special. Any other way we can help, just let us know. Denise and Olive from Lakeside Stitch and Knit are already ready to get out on the front lines to defend you to the end."

"Their kindness—everyone's kindness—has meant so much to me." Drake drew Rosa close as her emotions rose to the surface. "Thank you so much for letting us film in your building, Calvin. But I just want you to know that if at any point you feel uncomfortable with having a reality TV crew and cast here, we can figure out something else."

"Are you kidding? I'm the hero of the century right now." He winked at the pretty girl who was peeking in his office door. "You wouldn't mind signing an autograph for my sister, would you?"

"I'd love to." Rosa immediately walked over to the door and held out her hand as if she were meeting a peer instead of a child. "You must be Jordan." Drake had told Rosa that Calvin was raising his ten-year-old sister all by himself, after his parents had both passed away one after the other within a month of Jordan's birth.

Jordan's eyes were huge as she nodded, so star struck by Rosa that she was speechless for a rare moment in time. Going out of her way to put Calvin's sister at ease, Rosa said, "I love your bracelets." Drake finally noticed the half-dozen woven bracelets in a rainbow of colors on Jordan's wrists. "Did you make them?" When the girl nodded again, Rosa said, "Maybe you can show me how sometime?"

"They're really easy. There's a kit you can use, but I figured out how to make them on my own."

"Cool."

That was all it took for Jordan to start talking a mile a minute, and Drake loved the way Rosa kept up with every bit of it. "You don't think she'd be interested in babysitting sometime, do you?" Calvin asked Drake in a low voice.

"You know what? I have a feeling that might be right up her alley."

Calvin raised an eyebrow. "You know I was kidding, right? Rosa is an international superstar with a heck of a lot more important things to do than hang out with my kid sister."

"Trust me, she would much rather learn how to make those bracelets than go to some flashy premiere." Calvin still didn't look convinced, but Drake knew it would make perfect sense to his friend once Cal got to know her better.

Rosa gave Jordan a hug, then when the little girl headed back outside to play with her friends, she turned to Calvin. "Your sister is great."

"I know," he said with a grin. "Thanks for making her day."

"She made mine too." Rosa reached into her bag for a folder and handed it to Calvin. "I know you're busy, and I don't want to take up too much more of your time today, so hopefully the information here will answer most of your questions about the setup for tomorrow's live shoot. My mother is arranging to fly my brothers in right now, but I'll make sure she drops by to say hello before tomorrow morning."

"I'm sure you've thought of everything we need

to know." Calvin put the folder on his desk. "Anything else you and your family need, just give a holler. We're all on your side."

"Thank you."

Instead of leaving with another handshake, she threw her arms around him. Cal, of course, didn't look at all averse to holding her for a few seconds, even when he knew damn well that she was taken.

Once Rosa and Drake were out of the building, she said, "I like your friend. It doesn't seem fair that he had such bad luck with his parents."

"His love life has been pretty rotten too, unfortunately."

"How can someone that handsome, who also happens to be a great brother, have a rotten love life?"

"Handsome?" Drake teased.

"I barely noticed," she teased back. "But seriously, he's a major catch. What happened?"

"There was someone back in high school. Sarah. We all thought they were going to be together forever. I run into her in the city sometimes, but she never asks about Calvin. Just like he never asks about her." When they hit a fork in the path, he decided on a detour. "Want to see something beautiful?"

"I already am, but I'm always up for more."

He pulled her close and kissed her deeply before leading her up into the mountains.

* * *

Rosa spent plenty of time in the gym, but given

how hard her lungs were rocked by this mountain trail, she planned to spend way more time in the woods in the future. Especially when everything around her was so lovely and inspiring. She wanted to buy silk floss in a rainbow of colors to stitch the reds and yellows of woodpeckers and goldfinches, the pretty white bark on the birch trees, the deep green leaves of the maples in dozens of shades all around them.

The only thing that didn't quite fit was the buzzing of the phone in Drake's pocket as they climbed the final stretch to the top of the hill. He pulled it out and looked at the screen a few times, before finally shutting it off with an impatient sound.

"Used to be, you couldn't get reception out here. It was one of my favorite things about this place."

"I'm pretty good at chucking cell phones from high places," she joked, "if you want me to give it a go."

"I'd take you up on it if I thought it would get this gallery off my back. But since I owe them a dozen paintings in a week, I'm sure they'd find a way to track me down even without the phone." Before she could respond to this rather shocking new piece of information about the gallery needing all those new paintings, he said, "Right now, though, I want us both to forget about everything we've got to do and just spend some time appreciating this."

Pulling her up onto a large, flat rock, he brought her in against him, back to front, and wrapped his arms around her waist. Sensual warmth flooded her at his closeness even as she gasped at the stunning beauty laid out in front of her.

"Oh, Drake." She felt it again, that sense that she'd finally found where she was meant to be. "You've painted this, haven't you?" She recognized this vista from one of the larger canvases hanging in his father's cottage. "Standing right here, looking out over the lakes and rolling hills."

"It's always been one of my favorite spots in the world. And now that you're here, I honestly can't think of anywhere else I'd rather be."

"I feel the same way." She turned away from the view to look into his eyes. "Someone had to have seen me by now and sent a tweet or posted on Facebook. The paparazzi will be here by tomorrow morning. Maybe even by tonight."

"Let them come." Drake looked fiercely protective. "They'll find out soon enough that's not how we do things at Summer Lake."

"It was one of my worst fears," she said softly. "That they'd find me and drag me back into a life, a world that I didn't want anymore. And then when I started falling for you, I hated the thought of them dragging you in too." She wrapped her arms even tighter around him. "But even if those fears never completely go away, I refuse to let them hurt me anymore. And I *definitely* won't let anything hurt you." Her lips lifted into a smile as she told him, "You already have the paintings the gallery needs."

"Rosa..." He framed her face in his hands. "I made you a promise to keep the paintings of you private."

"Now I'm asking you to make me a new promise. A promise to show them to the entire world. I can't stand the thought of letting such beautiful art sit dusty and forgotten beneath tarps for thirty years. And I would never forgive myself if you kept something you created hidden because you were worried about hurting me. You were the one who saw my strength from the start. You were right, Drake. I am strong. As strong as the woman you painted on all those canvases."

He didn't answer right away. Instead, he looked deep into her eyes as if he needed to make absolutely sure that she wasn't just saying it to make him happy. Finally, he said, "I'll show them. All but the last ones."

Though she understood his instinctive desire to hold back the nudes, Rosa knew better now. It didn't matter how many clothes she had on—it was who she was *beneath* them that mattered.

"*Especially* those last ones." She tightened her hold on him, wanting to get closer. Always closer. "When people think of me in the nude, I want *your* paintings to be what they remember. But it's more than the fact that I'm finally ready for the world to see who I really am. More than anything, I want people to see that true love changes everything. That risking your heart for the right person can give back even the things that you thought were gone forever. I didn't think I'd ever be able to trust again. To love. But you showed me that I could own every part of myself—the good and the bad—without shame. Without fear."

"You're so damned brave." He tangled his hands in her hair and kissed her before saying, "You've showed me how to be brave too. How to stop running. How to let go of the past and fight for a future with my dad.

You brought me back here, back to the place I've always loved best but never thought could be mine." He smiled at her, that beautiful grin that always sent her heart flip-flopping in her chest. "*Ours*, if a his-and-hers art studio and gallery on the lake sounds good to you."

She'd cried more in the past week than she had for the past decade, but she didn't feel the need to stop her tears this time. Not when every single one came from pure joy.

"A his-and-hers art studio and gallery sounds like a dream come true," she replied. "Maybe we can even convince your father to build us a house."

"Something tells me he's already started drawing up the plans."

EPILOGUE

Rosa was strong and luminous in front of the cameras, and Suzanne couldn't have been more proud.

Rosa's brothers, Aaron and Lincoln, were seated with her and their mother on screen. The two boys reminded Suzanne of her own brothers at that age. How they were obviously overprotective of their sister, while also overrun with enough hormones that they homed in on any pretty girl nearby.

Everyone watching the live broadcast in the town hall obviously wanted Rosa to know how deeply they supported what she was doing today. Not just Drake, Harry, Suzanne, and her father, but also Denise and Olive from the yarn store, Christie from the inn, and Calvin and the city hall staff, as well.

The paparazzi had come in droves and had tried to park themselves and their cameras right outside the town hall—but the locals were having none of it, so the closest the photographers and cameramen could get to Rosa was the other end of Main Street.

Suzanne had always loved being at the lake, but after graduating from Columbia with a degree in computer science ten years ago, she'd worked in high tech in New York City ever since. Fortunately, now that she ran her own company, she had the flexibility to come here more often. Sure, she always brought several computers with her, but at least she could see trees, breathe fresh air, even jump into the lake if she was so inclined. But beyond the beautiful natural surroundings, it was the closely connected community that continued to impress Suzanne. She was all thumbs when it came to knitting, but Denise and Olive had been so enthusiastic about her joining in on their knitting nights that she'd gone several times over the years and pretended to knit while mostly drinking wine and laughing with the other women.

It was a testament to the Summer Lake community how quickly—and passionately—they'd rallied around Rosa.

Suzanne's phone buzzed in her pocket for the millionth time, and Harry shot her a look. Though she was always on call for her employees, she decided to shut it off completely so that she wouldn't distract anyone while Rosa was speaking.

"I've often heard people say that I'm famous just for being famous," Rosa said in a steady but emotional voice. "Today, whatever people might think of my choices, I'm simply glad that so many of you want to hear what I have to say." She looked directly at the cameras, while her mother held tightly to her hand and her brothers flanked them both. "For any woman, any man, who has been made to feel cheap or dirty or small on the Internet, whether it's with words or in pictures—I want to let you know that we don't have to feel ashamed. Because it isn't our fault. It doesn't matter what we've done in the past. It doesn't matter what we've worn, what we've said, who we've dated, what career we've had. None of us deserve to be attacked, either online or off." Rosa paused to let her words settle with the millions of people around the world who were watching the live broadcast. "Even if I can never get the pictures off the Internet, I'm not a victim. I'm taking my life back, right here, right now, and I'm going to make it better than it's ever been before. With art, with friends, with family, and with the foundation my family and I have created to support people who have been hurt by personal cyber-attacks."

When the cameras finally went dark, all of them gathered around Rosa in a big group hug. Suzanne had already spoken with her about the role she'd like to take as the lead technical volunteer in the Bouchards' new foundation, and she was excited to get going with it as soon as possible.

Waiting until she'd stepped outside the city hall building to turn her phone back on, she wasn't thrilled to see another array of phone calls from several random numbers she didn't recognize.

She was shoving her phone back into her pocket when Harry said, "He's still bothering you, isn't he?"

Suzanne should have known better than to tell her brothers about one of her tech competitors. The guy seemed hell-bent on annoying her in any way he could in the hopes that she'd lose her momentum on their newest security product, which was particularly groundbreaking, if she did say so herself. Lately, she was getting dozens of random phone calls each day, but no one was ever there when she picked up.

Though she knew it was nothing more than a mind game, she didn't want to lie to her brother and act like nothing was happening. "Don't worry, Harry. I've got it under control."

Unfortunately, he looked anything but convinced. "Have you looked into hiring a bodyguard yet?"

"No, and I'm not going to." *No* was the same reaction she'd always had to such a ridiculous suggestion. "My competitor is a pain, but apart from bombarding me and my servers with automated junk emails and calls and uploads, he's harmless."

For a moment, she thought Harry was going to press her further on it. Thankfully, Drake and Rosa walked out arm in arm just then and asked if they wanted to head to the Tavern for a drink.

No question about it, Suzanne would much rather bask in the glow of Drake and Rosa's love than argue with her brother about a bodyguard. Because if love could come for her youngest brother in the most unexpected way, that meant there was hope for the rest of them, didn't it?

Although she couldn't imagine how she would possibly meet the love of her life when she usually spent twenty-four seven with her computers. Especially if she gave in to her brother's concerns and actually hired a bodyguard to tail her every second of every day...

* * * * *

For news on upcoming books, sign up for Bella Andre's New Release Newsletter: http://www.bellaandre.com/Newsletter

And don't miss Suzanne Sullivan's book – SINCE I FELL FOR YOU (New York Sullivans, Book 2) – coming Fall 2016!